IT'S ALWAYS BEEN ME

IT'S ALWAYS BEEN ME

A Novel

MEGAN WALROD

SHE WRITES PRESS

Published by SparkPress, a BookSparks imprint,
A division of SparkPoint Studio, LLC
Phoenix, Arizona, USA, 85007
www.gosparkpress.com

Published 2025
Printed in the United States of America
Print ISBN: 978-1-64742-914-0
E-ISBN: 978-1-64742-915-7
Library of Congress Control Number: 2025900946

Interior design by Stacey Aaronson

To anyone who needs the reminder that
it's always been you.

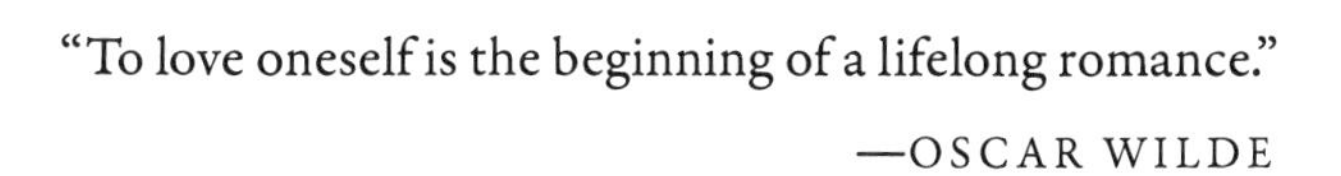

"To love oneself is the beginning of a lifelong romance."

—OSCAR WILDE

PROLOGUE

Santa Cruz, California

I BURST UP THROUGH THE SURFACE AND GASP FOR breath. My lungs want me to rest, but my mind doesn't. A lone seagull cries out overhead. My stomach growls. I put my head down and swim toward the sandstone cliffs. Thoughts of Nana spur me on. I kick harder, pull faster.

Sabinaaaaaa . . .

I pause and tread water while I scan the sea around me. Nobody's there. I yawn and tug at my ear to release any water that might be in there. Maybe that's what's causing me to hear things—that or lack of sleep.

Sabina, see? It's okay to be in the depths.

The voice sounds like a woman's—light, airy. Eerie, almost. A small wave lifts and then lowers my body as I think about what Nana and her BFF, Dora, would say. That it's a Selkie—one of the mythical, shape-shifting "seal-folk"—coming to offer me support. Ever since my first summer with Nana, back when I was ten years old, she and Dora had regaled me with stories about these magical beings. I heard all about how they shed their fur to take on human forms and loved coming ashore to dance. Because I'd already been obsessed with mermaids, I easily embraced the Selkies. Over the years, they became the equivalent of patron saints for Nana, Dora, and me.

My chest tightens. The thought of Nana not being at the cottage when I return makes it hard for me to take a full breath. During the nine summers I spent in Santa Cruz as a child, I never imagined there would come a day when I would have to live without her. Now, that possibility hangs over me like the fog bank that embraces the Moss Landing smokestacks. I can just barely see the bottoms of those towers on the east side of Monterey Bay as I turn and resume my overarm crawl back to the beach.

On the shore, I pull off my wetsuit and wrap myself in a towel. My fingers tingle but not from the cold. They ache to pick up a paintbrush and capture the early morning sunlight seeping into the fog like a runny yolk. A heavy sigh spills out of me. After a swim, when my mind is quiet, I can pretend that everything is okay. I take a deep breath. The briny air is so fresh, so different from the smog I'm used to in LA.

I bend over, grab my thick mop of hair, and squeeze the seawater from it. Then I pull off the elastic band and flip it over my head. Nana used to laugh when I did this. "You're just like the Little Mermaid," she'd say. "Both of you with your gorgeous red tresses!"

Thoughts of her laughter are interrupted by a line of pelicans flying close to the curl of a wave. One, two, three . . . eight in all. I don't know why I started counting these birds, but I've done it for as long as I can remember. It's comforting to perform an old ritual, like I'm returning to some part of me that's been buried for way too long. My stomach growls again. The last time I ate was yesterday afternoon—a few bites of a tuna sandwich at the hospital cafeteria. Between worrying about Nana and the disaster that is my marriage, I haven't wanted to eat.

A wave of heat rushes through my body as Reece's handsome face—his dark chocolate-brown eyes and square jaw—flickers before my eyes. I don't see how we can recover from this, but I can't picture my life without him. In an attempt to push him out of my mind, I focus on the sound of the small waves hitting the shore with a quiet thud, one after the other. They're so gentle—nothing like the dark crashing waves that woke me up around 3:00 a.m. "It wasn't okay to be in the depths last night," I murmur aloud, not sure who I'm actually speaking to. A Selkie? Myself? The nightmare had seemed so real. I was in the ocean, alone, with no shore in sight. There was a storm. Waves lifted me up, tossed me back and forth, and then pushed me down, threatening to drown me. No matter how hard I fought the tug of the current, I couldn't get my head above water. How could the ocean, the place that's like a second home to me, seem so scary? It's always been my sanctuary. I turned to the sea when my parents sent me to Nana's the first time, when I felt like they ditched me. I swam my way through the end of my first relationship, when I was fifteen and my summer love took off without a word. Anytime I've felt abandoned, I've always been able to find solace in the water and the thought of its magical creatures.

But now, with death and divorce looming over me, my nightmares have turned my source of solace into a source of torment. Are they trying to tell me something—like, maybe this time, it's going to require a whole lot more than the sea to fix this mess?

1

Los Angeles, California

WE'RE STANDING AT THE KITCHEN ISLAND. REECE HAS only been home from the band's West Coast tour for a few hours. He's showered and taken a nap, and we're in the midst of unpacking a bag of Ethiopian takeout.

"Shug," he says, using his nickname for me, "we need to talk."

He started calling me Shug the first year we met, when he came up from LA to visit me in Berkeley almost every other weekend. I was finishing up my MBA and counting the hours until he would knock on the door and whisk me away from the stuffy B-school world. He'd joked that, although I cursed like a sailor, I tasted as sweet as sugar—and Sugar eventually got shortened to Shug and Shugga. But he hasn't called me this in a while, and his voice is strained. He's gripping the edge of the island with both hands.

A question forms itself in my mouth, but I don't ask it. I

already know this is going to be bad. I feel nauseous and set the food down.

He pushes himself away from the island. "But not here. Let's go in there." He motions toward the living room, then turns and leaves the kitchen.

My heart is racing. As I follow him down the hallway, I can't help but feel like I'm walking the plank on a pirate ship. I reach out and run my fingers along the framed photos of us lining the walls—for luck or for reassurance, I'm not sure. My fingers stop on the picture of his proposal, the only time I've been onstage during a show. It was a fairy-tale moment: In the photo, he's down on one knee, and I'm covering my mouth with both hands. I remember the band cheering us on and the audience going nuts. Another wave of nausea hits me.

Once we're in the living room, I sit down cross-legged on the couch. He sits at the other end, as far away from me as he can get. As I wait for him to speak, he tucks one long leg under the other, glances out the window at our small backyard, and then looks down at the glass coffee table. Finally, he lifts his eyes and clears his throat. "I slept with Fee."

His words are like a kick in the chest. "Fee?"

"Fiona. Lead singer of the Pinks. The band that opened for us on tour."

"I know who Fiona is." She's the pretty, petite, dark-haired one I'd asked him about before. Every time I see them onstage together, it's like they're having sex. Not physically, but emotionally, energetically. But, when I'd mentioned that impression, Reece had brushed off my concerns. "Oh, it's nothing," he'd said. "She's a flirt. It doesn't mean anything."

Bile rises in my throat, forcing me to swallow before speaking the words out loud.

"You . . . slept with her." I try to focus on his face, but my head is spinning. It's like the floor just fell out from beneath me and there's nothing to hold on to. I suddenly have a need to know more, as if knowing the details will prevent my fall into the abyss. "Once? More than that? Just this tour, or has it been going on for a while?"

He shakes his head. "It hasn't been going on for a while. It just happened on this tour." He pauses. "Twice."

My skin goes cold, pricked with a thousand icicles. Then it burns hot. "Twice? What, were you drinking? Were you on the bus? In a hotel? Does Jaxon—do the other guys—know?" I don't know why I care if the band's lead singer or the rest of them know, but I do.

He looks away. I stare at the small silver helix hoop piercing in his ear. I had been with him when he'd gotten it to commemorate the band's first album. "We did it, Shugga! Come on, why don't you get one too? Or maybe another tattoo, somewhere sexy?" But I'd said no. It was his album, not mine. Sure, my life had been dedicated to getting that album out—as his had been—but I was just the behind-the-scenes support. He was the creator. It's his photo and name on the cover, not mine. Mine is down there in the fine print, with some boring title like Management Services. My attention is drawn to the muscles quivering in his jaw. He turns back to me. "I . . . I don't think it would help to share those details right now."

My body feels like it's on fire. My hands clench into fists in my lap. "So, what . . . you knew you made a mistake the instant it was over but couldn't help yourself and went back for more? And now you feel guilty and want to . . . to . . . make amends?"

"I'm sorry, Sabina." His voice is thin, like a string stretched too tight on his guitar.

"For what? For breaking my trust?" I reach for the golden band on my ring finger. "Breaking your vows?"

"Yes." He looks down at my hands. "But . . . but things here . . ." He moves his hand back and forth between us. "Babe, I love you, but you have to admit, we haven't been *us* for a while. You haven't been happy. We've been fighting over stupid shit." He looks at me pleadingly, as though if I agree, he'll be released from all guilt and blame.

I surprise myself with the force of my exhalation. "You're right. We haven't been *us* for a while." For the last seven years—basically, ever since we got together—we'd done everything we could to get his band a record label. He'd been his charismatic self onstage and with the music execs, while I hired and managed the team, dealt with booking agents, and pored over contracts. We had agreed to put off having kids until his band was more established. And I'd given up painting. Painting had been my thing ever since I was a little girl. It was a religion for me. A communion. The best way I ever knew to express all that moved through me. But I'd quit making art to focus on Reece and his music.

For the last few years, though, I'd been yearning to reimmerse myself in my passion. Maybe get some pieces into a gallery or do some murals. Every time I mentioned painting to him, though, he told me how much he needed me. "Shug, we just signed with Virgin Records. You know this is a freakin' huge break for us—the band, you, and me. We've gotta capitalize on this now! I need you backing me up more than ever." So I haven't lifted a brush in years, and my resentment has simmered beneath the surface, coming out sideways, contributing to the stupid fights he mentioned.

"That's exactly why we're in counseling with Brian. But what good is that doing us?" I throw my hands up in the air. "Brian told us just last month that I was supposed to try to be more trusting, and you were supposed to try to be more trustworthy. I held up my end of that. Guess that makes me a fool." I scratch at the scar on my forehead. "Are you trying to wreck us? 'Cause this is a deal-breaker for me, you know."

My mind flashes on Marco, my on-again, off-again college boyfriend. His intense honey-brown eyes blaze in my brain. Marco had been an architecture major who loved the design of women's bodies too much to be with just one. I'd given him second and third chances, but he had shown me who he was that first time and never changed.

Marco's face fades and is replaced with an image of my dad. He'd had an affair when I was a teenager and left to live with the other woman for a summer. I never got the whole story, but I know it broke something in my mom. I'd thought that was my dad's only affair until I started talking to my mom about Marco. Then she'd told me the truth. There had been—and still were—other women. When I asked her why she continued to stay with him, she'd said, "I made a vow for a lifetime, not just till it gets hard. You work on it. You stay with your husband."

"But it takes two to work on a relationship," I'd insisted, and Dad never changed.

"Fidelity isn't his forte" she'd acknowledged. Her acceptance had pissed me off. Did she think she didn't deserve his faithfulness? His loyalty? Did she think that what he offered was as good as she could get?

I'd given Dad a hard time about it, back when we still had heart-to-heart talks, but that just served to widen the gap between us. He'd literally put up his hand to stop me from speaking. "This is between Gwen and me. It has nothing to do with you." But it did have something to do with me. His unfaithfulness felt like a betrayal of our family. How could I trust or respect him knowing he didn't respect Mom enough to honor their vows?

I shake my head. "From the very beginning, I told you. I don't put up with cheating. Marco was a cheater. My father is a cheater. No more cheaters."

"Sabina, I'm not either of those men." He's angry too. I can hear it in his steely voice.

"No, Reece, you aren't. But it's looking like you have the same tendency of having sex with a woman you're not committed to. And that doesn't work for me when we both chose monogamy." We stare at each other. The air in the room feels sharp, edged with barbed wire.

He raises his eyebrows. "What happened to 'All good things are wild and free'?"

"Don't you dare use that to justify your betrayal!" I shout. That's *my* motto—the Thoreau quote I learned from Nana and came to love so much that I got it tattooed on my hip.

He lifts his hands up quickly as if to disarm the bomb he just dropped in our laps. "All right. You're right. But, Sabina . . . that's it then? You'd end our marriage over this?"

Would I? Does he want me to? I look away. My eyes fall on

the framed picture of him on the wall next to the bookshelf, a photo taken during the band's performance at the Roxy last year. He's in one of his iconic poses: knee up, hitting a power chord, mouth open wide, with sweat streaming down his face. With a sudden knowing, I look back at him and the words fly out. "You tell me. Is it over between you two? The Pinks are opening for you again here in LA this week. Then you're heading into the studio together. Fiona's featured in two of the songs you're recording. No matter what I say, you don't plan to end it yet, do you?" I cross my arms over my chest and glare at him. I know the answer. I know what's coming.

He breaks eye contact and looks down at his hands. "I said I was sorry earlier, not just because I slept with her but . . . because, well, it's more than that." He swallows. "I have . . . I have feelings for her. I think there could be something with her. Something more."

I snort. "Feelings? Those are hormones. You don't have to act on them."

He covers his face for a moment, then drags his hands down over his freshly shaven jaw. I notice a couple spots of blood. When he looks at me, I see the anguish in his eyes. "I don't know if it's the chemistry of us playing together or getting ready to record . . . that's why I just . . . I want some time to sort this out. To see what this really is."

Somehow, I keep my voice low. "You want to see what this is? With Fiona? You don't want to see if we can find our way back to us again?"

"I . . . I don't know, Sabina." He leans forward just a little bit. "Do you think it's possible?"

"Not if you want to 'see what this is,'" I say.

"I knew you'd do this." He falls back on the couch and exhales loudly.

"Do what?"

"Get angry. Push me away."

"Are you kidding me? Reece. You're sitting here telling me you've slept with another woman. Not only that, you want to see what this might become if you spend more time with her." I jump up off the couch and take a few steps toward the window. I want to break something, throw something. I spin around. "We know what will happen if you spend more time with her: You'll fuck her. And it'll feel like love at first. Especially when you're playing onstage together and recording together. Until it all fizzles out or blows up on you or . . ." I can't picture it becoming anything else right now but a big disaster.

The muscle in his jaw twitches again. "You can't tell me you've never had feelings for other men while we've been together."

"That's not the point!" I press my hands over my eyes and take a deep breath before continuing. "It's one thing to be attracted to someone. It's a totally different thing to act on it. You crossed a line. You know it, I know it, she knows it. You don't get to have both of us. That's not how this works."

I turn toward the window, seeking answers from our tiny backyard. What do you do when your husband sleeps with another woman? Not just once, but twice—and he's basically saying it's going to happen again? My hands curl and uncurl at my sides. I know what my mom would do—or does. But I don't think I'm willing to follow in her footsteps, not in my own marriage. So, do I just end it instead, right here and now?

The glare of the sun on the chrome grill we bought during our first summer here in Silver Lake suddenly makes the options obvious to me. I rush to speak, afraid that if I don't say it now, I'll chicken out. "Let me make it really clear. You stay here, commit to more therapy to see if we can repair us, and don't sleep with her again. Or, if you want to prioritize her over us, you leave now. But, if you leave, we're over."

His eyes go blank. "Don't do that, Sabina. Don't give me an ultimatum."

Damn. That's exactly what I'm doing. I hate ultimatums too. Dad used to give them to me. "An MBA or nothing. Which will it be?" No art school. No MFA. No support for what I wanted. Just what he wanted. His money, his way. This is different, though, isn't it? Rather than just kicking him out, I'm saying I'll work on forgiving him if he stays. But can I really do that?

Other questions flicker through my mind, quiet and fleeting, like fireflies in the night. Do I actually want him to stay? Do I want to work on us? Or is there something else out there for me?

He stands up and walks toward the window, his back to me. I can hear him taking a few controlled breaths. When he turns around, I feel like I'm looking at a stranger. The handsome face I know so well is tight. His mask is on. "If I stay because of the ultimatum, no one wins. You're just trying to control me rather than communicate with me."

"Oh, nice move, using Brian's words." But he's right. I feel utterly out of control, and so I'm trying to control him. I don't like it, but the truth of what he's done is tearing me up inside. He actually slept with another woman. Kissed her. Touched her.

Was inside of her. The images of them together are making it hard for me to breathe.

"What do you really want, Sabina?"

His question hangs in the air. I squirm and pull on a thread hanging from one of the throw pillows. Our therapist often asks us this question. I've had a hard time answering it. But, in this moment, I don't get the sense that it matters what I say. He's already made up his mind about what he wants.

"Seems more like the question is, 'What do you really want, Reece?'" I swipe at the tears in my eyes before looking back at him. "It sounds like you want both of us. You want to fuck her some more while not making any kind of decision about us. I can't stand by and do nothing in the meantime. That's crazy-making and cruel."

"It's not cruel, Sabina. It's just honest." For a moment his mask slips, and I think I see sadness moving across his face. But, just as quickly, it turns hard again, and he looks at me with eyes that match his flat tone. "Our marriage hasn't been working for a while. We both know it. Maybe this is just the . . . the thing to finally make us confront that. Maybe there is something real between Fiona and me. Maybe it is just . . . nothing. Maybe I'm making a mistake. I'm not doing this to hurt you, but I'm not going to stay because of an ultimatum. I have to find out what this is. With Fiona."

I don't say anything. I just watch as he slowly walks out of the room. I listen to him move around in our bathroom, turn on the water in the sink. I remember the debate we'd had with the contractor. He'd encouraged us to get the highly coveted "his and hers" sinks. But we wanted just one. "Couples who spit together stick together," we'd joked. So much for that.

Only after I hear the front door close behind him am I able to move. I stomp into the kitchen, where the takeout containers sit open on the island. They now feel like an insult. I pick them up, one at a time, and throw them into the garbage. I can't help but snort when I notice that the splatter of red, brown, and yellow sauces on the wall behind the bin kind of looks like art.

2

I KNOCK ON MEL'S DOOR, THEN DROP MY SMALL DUFFEL bag on the mat. Just beyond the house, the bright June sun is setting over the Santa Monica Pier. Although it was a scorcher of a day, I can't stop shivering. I wrap my arms around myself and stare at the pink bougainvillea growing next to the front window.

The door swings open. "Bina!" Behind her oversize glasses, Mel's tawny eyes are wrinkled in concern. Her bangs are pulled back from her forehead with two bendy clips—a sure sign she's been baking. "Oh, honey." She looks down at the duffel. "What's this?"

"Some clothes. Toiletries. I . . . I just can't stand to be at the house right now."

She picks up the bag and sets it down in the entryway behind her. Then she tucks me into her familiar hourglass frame. She claims her boobs and hips hide all the extra calories she consumes from her recipe experiments. "I've got you," she whispers.

With that, the sobs that have been pressing against my chest pour out of me. "He . . . they . . . she . . ." It's not until I hear the sound of a car driving by that I remember we're standing in the doorway. I lift my head from her shoulder. "Can we go inside?"

"Of course." She closes the door and guides me toward the living room.

Hhhk!

Damn. The sobs have receded and left hiccups in their wake.

Mel gives me a squeeze. "I'll grab you some water. And, oh! Do you want a slice of pear-and-cardamom cake? I just pulled it out of the oven."

The perfumed sweetness of her pre-gig ritual permeates the house. It's always this cake, always made the day before an important catering event. But I can't imagine eating anything right now—not even this heavenly treat with its maple–cream cheese icing. I shake my head, sink into the couch, and reach for her rainbow-striped throw blanket. She's had this ratty thing since our freshman year at UC Berkeley, thirteen years ago. When we first met, she had five different kinds of baked goods for sale spread out on this blanket in the quad. I quickly grew fond of her blueberry muffins and compassionate three-dollar therapy.

I drink the water Mel brings me, then hold my breath. *Hhhk!* Still. She settles down on the couch, places a pillow on her lap, and taps it with her hand. I take another gulp, hold my breath, and lie down with my cheek on the pillow and legs curled up in the fetal position. We're silent for a few minutes as she strokes my hair.

"Remember when we first met Reece?" I ask once the hiccups are gone. I drift back to that August day seven years earlier when I had first seen the man who would become my husband.

He'd been playing an electric guitar that I later learned was his most cherished possession: a blond 1957 Telecaster. His light brown hair was pulled back in a short ponytail. He sported a goatee, black T-shirt, and faded jeans, and he swaggered across the stage like he owned it. Sweat glistened on his forehead, and my sudden desire to lick it surprised me.

"Yep," Mel says. I can hear the smile in her voice. "It's funny to think about the Sunset Rangers playing a dive like the Silver Lake Lounge now. But it felt so good to dance after that awful bridal shower gig up in Topanga, right? We just let it all out."

I close my eyes, letting my memory of the scene unfurl.

It had been Miguel, Mel's boyfriend, who'd suggested we check out the band. I was wearing a curve-hugging dress I'd changed into after Mel and I both showered off the effects of the chocolate fountain—every caterer's nemesis. The three of us ended up dancing right in front of the stage. The lead singer's throaty voice, the hot guy's sinuous guitar, and the drummer's slow, languid beat made it easy to get lost in the music. I swayed back and forth, feeling all warm and melted, like the chocolate I had been cursing just a few hours earlier. At one point, I looked up and locked eyes with the guitar player—Reece. For a moment, I couldn't breathe. He shot me a sly smile. I flushed and looked away. Out of the corner of my eye, I saw him take a step closer to the edge of the stage, closer to me, as he stomped on his pedalboard and took a solo. When I looked up at him again, his dark brown eyes pierced mine as he joined in on the chorus, "Hey hey babe, don't go. Stay with me tonight." It was like he was singing directly to me, just for me. After that, I didn't look away.

"He couldn't take his eyes off you," Mel says. "And, yeah, he was in his element that night—crowd-surfing and all, remember? Then, when he invited us to come hang out after the show and meet the rest of the band . . . yeah, I remember thinking that promise you'd made didn't stand a chance under the full light he beamed on you. And, well. I was right."

"You were." When I'd first met Reece, I'd sworn off men for at least six months. It had only been a few weeks since ending things with Marco. Yet that night, backstage, the air between us had crackled like a summer sky before a lightning storm. I tried resisting it—him—at first. But he was so charming, and a perfect gentleman too. He asked me what famous people I'd like to have dinner with and what I'd do if I inherited a million dollars. Then he shared with me the story of how he got started playing music and told me about his top five favorite guitar players. Our fingers grazed once, as he handed me a bottle of beer. But there wasn't any other physical contact. He never made a move except to ask for my number before I left. He called the next day and invited me to go on a picnic with him before I headed back to Berkeley.

A sob catches in my throat as the memory of sitting next to him in the Exposition Park Rose Garden is usurped by an image of Reece onstage with Fiona, sharing a mic, singing the chorus of the Sunset Rangers' latest song, "Love's Leftovers."

"Want to tell me about it?" Mel's voice is gentle. "All you said in your text was that you two had a fight and you were coming over."

Mel has had my back throughout my relationship with Reece, starting with our long-distance courtship and continuing through my move to LA, our engagement, and the wedding. She's also heard me talk about our struggles over the last few years—sometimes at a bar over cocktails and other times at a prep table, when I've pitched in to help her get ready for the weekend weddings that make up the bulk of her growing business. But what Mel doesn't know yet is what I found out a couple hours ago. I roll over, stare up into her eyes, and tell her everything.

3

IS MY MARRIAGE REALLY OVER? IS HE WITH HER RIGHT now? The questions squawk mercilessly, like gulls descending on picnic blankets. As I walk over the pedestrian bridge that crosses the Pacific Coast Highway and leads to the sea, I take several long swigs of the cheap red wine I poured into Mel's travel mug. I'm hoping it'll quiet the cacophony in my head.

The chill of the ocean greets me like a damp caress as I step off the bridge. For the first time since that conversation with Reece, I'm able to take a full, deep breath. I kick off my flip-flops and stride toward the ocean. I know it's there for me—ready to accept whatever I have to unload.

I sit down in the sand and open the pack of American Spirit cigarettes I picked up on my way over to Mel's. A whiff of the tobacco's earthy richness hits my nose. I take another deep breath and eagerly pull a cigarette from the box. Its filtered end feels comforting between my lips, kind of like a pacifier. The click of the lighter, the bright flame so close to my face . . . each step of this ritual feels like a rebellion against my failing marriage. The first inhale is short, stuttering, and followed by a cough. The second inhale is longer, deeper. The nicotine immediately makes me feel lightheaded while also melting some of the tension in my shoulders.

As I exhale a long ribbon of smoke, I remember the last time I had a cigarette. It was over a year ago, at Reece's thirty-second birthday party. The look on his face when we walked into the rooftop bar and everyone yelled, "Surprise!" had been worth all the planning. "Best birthday ever, Shug," he'd said.

When he started dancing with other women, it wasn't a big deal—at first. Some of them were our friends; others I didn't know so well. Like Holly, a blond wearing a little red dress. I'd sensed something more was going on, but he'd laughed me off. I'd felt guilty for suspecting. But I saw the looks and the hand that slipped down a little lower, then back up again less quickly. I knew there was nothing wrong with flirting. I did it. But for me, flirting was about getting into my own sexiness, not about the other person. Then I'd bring all that turn-on home to Reece. But was he leaving me a little bit every time he flirted with another woman? Was it about the other woman for him?

I push my way to standing and wobble for a moment before finding my footing on the sand. "You fucker!" I yell. "How dare you! How could you? We were going to have kids. We were going to do the whole big-family, happily-ever-after shebang. To love and to cherish till death do us part." I kick at the ground, releasing a spray of sand. Have these seven years with him been a total waste? I take one last drag—how can this guilty pleasure be over already?—and then pause, unsure of what to do with the butt. I'm not going to add littering to my list of sins. So I finish the rest of the wine in a few swallows and toss the remains of my cigarette into the travel mug. "Sorry, Mel."

Then another face crashes into me: Fiona. "And you! Back-stabbing bitch!" She had actually befriended me on a recent tour, when I joined them in Vegas for a four-night run there. I whirl around and throw the mug into the darkness. My hands clench. I kick at the sand again, only, this time, it's firmer and catches my toes. I trip and land face down in wetness. "Fuck." I pound my fists, feeling satisfied that they actually make an impression in the sand here at the waterline. "Aghhhhh!"

Exhausted, I flip over on my back and close my eyes. A cold trickle of water touches my bare feet. I don't move. The next wave wets my ankles. I shiver, wondering if the next wave after that will soak me entirely if I don't get up. But I don't care. Giving up and letting the waves carry me off sounds pretty good right now—easier than dealing with the sinking feeling that I made a huge mistake when I married Reece. I wish I could go back in time and not go backstage to meet him. Not give him my phone number. Not answer the phone when he called. Not go on that first date with him. Hell, not even go to the lounge in the first place. There are hundreds of other bars in LA we could have hit; why did we have to end up at that one? I groan. It's too late to undo any of it. So many little moments leading to such a big debacle. There's no way out. I might as well just stay here, lying on the sand.

Sabina, get up. A voice tugs at me. A woman's voice.

I open my eyes and shift my head side to side on the sand but don't see anyone. "Mel?" I call out, but there's no answer. My legs are wet now, almost up to my knees. The beach seems to be dropping away beneath me, pulled away, bit by bit, with each retreating wave.

Sabina, get up. The words beckon like a whisper in my ear.

I lean up on my elbows and look around. "Are you a Selkie? Here to save me?" I still don't see anyone and lie back down.

Sabinaaaaaaaa. The voice pierces me with its high pitch. I must be really drunk. But I didn't have that much wine. Or did I? "All right, all right." I push myself up just as a wave splashes my shorts.

There you go. The voice is quieter now. *Keep going.*

"Who are you?" No response. I sway as I stand up, a little more buzzed than I thought. I head toward the footbridge, then turn back, remembering the mug. It takes me a few minutes, but I find it. I remember to grab my flip-flops too. Then, as I walk toward the highway, I light another smoke. One for the road.

"BINA."

I lift my head at the sound of my name and . . . oh, crap. There's a vicious pounding behind my eyes. My mouth is dry and nasty. "Leave me alone . . . I just wanna sleep."

"Sabina." The voice is a bit louder this time.

"Wwwwhaaaat?" Suddenly, I remember I'm at Mel's house, in her guest bed, because my husband is sleeping with another woman. I think I might vomit.

"Your cell's been ringing. When I saw it was Dora calling you for the third time, I went ahead and picked up." I can tell by the sound of Mel's voice that the worry line between her eyes is activated. "It's . . . she said it's Lia—your Nana."

"Dora? Nana?" I shoot my arm out from under the covers, keeping my eyes closed against the bright light coming through the window. Mel presses the phone into my hand, then sits down on the edge of the bed. "Dora?" I practically shout. "What's going on?"

"Bina Bell, it's your Nana. She's . . . she's had a stroke." My grandma's best friend's voice sounds ragged. "She's in the ICU."

I bolt upright. "What happened? Is she going to be okay?"

"We were at Rosie McCanns, the Irish pub, with Ruth and Roo—all of us Library Ladies—enjoying mimosas. Lia almost dropped her glass, then she started talking all garbled. Thank the gods we were with her." She pauses. "We called an ambulance. And, well, Bina . . . they're not sure if she'll make it through the night."

For the second time in less than twenty-four hours, I feel like a bowling ball just hit me in the stomach. It takes me a moment to catch my breath. "I'll drive up to Santa Cruz now. I'll be there as soon as I can."

"Good. Just so you know, I called your folks too. Craig's actually in San Francisco for a meeting. He said he'd come right down."

Even though Nana is Dad's mom, "right down" most likely means as soon as it's convenient for him—and before he catches his flight back to New York City, where he and Mom live. I'll be surprised if he stays the night in Santa Cruz. He's always played the "business calls" card anytime he doesn't want to be present for something. As an investment banker, he claims to have important clients to woo at all times.

"And Mom?" My guess is she won't be able to make a trip out.

"She's having another flare-up. Hasn't been able to teach for the past couple of days. Poor Gwen."

The first few times Mom's rheumatoid arthritis flared up when I was a kid, I was terrified. It made no sense to me how one minute, Mom was up and about with lots of energy, and the next minute, she was knocked out, unable to talk. I was afraid she'd never get out of bed. Instead of asking her for help, I slowly became the one doing the caretaking. As I got older, the flare-ups happened less, but they seemed more intense when they did occur, as if making up for lost time. Mom probably feels awful about not being able to come to California. She and Nana bonded over their shared love of teaching the classics, especially Jane Austen's novels, long before I was born. They became even closer when I was a baby.

"Oh, Dora . . . is Nana conscious? Does she know what's going on?"

There's a pause before she answers. "She's in and out, Bina love. In and out."

After hanging up, I fill Mel in and head to the bathroom. Before I make the six-hour drive north, I've got to wash off the grit. I'm pretty sure it's not just the sand between my toes that's making me feel filthy. She follows me in and sits on the toilet. As I pull off my nightshirt and yank back the shower curtain, she says, "Lia was always like a fairy godmother to us when we visited her during college. It was amazing, you know? Within an hour of greeting us, after serving us tall glasses of her yummy lavender lemonade, she'd ask just the right questions. And she listened in that special way she had—the one where she put her eyes on you and tilted her head. Dang, one visit with her was more nourishing than a decade with my mom."

"I know. That's Nana's magic. But hey, no past tense." I've

thrown my hair into a messy bun. No time for washing and conditioning it, let alone drying it. But the hot water on my body is soothing, even as I become aware of my aching chest. Nana's my person. She can't go. Not yet. "She's still with us."

"Right. Sorry!" Mel calls out. "I'd offer to go with you but . . ."

"Shit! Your big celebrity wedding is today!" I pull the curtain open to look at her. "I was going to run food for you." Mel's been prepping this thing for weeks. She's been catering events in LA for eight years now, slowly getting more complicated, higher-paying contracts. But, up until this point, she hasn't gotten real high-profile gigs—the ones she's dreamed of orchestrating ever since we were nineteen and addicted to *People* magazine. This one is her big chance to break into the scene, and I was supposed to be there to support her.

"Ahh! I don't want to get wet!" She swishes the curtain closed and talks a bit louder. "I have Minh on standby. This thing is too important for me to not have backup plans. So don't worry. I'm just sorry I can't come with you. Hey, wait!" Her voice takes on a more excited tone. "James is in Santa Cruz, remember? He just took that job at the hospital—he might even be one of Lia's nurses. How wild would that be?"

"Oh, wow. James tending to Nana. Talk about a role reversal." As I turn off the water, I flash back to last night. "I'm sorry I used your travel mug as an ashtray."

"Yeah. I was gonna give you shit about that. I bet your mouth tastes sublime this morning."

"It's gross." I pull a towel off the rack and wrap it tightly around my body, as if it can protect me from what's coming, what I have to deal with when I step out of this brightly tiled safe zone. "Can you grab my toothbrush for me?" As Mel digs through my toiletry bag, a queasy sensation moves through me. Reece. Fiona. He slept with her. "Mel. What am I going to do about Reece? Us? Our marriage?"

She hands me my toothbrush with toothpaste already smeared across the bristles. "You don't have to figure any of that out right now. Get dressed, get that nasty taste out of your mouth, and get on the road. Go see Lia."

4

Santa Cruz, California

"JAMES!" I SPOT MY OLD FRIEND'S SOLID FRAME AND PERFECT crew cut at the nurse's station. He looks just as handsome as he did when I introduced myself to him in our freshman dorm. Back then, I was checking him out for my roommate. She was crushed to hear she'd never have a chance.

"Beans!" He comes out from behind the desk and wraps me in his strong arms. "Oh, girl." After holding me for a while, he steps back and frowns. "Why do you have grease on your face?"

"Oh, right. I blew a tire north of Bakersfield on I-5. Some guy pulled over, probably with a hero complex, offering to help. But I waved him off." I shrug. "Changed it myself."

He raises an eyebrow. "Well done. I can get you something for that. The grease, I mean."

"Thanks. But I want to see Nana. Is she . . . still . . . ?"

"Yeah. Lia's still with us. I'll walk you to her. Give me a second." He steps back behind the desk and talks in low tones with another nurse. Then he loops his arm in mine and guides me down the tiled corridor. "You just missed Ruth and Roo. It was a blast from the past seeing the Library Ladies again. I don't think I've seen them since . . . well, college, I guess."

"I bet." I glance at the name badge on his chest and spot the brown mala beads around his neck, tucked under his navy blue scrubs. A hospice nurse gave the strand to him when he was twelve years old. He once told me how holding and counting the beads had kept him from going over the edge as he watched his younger sister die of leukemia. That experience—the kindness of the nurse—was what led him to his career path.

"Not the greatest way to have a BFF reunion, though." He pulls me a little closer. "Beans, Mel told me about Reece too."

"Yeah, Reece." I rub my forehead. Luckily, James knows me well enough not to ask me more about that right now.

We stop in front of a closed door with the number 12 on it. He pauses with his hand on the knob and turns to me. "Before we go in, just know, this stroke hit her kinda hard." He must see the shock in my eyes because he squeezes my fingers. "She's still Lia, but different." He explains that a weakened blood vessel in the left side of her brain started bleeding. She's having difficulty moving her right side, and her speech is also impacted—a condition he calls "dysarthria." But he tells me that she knows what happened, who she is, and what year it is, and that these are good signs. "Ready?"

I nod, and he opens the door. Before I can fully take in the sight of Nana, Dora stands up from a chair next to the bed, her long silver hair frazzled around her face rather than hanging over one shoulder in its signature braid. She opens her arms to me. "Bina." I step into her embrace and get a whiff of the rosemary shampoo she's been using for years. For a few moments, neither of us speaks. Then she pulls back, and I look over toward the bed where Nana lies under a pale yellow hospital blanket.

"Sabina," she says—but she pronounces my name more like "Sawina." She's always been so articulate, so careful in her speech, that even with James's advance notice, I'm taken aback. Dora steps aside so I can move closer to Nana. I slide down into the chair next to her bed and take her in. She looks so fragile, with her chin-length white hair fanned out behind her on the pillow and her long arms motionless next to her slender frame. The wrinkles that I've always thought gave her face extra personality now make her look older than her seventy-six years. The machines connected to her on both sides of the bed beep and click.

"Nana." I reach out to hold her hand in mine, careful not to bump the IV, and notice her wedding ring is still on. She's never taken it off, even after Pops died seventeen years ago. "He may no longer be in physical form, but he will always be my beloved," she often said. I always hoped to find that same kind of love—and I thought I had. Who knows now. I look up and notice her lips are trying to curve into a smile, but only the left side lifts, like a one-sided mermaid tail. I bend down to kiss her cheek. "How do you feel?"

Her head makes the smallest of movements. "I . . . in a dream."

I scrunch my face up. "Not a really fun one, though, yeah? Not like the kind where you fly." I notice that her usually clear and bright topaz eyes are cloudy and dull. When she doesn't offer anything further, I look over at James.

"Dr. Patel will be in soon to give you an update," he says. "Meanwhile, Lia, we're all—the nursing staff—rooting for you. With prayers to all of our different gods and miracle-makers." He presses his hands together in front of his heart and bows to her. "You know it's karma, don't you, Lia? The fact that I'm here to take care of you." Nana makes her little one-sided smile as James turns to Dora. "Dora, you know it was Lia—not my parents—who encouraged my choice to become a nurse, don't you?"

Dora nods. "That sounds like her. Your parents were against it?"

He laughs a sad laugh. "They were against most things I chose. They wanted me to become a doctor and marry an old family friend, Wendy Clark. They were not so happy when I chose nursing and informed them I was more interested in dating people named William or Daniel."

"I remember that," I say. "It was during one of our 'Just Because' dinners. Nana slammed her fork down and said you couldn't go through life letting other people's decisions and opinions determine your path."

During the first semester of our freshman year, Nana had invited me to bring Mel and James down from Berkeley for a "Just Because" dinner—a tradition she had started with me during our summers together. "Just because we can," she'd said.

Mel had a beat-up Honda Civic, so the three of us had piled in and made the two-hour drive south for a dinner that turned into a weekend visit. After that, those dinners became a regular pilgrimage for us. We'd make the trip a few times each semester.

"'You're responsible for your own happily-ever-after,' she

always told us—didn't you, Lia?" James pats his chest, and I see her lips move slightly.

I think about Reece. About the decision he's making that's determining the fate of our marriage and what I thought would be the path to my—to our—happily-ever-after. I sigh, and the gush of air that comes out is much louder than I intended. At that same moment, I notice that someone is missing. "Wait, where's Dad?"

Dora gives me one of her looks that has genuine sympathy, annoyance, and *Well, you know him*, all rolled into one. "He was here. After an hour of sitting at Lia's bedside and charming all the nurses—"

"Hey, except for me," James interjects.

"I stand corrected." Dora smiles. "After he charmed all the nurses *except* James, he said he was sorry to miss you, but, since there was nothing he could do, and she was in good hands . . ."

I already know what she's going to say. "He left."

James nods his head.

"Did he say when he's coming back?"

Dora shrugs.

Of course Dad was schmoozing with the nurses. Women have always been attracted to his athletic six-foot frame, piercing green eyes, and carefully groomed red hair. I look back at Nana, whose eyes are closed. She and Dad were never very close when he was young, which she judges herself for. I've never been able to figure out why. As he got older and showed a preference for finance over family and making a profit over being of service, they grew even further apart. Around the time I was born, they had a big blowout. He was furious when Nana and Pops sold their three-bedroom farmhouse in Watsonville, a small agricultural city about twenty miles south of Santa Cruz. They'd let a cousin have it for a bargain. "They could've gotten a fortune from one of the big strawberry farms. Instead, they got just enough to buy a seaside shack in a college town. Ridiculous."

Before I can ask anything else about my dad, a man with bushy black hair and a white coat appears in the doorway. "Dr. Patel," James greets him. "You've already met Dora. This is Lia's granddaughter, Sabina." Dr. Patel's eyes narrow as he looks at me, probably noticing the grease on my cheek. I squirm in the chair. James continues, "If you'll excuse me, I have some other patients to check on. I'll be back later." Before stepping out, he gives the three of us a smile that seems to wrap us in a hug. He's a natural at his job. Even in the midst of all this, I'm glad I'm getting to see him do it.

Dr. Patel steps to the bottom of Nana's bed and explains that although they don't have to do surgery to relieve pressure around her brain, she's not out of the woods yet. He runs through a list of the different risks she faces, but I'm not able to take in all the details. I do hear him when he says that what she needs most right now is rest. "This is why I'm limiting visitors to one at a time and only from 11:00 a.m. to 2:00 p.m.," he states forcefully.

My mouth falls open. Dora jerks her head around and gives me an incredulous stare. "But, Dr. Patel!" I look back up at him.

He raises his hand. "This is the best way to help her right now. Depending on how she's doing tomorrow, we may start her rehabilitation with speech and occupational therapists. She'll need any remaining strength she has for that. I know you've just arrived, so you can stay for thirty minutes. But, after that, I must insist you leave. You can come back tomorrow."

"Well then," Dora says, her voice uncharacteristically thin, "I'll leave you to be with your Nana." She kisses me on my cheek—the one that doesn't have grease on it. "And Lia," she says as she pats Nana's leg, "I'll bring that book of Dickinson's poetry you love tomorrow to read to you. So, you best be here." She collects her purse and heads out the door.

Dr. Patel taps his gold watch. "Thirty minutes." Then he's gone too.

I slump in the chair and turn toward Nana. So much for being with her 24-7. I take a deep breath. She still smells like home—even here, amid the antiseptic scent of the hospital—like vanilla and lavender and a hint of something I could never name. "The Wild" was what she called it. I whisper the words I've been saying to her for as long as I can remember: "I love you, Nana. Like the ocean loves the shore."

"I love you, Sabina, like the shore loves the ocean." Even though she sounds like she's talking with sand in her mouth, her familiar reply soothes me.

She surveys my face for a moment before closing her eyes. I stroke her hand. Her skin is soft, thin—like the petals of a California poppy—and cool to the touch. I lay my head down next to our hands, wishing all of this were a nightmare I could wake up from. "Oh, Nana," I whisper. I'd like to tell her all about Reece but don't want to burden her. Suddenly, my entire body aches, like someone has pounded me all over with a meat tenderizer. My nose starts running, but I don't have the energy to look for a tissue. I tilt my head to the side so I can keep breathing and let the snot soak into the blanket.

I'd do anything to feel Nana's hand on my head right now,

hear her reassuring me that everything will be okay, somehow. But she doesn't move. All I hear are the sounds of machines beeping—steadily, mechanically, relentlessly.

5

I WAKE UP GASPING AND SUCKING IN AIR. I'M REACHING for someone, something, anything—but nobody is there. I blink. Wait; I'm not drowning in a raging sea. I'm not thrashing around in the huge waves I just saw and felt. But where am I? I reach above me, and this time, my hand hits something hard. I look up and can just barely make out my name etched in large letters across the headboard Pops and I made from recycled wood. Then it registers: I'm in my bedroom at Nana's—the bedroom that's been mine since I was ten years old. I'd crawled up here after almost falling asleep on the wicker couch on the front porch. Even though I love Nana's place, I had a hard time walking through the door of her vacant cottage after leaving the hospital. Until last night, I'd never slept here alone.

I roll over and look at my phone. It's 3:17 a.m. I hug a pillow to my chest and close my eyes, pretending for a moment that Reece is holding me from behind, his arm tucked around my waist. We used to sleep like that every night when we first moved in together, in our apartment in Los Feliz. But once we moved into the Silver Lake house and converted the garage into a studio, he stayed up most nights working in there. He'd come to bed late and not spoon me, saying he didn't want to wake me up. I strain to remember his smell, feel his warm breath on my neck. When did he stop holding me close? When did I stop reaching for him? Is that why he started reaching for her instead? Is he spooning her right now . . . or worse?

"Fucker!" I bolt up and throw my phone across the room, experiencing a strange sense of satisfaction as it hits the wall and falls into my open duffel bag. I plop back onto the pillows and scissor kick my legs in the twisted sheets. "Urggghh. You're supposed to be with me."

The burst of anger fizzles in my chest and dissolves into a long, shuddering sob. I curl up, fist to mouth. There aren't many tears—I must have dried myself out at the hospital yesterday—but the chest heaves keep coming until I'm choking and gasping for breath, like I'm in the nightmare all over again. Which I guess I am—only, it's not one I can wake up from. I cover my face with my hands. My head aches, right behind my forehead. When I cough, the pain is like a vise around my temples.

It's clear that sleep isn't going to come, so I slip out of bed and head downstairs, stumbling over a pile of my discarded clothes in the dark. Nana's cottage is as familiar to me as my parents' three-story brownstone in New York City, but there are no Persian rugs or antiques here. Even in the dark, I can weave my way through the hallway and around the overflowing bookcases that Pops made. In my mind's eye, I can see his initials carved on the top shelf: "PB" for Patrick Bell. I've memorized, too, the assortment of photographs hanging on the wall across from the couch. I know the smiling faces that watch over this room.

I'm drawn to the crystals hanging in the big bay window. They seem like ordinary pieces of glass floating in the dark, but I know their secrets. As I touch each one, I remember when and why Nana and I hung them. A small moon-shaped one after my cat, Luna, died, when I was eleven. A large round one after Pops died, when I was fourteen. A teardrop-shaped one the summer Mom and Dad separated temporarily, when I was fifteen. I can almost hear Nana's voice saying, "Even when it looks like the world has ended. Even when the tears keep coming. Look for the light. Look for the rainbows. You'll find them." Hanging these crystals was her way of making me commit to that. And here they are, carrying her voice now, even though she can barely speak in her hospital bed.

"Nana, I don't see any rainbows in this situation. Not with Reece. Not with you." My voice is hoarse. "Well, okay. You're alive. That's a huge rainbow. But for how much longer?"

I drag myself into the kitchen, past the butcher-block island to the fridge. It's covered with magnets whose sayings I know by heart: "Keep calm and read on." "The book was better." "We lose ourselves in books. We find ourselves there too." I reach up to a high shelf and find what I'm looking for: a bottle of Teeling Irish whiskey. Pops's favorite tumbler with the weighted bottom is next to it. I pour a couple inches of the amber liquid into the glass, then pause to breathe in the fumes before taking a sip, just like he used to do it—slowly and with great appreciation. After holding the fire in my mouth for a few seconds, I swallow. It slides down my throat, a river of heat.

The air seems to shift around me, like the house is sighing. "I know. You miss her too. I wish I could tell you for sure when she'll return, but I can't." Although Dad was upset with them for buying this place, Nana and Pops had always dreamed of having a "cottage by the sea" when they retired. I couldn't picture Nana ever being anywhere else.

I rest my forehead on the cool glass of the sliding doors and stare out at the backyard. The studio, a separate building about ten yards from the back deck, seems to glow a little in the darkness. My easel is in there. I can see it clearly, as if I have X-ray vision: it has been in the back corner, covered with a paint-splattered drop cloth, since I left it there. Seven years ago. The window fogs up in front of my mouth. Out of habit, I draw a heart in the little cloud left by my breath.

I grab an ivory cable-knit sweater hanging next to Nana's apron and pull it on over my nightshirt. With one last gulp of whiskey, I set the glass on the counter and open the door. The grass is soft on my bare feet. The studio is locked, but the key is in its usual spot, under a big clamshell next to the entrance.

Opening the door and stepping inside, I'm transported back in time.

I WAS fifteen years old, pouting at the breakfast table, when Nana sat down next to me wearing one of Pops's faded denim shirts. "What's the one thing in the world you love the most besides the ocean—not including people?" she asked.

I responded without hesitation. "Painting."

Her twinkling eyes told me she was up to something. "What's the one thing in the world your Pops loved the most, besides you and me and your dad?"

"Working in his shed. Building things. Fixing things. Making them whole again."

"And . . . what was one of your favorite things to do with your Pops?"

"Hang out in the shed with him."

She reached out and placed her hand on mine. "How would you like to help me clean out the shed and turn it into a studio for you to paint in?"

A smile spread across my face for the first time since Graham—my summer romance and first love—had gone MIA five days earlier. "I'd love that. I think Pops would too."

"I think you're absolutely right." She raised our hands to her mouth and kissed my tanned fingers. "And, given that you have a big sweet sixteen coming up, I'll take you to the art store to get that wooden easel you've been checking out. It's time, Sabina. Time for an easel upgrade. Just like every woman needs a room of her own, so, too, does every painter need the accoutrements of her craft."

I SLOWLY adjust to the lack of light and look around the studio. During my summers, I spent so much time here the space began to feel like a temple. I kept coming here even when I was living in Berkeley. The studio was my place to retreat to on weekends and during breaks—a way to get out of the city, out of dorm life, out of the logical, methodical world of business classes. Up until I moved down to LA to be with Reece, that is.

Now, it smells musty. There are boxes of books sitting on the counters and stacked on the floor. Donations from the Library Ladies, I bet. I wonder if all of my summer beach reads—the Harlequin romance novels I'd coveted so much as a teen, much to Nana's chagrin—are in one of these boxes. They're really just grown-up versions of the fairy tales I grew up with—*Sleeping Beauty*, *Cinderella*—all those formulaic stories that suggest a woman can't be happy or survive on her own. I've always had mixed feelings about them. I loved the drama, and I loved skimming through to get to the sexy scenes. But I hated how even the strongest heroines seemed unable to rescue themselves from horrible situations. All they could do was wait for a man to show up and save them. And then marry them. That was what made for a happily-ever-after.

I push a stack of books out of my way to reach the easel. The drop cloth is covered with a thick layer of dust. I fold it back slowly, carefully. At the sight of my heavy-duty H-frame friend, a strange sound erupts out of me—part cry, part laughter. "Hi, you," I whisper, not caring how foolish it is to be talking to my easel. I stroke the smooth wood. "It's been a long time. Too long."

The day Nana and I went shopping, I thought we were going to get the simpler A-frame design. It was less expensive and would have been fine. But Nana had surprised me. She'd done some research and knew the H-frame was better suited for larger canvases. She encouraged me to go as big as I wanted. That had reminded me of Graham's sweatshirt—the one that said GO BIG OR GO HOME in big capital letters. The one I had somehow ended up with.

My attention is drawn to the small nine-by-twelve-inch canvas resting on the easel. It was one of the studies I'd done in preparation for a much larger mural Dora had invited me to paint on the outside of her gallery in downtown Santa Cruz. I pick up the canvas and reach over to flip the switch on the table lamp. As the light flickers on, the painting in my hand seems to come to life for a second. Four women dance around a fire on the beach. Their hips are mid-sway. Their arms and faces are raised to the full moon. Long hair streams down their backs—brown, black, red, blond. Nearby is a pile of furs, a mound of russet, charcoal, and light gray. The cobalt blue water laps at the shore. The mood of the painting is dark and mysterious, yet there's a warm glow to it too. I'd added a thin, almost translucent, layer of gold and Naples yellow paint over and around the dancers to both soften and lighten them. I wanted to show their otherworldly nature. Looking at the painting now, I actually think I succeeded.

I sit down on the stool with the painting in my lap. I hadn't yet gotten to working in Thoreau's quote, "All good things are wild and free," in large cursive letters along the bottom. It felt right to include it, though, given how wrapped up this saying had become with the story of the Selkies. I lean my head back on the wall and close my eyes to savor the memory that surfaces.

"HAVE YOU told her about the Selkies yet?" Dora asked Nana in a conspiratorial whisper. It was my first summer staying with Nana and Pops, and I was just getting to know these women who would become such fixtures in my life.

I looked up from my corn on the cob. "Selkies? What're they?"

"It's not what they are." Dora waved her glass in the air, not noticing—or minding—that a few drops of her watermelon martini splashed out of it. "It's *who* they are."

I looked back and forth between them where they sat at the picnic table, taking in Dora's pink feather boa and the sparkly tiara she'd insisted Nana wear for our special girls' night. She'd adorned me with a smaller one with purple glass gems, right after Nana had French braided my hair. *They are the most extraordinary women I've ever met*, I remember thinking. Dora's cackle was loud, like a sea lion's bark. And she could get Nana laughing so hard that tears streamed down her face. They didn't talk down to me or treat me like a visitor. They treated me like I was one of them, one of their special club—like they'd just been waiting for me to join them for their summer shenanigans.

Dora set her glass down, then said, as if sharing a secret with me, "The Selkies are 'seal folks' who are able to change from seal form to human form by taking off their fur. There's a Celtic story about these mythological beings, about how a fisherman came upon a group of women dancing on the shore under a full moon. He was so mesmerized by their beauty that he wasn't watching where he was going and tripped over a log, making a loud noise."

Nana continued the story. "The women fled to their pile of furs, pulling them on and diving into the ocean one by one. But the fisherman was able to grab the last fur. Even though the remaining woman begged for him to give it back to her, he refused."

I leaned over my plate, my corn on the cob forgotten. "What happened to her?"

Dora shook her head. "The woman had no choice but to stay with him. She couldn't return to the sea without her fur. On land, without her fur, she had two legs and could pass as human. So she stayed with him, forced to be his wife."

"Some say she fell in love with him," Nana interjected.

Dora clucked in agreement or disbelief; I wasn't quite sure which. "They even had children. But no love could compare to the love she had for her true home. One day, she found a key. She didn't know what it opened but had a feeling it was important. She searched all over the house and finally found a chest in the basement, sitting under a pile of blankets she'd never noticed before." She paused for dramatic effect. "And guess what? The key fit the lock perfectly. Inside the chest, she found her fur. It had been hidden there all those years. She pulled it out and held it in her hands. The fur was the real key to her freedom. But what was she going to do? She loved her children and didn't want to leave them. She knew she had to make a decision quickly, since the fisherman was expected home soon. So, even though it pained her, she said goodbye to her two children and returned to her true home . . ."

"The sea?" I asked. Dora and Nana nodded their heads in unison.

"The moral of the story being," Dora said, raising her glass to Nana's as they both said together, "'All good things are wild and free.'" She swirled her cocktail. "Your Nana and I have been calling upon the Selkies for help and guidance since before you were born."

"But they're not . . . real . . . are they?" My eyes must have been as big as a seal's.

"Selkies are like mermaids," Nana said, tapping her heart. "They're real in here."

I noticed the end of one of my braids was dangerously close to a pool of melted butter on my plate and swung it over my shoulder. "Have they actually helped you?"

Nana took a bite of watermelon before answering. "Absolutely. The Selkies have helped us when we're in the ocean and drifted too far from the shore or have gotten caught up in a strong current. They seem to know everything about the sea."

"And emotions. Isn't that what emotions are like?" Dora reached her arms out wide. "The ocean? Big waves that move through us." She patted her chest. "The Selkies always seem to find a way to help us navigate heartbreaks and tough emotional things too."

"The important thing to remember, Sabina," Nana waited until I looked her in the eyes before continuing, "is that the Selkies work in mysterious ways. Your job is to ask for help and trust that they'll show up for you, one way or another."

In the days following that dinner with Nana and Dora, I began to call upon the Selkies. My mom prayed to some invisible god at night, so why couldn't I talk to these magical beings? When I was out in the ocean and felt afraid, heck, when I was anywhere—even back in New York—and felt afraid, I called to them and asked for help. Support always showed up, often in the form of courage. I began to think of the Selkies as my own personal guardian angels. Who needed Prince Charming?

But I'd been upset that the Selkie abandoned her two children. I had so many questions. Wouldn't she miss them? Could they go with her and survive since they were part Selkie themselves? Did she ever return to visit them? Did she have another family in the sea?

I'd also been angry. I wanted to know why the fisherman stole her fur and took her from her true home. How could she have fallen in love with someone who did that? Or had she just pretended to? Why hadn't the other Selkies who knew what had happened to her tried to help? Nana had listened to my concerns, and we'd spent hours discussing possible answers to these questions, though we never settled on any.

Later in my teens, another story, the one that inspired my mom and dad to name me Sabina, troubled me as well. My parents took turns sharing it with me year after year on my birthday.

"Your dad and I were in the same classical mythology class at NYU," my mother began. "When it came time to write a paper about a controversial myth, we both chose the Sabine women. There was only one book in the library about them, and I had it."

Dad would jump in. "So I asked your mom out for coffee. By the time we were done, we'd debated the Romans' motives and the reasons why the Sabine women stayed, and I wasn't going to let this blue-eyed beauty go until I knew when I could see her again."

No matter what issues these two had with each other over the years, my mother always blushed when she told this part. "I'd had a crush on your dad, who was a year ahead of me, all semester. I was thrilled when he wanted to go out with me. One date led to the next, and, well, when I became pregnant with you, we thought about naming you after the Sabine women since they had brought us together. When you were born, with your red curls and big kicks, we knew you were going to be strong, just like them."

But how did choosing to stay with their captives make them

strong? My curiosity drove me to learn more. I discovered that the Roman men had abducted women from the Sabine tribe to make them their wives. When the Sabine men came to rescue them, it's said that the women intervened, demanding that the men put down their weapons. They didn't want to lose their fathers and sons, nor their new husbands. So they negotiated a peaceful settlement and chose to stay with the Romans. Both my mom and dad thought the Sabine women stayed because they were able to enjoy certain privileges they hadn't had before, like owning land. Dad viewed them as smart businesswomen: they knew they were being treated as commodities, yet when they saw their options, they chose the men who could offer them a better life.

A YAWN erupts from me. I lift my head from the studio wall and rub my eyes. With the Sabine women as my namesake and the Selkies as my patron saints, I've secretly wondered if I'll ever find peace with men—or myself. Does my strength come from my ability to fight or surrender and give others what they want? Do I have to stay away from men to have what *I* really desire? Can I be with a partner in a way that allows us both to chase our dreams, or am I cursed by my birthright?

I shake my head, remembering how Reece had used "All good things are wild and free" to justify his infidelity. It felt like he was taking all that I held as sacred and turning it into a permission slip to do what he wanted without considering—or caring—about the impact of his actions on me.

My belly twists into knots as the extent of this cosmic joke hits me. When I was working on the study sitting here in my lap, I was preparing to share the story of the Selkies with all of Santa Cruz and launch my painting business with a mural project. Instead, the Selkies were left behind, forgotten. The reality of this deflates me.

When I'd announced my plans to put the mural project on hold, Dora had given me one of her "strong talks." Nana had remained silent while Dora warned me against making a man my first priority. But then Nana piped up and asked, "Sabina, is this what you really want?" I'd said yes. I was falling in love. Reece was inviting me into a whole different life that had seemed exciting and promising. All I wanted was to spend time with him and give him everything I had to support his dream. It really did seem to make sense at the time. Why does it feel like a punch to the gut now?

I turn off the light and lock the studio door behind me. Why does falling in love feel like a form of captivity? Why does someone—and isn't it always the woman?—have to give something up?

6

"EXCUSE ME?"

I whip my head around toward the sound of a man's voice. He's standing several feet away from me on the beach with a camera in his hands. I'm in my bikini and wrapped in a towel, having just taken off my wetsuit. Although I'd finally been able to fall asleep after the nightmare and my visit to the studio, I'd woken up feeling restless. So I decided to come down here for a swim as a strip of dusty rose light glowed along the horizon.

"I'm sorry to disturb you . . ." He's looking at me in a strange way—like I'm a mirage. His eyes are the color of the ocean on a stormy day. Unable to find my words, I nod at him. He smiles, and several small lines appear around his eyes. "Bella?"

The way he says that old nickname sparks a glimmer of a memory—big waves, a surfboard, the Selkies. I scratch the scar on my forehead. "Yes." I say it almost as a question. Then a name I haven't heard, let alone said, in a long time slips out of my mouth: "Graham."

His face lights up. "Bella, it's . . . it's so good to see you again. It's been . . ."

"Ages." His laugh is big and rumbling, but I can't return his smile. I feel scattered, disoriented. Memories of our summer together fly through my mind: Graham and I running down the cliffs together, diving into the water, racing to see who could reach the lighthouse first. Eating ice cream on the wharf. Riding the thrill rides at the boardwalk. The ache in my chest when I woke up one morning to discover his Jeep was gone from the driveway next door, that he'd left Santa Cruz—that he'd left me—without saying goodbye.

And then he's wrapping me in his arms. "I'm all wet," I protest. But he either doesn't hear me or care, and I find my arms slipping around him, breathing him in. He smells earthy, like pine.

"I never thought I'd see you again," he whispers. I pull back quickly. "Bella, you look great." I step back and reach down to pick up my fallen towel. *Bella.* He'd given me that nickname when I was fifteen. We'd been sharing cool words we knew in other languages when he'd mentioned that Italian, Spanish, and Portuguese all shared the word "*bella.*"

"Your last name is Bell, your laughter sounds like bells, and you're beautiful," he'd told me. The nickname stuck. I smile at the memory.

"There it is. I've missed your smile." Gazing at him, I take in the familiar face, and yet, the rest of him . . . there is no more boy here. He is all man, from the scruff-covered jaw and the thick brown tousled hair to the strong shoulders and lean build.

He pulls his eyes off of me and scans the beach. I watch him take in this half-mile stretch of sand, bordered by the lighthouse at one end and a long sandstone cliff on the other. I wonder if he's picturing all the picnics and campfires we had here, or the countless times we walked around the cliff at low tide to get to the boardwalk.

Before I can utter a word, he's doing that thing he used to do: answer my unspoken questions. "There are a lot of memories here."

"Mmm." Is it shock or grief or something else that's keeping me from saying more?

Graham cocks his head to the side, returning his attention to me. "How are you, Sabina?"

Do I tell him how my entire world is a wreck? First Reece and now Nana and . . . no. I can't go there. Besides, I've just barely gotten myself together enough to go for a swim. "Well, right now, I'm curious to know what brought you back to Santa Cruz and this cove."

He gives me one of his looks that lets me know he sees through the deflection. But he lets me get away with it, just like he used to, and answers. "Well, that's a bit of a long story, but the short version is family and . . . work." He raises his camera. "I turned my passion for photography into a business. My home base is Anchorage, but I've been invited to do a workshop at Esalen this month—you know, the hippie retreat center down in Big Sur."

"You must be pretty good to receive that invitation." I decide not to ask about his family.

He shrugs. "I've done okay for myself." My belly growls, and Graham laughs. "Do you want to grab a bite to eat? A coffee? Or maybe an ice cream like old times?" He grins. "I'd love to catch up."

I'm tempted. An outing with him would help distract me from the mess that is my life, at least for a little bit. But, between the way he's looking at me and the fluttery sensation in my chest, I'd better not. I sense that I could get caught in a riptide when I've just found a little bit of ground to stand on. "I . . . I've actually got to get going."

"Then, maybe another day this week?" His voice is deeper than it used to be.

Let him in, I can imagine Nana whispering to me. *For goodness sakes, Sabina. Let him in.* Nana always did have a soft spot for Graham. "Remember my grandma's—Lia's—place?"

"Your Nana!" His eyes get big. "Of course! Yeah, of course I remember her cottage on Seabright Avenue."

"Well, I'm staying there right now." I reach down to grab my wetsuit. "You can stop by this week. If I don't answer the door, come around back. I might be in the studio." The words come out of nowhere, taking me by surprise. *I might be in the studio.* And yet they feel so natural, so right.

"The studio?"

"Oh. Yeah." It dawns on me that he never knew the building as a studio. "The old shed."

His smile broadens. "So, you're still painting."

I bite my lip and offer a noncommittal shrug. "Anyway. Like I said, I have to go." I'm suddenly aware of how abrupt I'm being with him. But this man's not the one I loved so many years ago. Or the one who left without saying goodbye. That was young Graham. Seventeen-year-old Graham. A boy. I don't know this man. And yet, as we lock eyes, I can almost feel the firm touch of his hand holding mine, his full lips brushing across my mouth, the way we pressed against each other in the water, teasing, tempting, curious. Damn. There's that riptide again.

As I take a step toward the path that leads up the cliff, I remember the voice I heard while I was swimming—the woman's voice that had called my name and told me it was okay to be in the depths. The one that I've been holding on to for the last twenty minutes, since I almost melted down about Nana, Reece, and the disaster that is my life. I was probably just imagining things. But, still. The timing is curious. I turn back to Graham. "The Selkies still visit here. Perhaps you'll be lucky enough to see one again." I wave goodbye and walk away.

"I think I just did," I barely hear him say.

7

Sixteen Years Earlier

I TURNED MY SURFBOARD AROUND AND STARTED paddling for the shore.

"Paddle like you mean it!" Zach shouted.

My heart was pounding. I looked back over my shoulder. From down on my belly, the wave looked bigger than any wave I'd ever seen.

"Pop up! Now!" His voice carried through the roar of the ocean. The wave was rising beneath me. I was trying to remember everything he'd taught me back onshore. Lift my upper body off the board. Keep my hands in cobra position. Slide my legs up to my hands. Don't let my hips go higher than my head.

For a second, I felt my feet land flat on the board. But then, the back of the board lifted up, and I was staring down the steep face of the wave. The nose of my board plunged into the water, and I followed, tumbling headfirst. After that, everything went dark. The wave crashed over me, pushing me down. My board, connected to my ankle by a short cord, tugged me in some direction—upward, I hoped. I paddled fiercely, trying to get to the surface. But more water pressed down on me. My chest felt like it was going to explode. I kicked as hard as I could.

Finally, I found air and gasped for breath. Then another wave came right at me. I closed my mouth just as it hit and pushed me under again. *Selkies! Nana! Help!* I screamed silently. The cord on my ankle jerked, twisting me around. Then something smacked my forehead over my right eye. A stabbing pain radiated through my head and into my jaw, my neck. Something rough scraped along my side. *Selkies! Please get me out of this!*

My arms felt weak. I couldn't seem to kick anymore. I thought about how easy it would be to stop struggling.

Then someone was pulling me up onto a board. "Hold on to this," a voice said. I felt the cuff of the leash on my ankle release. "Hey, really. You gotta hold on, okay? Another wave is coming."

I coughed and reached for the edges of the board as the water lifted me. The voice didn't sound like Zach's. I tried to turn around to see who it was but winced at the pain in my side.

"It's okay. Let the wave carry you. I've got you."

I wondered who this stranger was yet closed my eyes until we reached shallower water.

"Can you slide off the board and walk to shore?"

I started to nod but winced again at the lightning bolt of pain that shot through my head. I slid off the board, put my feet down on some slimy rocks, and tried to stand up on wobbly legs. I managed to make my way up to the wet sand and sink into it. After a couple of deep breaths, I looked back toward the water.

He was carrying both of our surfboards. Bleary-eyed, I watched him. Tall. Lean. Water streaming off his brown hair and black wetsuit. He looked a little older than me but not by much. It was hard not to notice he was hot, even in my condition. He set the surfboards in the sand and squatted down next to me.

"Are you okay? How many fingers am I holding up?"

"Seriously? I'm not that messed up." But my head throbbed and my body ached.

"Seriously." He wagged his fingers at me again. "How many fingers am I holding up?"

"Twenty-nine." I bit my lip to hide my smile.

"Ha. Very funny. Really." There was laughter in his voice, but he kept a straight face.

I guessed he thought I might have a concussion. "Three."

"What's your name? What year is it?"

I answered, figuring he'd taken a first aid class and was being thorough.

He sat back and let out a big breath. "Okay. You're right. You're okay. But you are bleeding. We should get you to the hospital. You might need stitches."

"I'm bleeding?" I reached a hand up to my forehead and felt wet stickiness near my hairline. The cut wasn't gushing, but it was tender to the touch. When I pulled my fingers away, they were covered in blood.

"Hey, Sabina! What the heck happened? Are you okay?" Zach was running up then, looking back and forth between the two of us. His gaze settled on my rescuer. "Who are you?"

"I'm Graham." He stood up, rising a few inches above Zach. "Who are you?"

Zach puffed his chest out as he narrowed his eyes and responded. "I'm Zach. I was giving her a lesson and—"

"What? A lesson?" Graham looked down at me and asked, "Was this your first time out?"

I started to nod, but it hurt. I grimaced. Graham's face contorted. He turned to Zach, looking like he might hit him. "You're an absolute idiot. You let her go out in this swell for her first time? Her board is too heavy and way too small. This break at four or five feet is not for beginners." His voice got even sharper. "What, were you trying to impress her or something?"

Zach looked over at me, then back at Graham. "Dude, who do you think you are?"

"You guys, cut it out." I tried to get up but couldn't push myself off the ground.

"Hey, wait. Let me help you." Graham dropped down beside me and looped his arm around my waist. With his support, I was able to stand up, slowly. I got a little dizzy and reached out to grab his other hand. Something passed between us then like an electric shock. "I . . . I'm okay now."

He was looking at the gash on my forehead with obvious concern. "You really need to get this checked out, Sabina." I shivered at the sound of his voice saying my name. *Get a grip*, I chided myself. I was acting like a character straight out of one of my romance novels. Luckily, he misinterpreted my response. "Are you cold? I've got towels in my Jeep. I can take you to the hospital."

Zach put his board down in the sand, as though getting ready for a fight. "What are you, her savior or something? She just had a bit of a wipe out. No big deal."

"No big deal?" Graham pressed his lips together and shook

his head. "You weren't there. You didn't see her board whack her on the head." He waved his arms as he talked. "And drag her against those rocks over there. She could have a concussion. She's probably going to need stitches. All thanks to your stupid recklessness."

"Hey, Graham," I said quietly. "I really appreciate your help with not drowning and all, but I don't even know you."

"I'm Graham Gray. I'm from Anchorage." My legs started to buckle. He reached out to steady me and there it was again—that electric shock. "I just graduated high school. I'm here for a summer course at the university. I'm staying with friends of the family over on Seabright Avenue. My mom's name is Sarah. My sister's name is Sam. I've got a battered old Jeep parked right up there." He nodded his head up toward the top of the bluff where the stairs led to a small parking lot. "There. Know me enough now to let me take you to the hospital?"

I started to laugh but grabbed my side. "Okay. Yes. You can take me to the hospital. But we'll need to call Nana—my grandma. She can come and meet us." Oh, Nana. Hadn't I promised her I'd curb my impulsive risk-taking?

"But, Sabina—" Zach protested.

"Zach," I wrinkled my nose. Why did I say yes to him? Ever since I'd met him a couple weeks before, I'd been telling him I was a swimmer, not a surfer. But he'd been so persistent, telling me I'd love it, and that this was our last chance to get out on the water together, since his family was leaving town soon.

The throbbing in my head worsened, like someone was using my temples for a drum. So much for falling in love with surfing. "Since neither of us have a car, let alone a driver's license, I'm gonna go with Graham. It'll be fine. You'll get the board, yeah?" He nodded reluctantly. "Oh, and my bike."

"The Jeep's got a bike rack," Graham said as he grabbed his board.

Zach scowled at Graham but didn't say another word as we turned and made our way across the sand.

Up at his Jeep, Graham helped me pull off my wetsuit and gave me a towel and a sweatshirt. "GO BIG OR GO HOME, eh?" I read the words that were emblazoned across the sweatshirt before pulling it over my head.

He shrugged and smiled. "Yeah. It's an Alaskan thing." He grabbed my wetsuit from where it hung on the door and threw it in a plastic tub with his. "But when you're first starting off with surfing, better to go small. Small waves. Big board."

"Or just go to the hospital."

He laughed then, a big rolling sound that vibrated through my chest and made me smile.

"Don't make me laugh again," I groaned, clutching my side.

"Hey, you're the one who said it!" We grinned at each other. But then the smile faded from his face as he said, "Come on, let's go. I wasn't kidding back there. You really might need stitches." He strapped his board on the roof, fins up, as I stood there rubbing my arms to warm myself up. "Where's your bike?"

I pointed to my red cruiser leaned up against the fence next to the stairs. He lifted it onto the bike rack then helped me step up into the Jeep and closed the door. From the driver's seat, he paused with his hands on the steering wheel and turned to me. "Okay, point me toward the hospital or urgent care, whichever is closest."

After I gave him directions to the urgent care on Soquel Avenue, I rested my head on the seat, closed my eyes, and breathed in the warm air flowing through the top and open sides of the Jeep. But then I saw glimmers of the dark water again, felt the knot in my belly, and tasted metal. I gasped and sat up a bit more and then gasped again when the small movement triggered pain in my side. Tears flooded my eyes. What might have happened if he hadn't pulled me out of the water? I shuddered. *Thank you, Selkies, for getting me out of there.*

I could feel his eyes on me. "It really hurts, doesn't it?"

"Yeah."

"I've had a few wipeouts myself. They can be nasty."

I wiped the tears from my eyes with the soft cuff of his sweatshirt and looked out the window. The buildings and palm trees on Forty-First Avenue blended together, blurry and familiar. Nana would be concerned but not angry. I closed my eyes again and breathed in and out slowly, counting to myself, "One, two, three," like Pops taught me to do when I'm hurting.

"We can call your . . . your Nana . . . from the urgent care."

I looked over at him, taking in his profile. "Are you a mind reader?"

His laughter set off another thrumming vibration. "What makes you say that?"

"I was thinking about her right when you said that." I remembered his introductory speech on the beach. "I live in New York City with my folks, Craig and Gwen Bell. But I've spent my summers here with Nana since I was ten. I'm fifteen now."

"Cool. New York City, huh? Do you like it there?"

"Yeah, I like the city—there are so many great art galleries.

And it's so alive. So crazy. But I love spending summers here with Nana. She'll tell you to call her Lia. She's cool. She's . . ." I glanced over at him. Suddenly, my head didn't hurt quite so much, and I wanted to tell him about the Selkies.

He looked over at me and nodded, encouraging me to keep going.

"Well, Nana, she's . . . she used to tell me stories of the Selkies growing up."

"The Selkies? What are they?"

When we reached a red light, I remembered he didn't know where he was going. "Oh. Turn left at the light." He put on his turn signal. "So, the Selkies . . ." I began. And I ended up telling him the story of the magical, mythical shape-shifters I'd come to believe in. He really listened, like Nana always does. And Mom occasionally does. He wasn't dismissing me like Dad would. "And, well, I know this might sound weird, but I called out to the Selkies today, asking them for help. And then . . ."

"I showed up?" He glanced over at me.

"Yeah," I said quietly.

"Hmm." Green light. He made the turn and then glanced over at me. "But they're just a myth, right? Do you believe in them?"

"I used to, when I was younger." I twisted a wet curl of hair between my fingers. "And even now, the Selkies don't feel made-up to me, like Santa Claus or the tooth fairy. I sense they . . . that even though they don't exist as actual seal people, there's a magic about them. Like there's a mystery in the depths of the ocean. Something beyond what we can see and experience with our eyes, I guess. So yeah. It's that—the magic and mystery of the wild—that I believe in." I suddenly got a bit self-conscious about how that must sound to someone other than Nana and Dora. But it was the truth; it was what I thought.

To my surprise, he didn't scowl or look at me strangely. Instead, he nodded thoughtfully. "The magic and mystery of the wild. Yeah. I believe in that too."

Before I was even out of the urgent care's treatment room, Nana had asked him all about his passion for photography and the course he was taking and invited him over for dinner. He'd accepted. And as it turned out, he was staying right next door. That began what I called "The Summer of Graham."

8

"BINA?"

"Beans!"

Voices call to me from the front porch, but they don't quite penetrate the daze I'm in. I'm entrenched on Nana's couch, staring at the crystals hanging in the window. I've barely moved since visiting her in the ICU. But when the door opens, and I see James's and Mel's faces, I snap out of my fog.

"Hey, honey," they both say at the same time. Mel sets down a cooler, slips off her sandals, and comes over to the couch, sitting down beside me and wrapping me in a hug. James kicks off his All Stars, plants a kiss on my head, then flops down on the floor in front of us.

"Mel, you drove up all the way from LA? What . . . why?"

She grabs a throw pillow to put behind her on the couch. "Well, after the celebrity wedding—which went great by the way!" She stretches out the word "great" into several syllables while raising her hands in the air in triumph. "I was chatting with James and when I mentioned that I had to meet a couple in San Francisco tomorrow morning, for another gig, he suggested this . . ." She waves her hands at the three of us.

James wiggles three of his fingers. "We decided it had been too long since the three musketeers had been together."

"I just delegated the cleanup to my staff," Mel says. "You know, now that I'm a caterer to the stars and all, I don't do dishes anymore." James makes a face and raises his hand like he's holding a teacup, pinkie finger sticking out straight and proper. They've never failed to make me laugh.

They both look around, taking in the room they probably remember. I glance over at the photos on the wall—one of them features the three of us during a summer campout in the backyard. "When was the last time you were both here?"

"Uh," James taps me on the leg as though that helps him remember. "It was . . . wait for it . . . our college-graduation party nine years ago?" He furrows his brow. "Could it have been that long?"

"Yeah! It was. Wow." Mel whistles. "But we've seen Lia since then. At your . . . wedding."

"Oh, yeah." The mention of my wedding is like a paddle, stirring up the nostalgia I've been wading in ever since my drive up here from LA. An image of Nana lifting her champagne glass to make a toast to Reece and me flashes in my mind. What had she wished for us? Something like lots of laughter and the right amount of challenges to help us grow, I think.

"James gave me an update," Mel says. "Said Lia's hanging in there. How are you doing? Have you heard from Reece?"

"I'm not sure how I'm doing, honestly. I've been in a strange, altered state. Like . . . is this all really happening?" That's the best answer I can provide. I'm trying to not pay too much attention to how I'm doing for fear of what I might find. Mel squeezes my toes. "Radio silence with Reece. Both ways. I thought about letting him know about Nana, but I just couldn't bear to have him come up here out of, you know, a sense of obligation or . . ." I can't bring myself to say the word "loyalty." "Whatever. And I . . . I had another nightmare last night."

"Ugh. What's happening in them?" James asks.

"Every night, I get tossed around by these crazy ocean waves. I feel like they're coming after me, wanting to swallow me up. I wake up feeling like I can't breathe. Like I'm going to drown. They're really intense." I take a deep breath. I love the ocean. I've so often found relief in it. It's really troubling to feel like it's tormenting me.

"I wonder what's asking for your attention," James says, as though talking to himself.

"What do you mean?"

He reaches out and puts his hand on mine. "You know, nightmares are often unconscious fear and anxiety bubbling up. So maybe there's some kind of message your psyche is trying to convey to you."

"Like what are you thinking, James?" Mel asks as she massages my feet.

"I don't know." James shrugs. "What if you didn't resist them? What if you let them . . . have you?"

"You mean, like, let go into the waves?" A dream fragment from last night pulses through me. "They're so menacing. I feel like the only thing I'll find in there is . . . death."

Mel raises her eyebrows.

"Well, what do I know?" James says. "Maybe you should keep resisting them. Maybe they do just want to have their way with you and drown you." He gets a mischievous look in his eyes as he moves closer to me and walks his fingers up my arm. "Or maybe," he continues in a Casanova-like accent, "They just want to make love to you and are upset that you keep rejecting their advances." Mel throws a pillow at him, but he ducks, and it lands on the floor behind him. "What?! What did I say?"

"Oh, James." I give him a playful shove. "Go take your lustful fantasies and share them with Caleb. I'm sure he'd enjoy them." Although I haven't met Caleb yet, I've heard all about him. He and James were introduced by a mutual friend at a New Year's Eve party last year and have been dating exclusively pretty much since then, which is a big deal for James.

"Don't worry, Beans. This isn't going to be your life forever. It's just right now. That's why we're here tonight," he says, raising his eyebrows up and down.

I squint and look back and forth between them. "What do you mean?"

Mel rubs her hands together. "We're taking you out tonight, Bina."

"You guys," I groan. "I don't want to go anywhere."

"Oh, come on. It'll be good for you to get off the couch. In fact," James leans over and sniffs me. "Good thing we got here when we did. Had we waited till you responded to our text messages, you might've just rotted away here. You're smelling pretty ripe, you know that, girl?"

Mel stands up. "Off to the shower with you. We can't have

you stinking to high heaven when we take you out. It's First Friday, baby," she purrs. "Gallery night!"

A spark of light ignites in my chest. First Friday. Art. Galleries. Cheese and crackers everywhere. This ritual is one of the things I love about Santa Cruz.

"We won't make you talk with anyone. You can just drink the free wine and mope around in the galleries." James stands up and reaches for my hand.

I take it and let him pull me off the couch. As I make my way upstairs, I hear Mel call out, "I'm stocking your fridge with lots of juices and food!"

"I don't promise not to eat any of it!" James's laughter follows me into the bathroom.

AS HOT water pours over my body, I remember how Nana, Pops, and I used to go to First Friday together every month during my summers here. I was so inspired by everything I saw that I'd come home and stay up late painting in my bedroom. Although Nana and Pops had gotten me watercolors and oil paints to play with, too, acrylics were my favorite—more flexible, and no fumes. I could water them down or layer them on thick and texture them with the different tools and palette knives I'd begun collecting.

Then we'd have what we called "Fourth Friday" at the house with the Library Ladies, where I displayed all the art I'd created during the month. At first, it was just for fun, and I'd paint over my canvases the following month. But there were times when someone wanted to purchase one of my paintings and hang it in their home or give it as a gift. They'd ask me, "How much?" and, after much hemming and hawing, I'd finally give them a number. I was amazed every time someone paid me, but it made me feel so powerful.

When anyone asked me to describe my style during those Fourth Friday conversations, I could never find one specific word to capture it. "Expressionism" came close. I painted the feelings, images, and inspirations that moved through me, letting them all pour onto the canvas however they wanted, guided by my muse. That continued to be the case as I painted throughout college and business school. I never felt like I belonged in one particular stylistic niche.

I put some jasmine-scented shower gel onto the loofah and slide it over my body. Ever since modeling nude for life drawing classes in college, I've had a greater appreciation for my curves. I like the roundness of my small breasts, the way the right one is a little heavier than the left. Reece loves to slide his hands from my narrow waist out to my hips and my butt. In our early days, we'd shower together and take turns washing each other. Inevitably, the washing led to kissing, which led to more. I shake my head. Reece *used* to love doing that.

I squeeze the loofah, then rinse off, thinking about my muse, whom I haven't heard from in a while. I suppose I stopped hearing her when I became Reece's muse. At least, that's what he'd called me in the beginning: his muse. He said I inspired a resurgence of new lyrics and melodies. Of course, that made me feel so special, so important. Who doesn't want to be a muse, right?

When it came time for his band to choose the cover art for

their first album, I'd offered up a few different designs. Reece had taken time to look them over, but, in the end, they'd gone with someone else's art. I thought the cover they ended up with was too dark and polished for their acoustic-driven rock music, but it wasn't my choice to make.

I roll my shoulders a few times before tilting my head back into the spray of water. I can see it so clearly now: The more I supported Reece and the more time I spent on his music business, the less time I spent on my art and the quieter my muse became. It's like she's been upset with me for turning my back on her. During Reece's last tour, when I was home with some extra time and energy, I'd thought about pulling out my paints, just like I had a handful of other times when he left for a while. But just like those other times, I felt dried up. There were no images to guide me. No sense of purpose or upcoming show to light a fire of inspiration. My muse was silent.

After drying off, I dig through my duffel and pull out a pair of flowy black pants and a fitted black scoop-neck top. A memory pops to mind of standing behind Reece's band during a concert, tucked into the shadows backstage, wearing a black Sunset Rangers T-shirt and black skinny jeans. We'd joked afterward about how I fit right in with the roadies. Ugh. I'm so over my LA-music-scene look, but I don't have much else to wear. I put them on but make a mental note to go thrifting sometime soon and find something—anything—with color.

Before heading downstairs, I linger in Nana's bedroom. Her familiar smell—the smell of The Wild—is especially strong here. "Nana," her name escapes my lips as I collapse into the chair at her dressing table. How many times have I stood here, next to her, helping her pick out her jewelry for the day? Watching her brush her hair or adjust a scarf around her neck?

I turn to the collection of scarves and shawls hanging from her closet door. The blue cashmere one with the cool ombré effect, the one I'd given her for her last birthday—her seventy-sixth—is draped on top. I pull it down and wrap the soft fabric around my neck and shoulders. As I look into the mirror to adjust its folds, I see my green eyes shadowed by long nights spent staring at the ceiling. I look like I've aged a couple of years this week.

"Beans?"

James's voice pulls me away from the mirror and down the stairs. Maybe being around art will resuscitate my muse—or, better yet, my life.

9

AT THE THIRD GALLERY WE VISIT, I STAND FOR A WHILE, mesmerized by a painting that captures the curve of beach by the Santa Cruz boardwalk. I know this spot. I've walked that beach and ridden every ride, from the swings to the roller coasters and everything in between. The lights from the park at night are mirrored back in the water, captured in swirls of thick oil paint. The double image of the park seems to waver in front of me; it's as though I'm standing on the beach watching the reflection shimmering and shifting in the moving water.

As I turn to the next piece, I'm transported out of the gallery and onto the craggy coastline in the photograph hanging there. It perfectly captures the waves of my nightmares. I feel the movement of the water in my belly, my womb. I hear the crash of the ocean on the rocks, smell the pungent sea air, taste salt on my lips, and feel the warmth of the setting sun fading away. But instead of feeling afraid, now I want to move closer. I want to dance with the sun that is sparkling and reflected in each drop of water.

"Bina?" Mel's voice calls to me as if from far away. I register a hand gently placed in the crook of my arm. I glance at her and look back at the image. "It's stunning," Mel says. She bends forward to read the placard beneath the photo. "Ooh. It's called *Her Power*. By Graham Gray. Why does that name sound familiar?"

Startled, I look down at the name to see it for myself. Graham Gray. After not seeing him for sixteen years, he sure has shown up a lot over the past two days.

"You know him, don't you?" All I can do is nod. "Let me go see if he's here tonight and if he has any more photos in the show."

The moment she walks away, I'm back on the coastline. Fortunately, I'm not drowning. I hear something, something beyond the crashing. Is it someone . . . singing? *Sabina, come see us.* The voice sounds familiar. I step forward and reach a hand out.

"Hey, girl. Earth to Beanie-babes," James sings out, draping his arm around my shoulders.

I'm drawn back into the brightly lit room. Right, First Friday. This is where I am. I drop my hand and turn to James. "Were you singing for a little bit before coming up to me?"

"Nope," he says, looking at the photo and then at me. "I just got here. But from the looks of things, you've been somewhere else."

"Yeah." All I hear now is the white noise of people chatting behind us. What does Graham know about "her power"? Who is *she*, anyway? And how is it that his photo is here? My heart thumps, almost tripping over itself. Is he here as well?

Mel comes up and gives me a hip bump. "Well, turns out the photographer, Graham Gray, left for the night. He just has this one piece here. The majority of his stuff is in a gallery down in

Carmel." She looks at me curiously. "Bina, what has you so transfixed by this photo?"

"It's, well, the waves. They look so familiar, like the ones in my nightmares. Only, they've been totally transformed and turned into art."

James's eyes get wide. "Whoa."

"Yeah, wow," Mel adds. We all stand there, side by side, staring at the photo.

"And the guy? Graham Gray?" James asks. "How do I know that name?"

I briefly remind them both who he is—my first love—and tell them how he turned up again just yesterday, a coincidence that still has me off-balance.

"Wowzer. Looks like your past is leaking into your present, Beans," James says.

Mel shakes her head. "That's weird timing." Then she grabs my hand. "We still have one more gallery to take you to. But before we go, did you want to get this piece?" Mel bends down and looks at the placard. "Oh, never mind. The red dot is on it. It's already been sold."

I look at the photo one more time, tucking this moment into my heart, like a Post-it Note reminder: crashing waves can inspire awe instead of fear. *Her power.* Maybe there is something in the depths of my nightmares that's worth exploring.

Next up is Dora's gallery, Soul Whisper. The whole place is a Dora hug, from its red door and the bells that jingle overhead when we walk in to the sound of jazz playing on the stereo and the scent of sandalwood. Although she claims not to have a creative bone in her body, I know better. She has a gift for making warm, inviting places like this. I scan the familiar interior, taking in the sculptures placed around the room. They're each unique, and yet they have a common theme: they're all made out of found objects. I move toward a sculpture of a dolphin composed entirely of driftwood. As I run my fingers along its smooth surfaces, a movement catches my attention. I glance up to see my own reflection in a round mirror. It's encircled in driftwood, with each piece radiating out, long and thin, like an individual sunbeam. Next to the mirror is a seahorse, made in a similar fashion.

As I wander among the creations, I'm reminded of the long summer days I spent on the beach as a young girl. I'd wander around, gathering shells, driftwood, seaweed—even pieces of plastic—and place them all in a big pile. Then I'd sit with the treasures to see what they wanted to become. Once a vision came to me, I'd create sculptures. Some simple, some elaborate. Some lying flat, others rising up out of the sand. As the bright day faded into twilight, I stepped further and further into the stories the sculptures shared with me. Everything was safe and exciting and magical. Creating something with my hands, turning what I saw inside into something tangible outside of me, gave me a sense of power. I would let the tide take my artwork away at the end of the day—except for the plastic bits, which I'd toss into a recycling bin on my way home.

In time, I came to realize that making art, whether it was on the beach with those sculptures or on the canvas with my paints, had been my way to escape Dad's moods and the heavy presence of his absence. It hadn't always been like this, though. When I was younger, he took me to Central Park on the weekends to ride the carousel. Or we'd hop on the Staten Island Ferry to see the Statue of Liberty and go out to lunch on the other side of the river. As I got older, we'd go to the National Museum of Mathematics together. The place satisfied both Dad's love of finance and my emerging passion for art, although swiping a brush across a digital canvas didn't give me the same satisfaction as I experienced with real paints. But by the time I was in middle school, Dad had started to check out. He put his work above everything else, including his family. When I suggested we do something together—anything, really—he'd either snap at me or ignore me. I'm not sure which was worse. Both his impatience with me and his indifference left me feeling confused and unimportant.

As I reach out to touch a sculpture of a sea lion with eyes made of blue sea glass, I remember Mom going all out for my tenth birthday party. She made a mermaid cake and took a small group of my closest friends to the aquarium, where we got to watch a sea lion show. Mom always did that sort of thing, and she attended my swim meets and other events at school when she was able to as well. Yet, even though she was there physically, she often seemed distant and vacant. When I tried to talk with her about difficult things, like a fight with a girlfriend or a barely passing grade, she'd seem overwhelmed and unsure of how to respond. Then she'd withdraw even more into her shell. Eventually, I stopped turning to her for any kind of emotional support. When I was in high school, her flare-ups worsened, and her health took center stage at home. Then, I felt like it was my job to support her.

I turn away from the sea lion sculpture and dip my head under a chandelier that's dripping strings of oyster-shell pendants. Another movement catches my attention. Outside the front window is a tall man with light brown hair, half of it pulled back into a man bun. Reece. And he's not alone. He's holding hands with a woman with blue-black hair. Although she's recently dyed it, I recognize Fiona's pixie cut. And I'd know that petite, curvy body anywhere. I watch as they look at each other, laugh, and then cross the street.

All the air rushes out of me. I want to flee, but I don't want to go out into the street. I can't be close to them. Then I remember the courtyard behind the gallery. I take long strides toward the back door. As I pass Mel, I whisper, "I just need some air," and keep walking.

I slam the door handle down and forward and am met with a cool breeze. I pull Nana's shawl tighter around my neck and make my way to the bench next to the four-tier cascading water fountain. What are Reece and Fiona doing here? My hands curl into fists in my lap. Is he here for First Friday? Since when is seeing art his idea of a good time? I dragged him to the LA County Museum of Art once during one of my first weekend visits. We'd spent so much time making out against one of the pillars out front that we'd almost missed the special exhibit I wanted to see. The picture of us intertwined together, acting like horny teenagers, is like a weight on my chest, making it even harder to breathe.

The sounds of music and people laughing and talking drift through the open back door. I look up and see Dora's familiar form. She closes the door behind her. "Sabina? Is that you?"

"Hi, Dora." I look at her through blurry eyes.

"Oh, dear." Dora comes and sits down next to me, pulling me into a hug. I breathe in her familiar scent—rosemary and mint. She releases me from the hug but keeps an arm wrapped around my shoulders. "Tell me about this," she says, touching my fists.

"I want to throw up. Or break something. I just saw . . ." I take a breath then blurt it out. "I just saw Reece and Fiona."

"What?" Her puzzled face reminds me that I haven't said anything yet to her or Nana about my marriage. I've just wanted us to focus on Nana getting better and returning home. But now it's clear I need to fill her in. "Oh, Bina Bell," she says when I'm done. "What do you think they're doing up here?"

"I have no idea. Seeing art, maybe. Something he never wanted to do with me."

We lean into each other, the fountain gurgling beside us. "Heartbreak can be such a miserable storm." She cradles one of my fists in her warm, wrinkled hands.

"And I'm scared, Dora. Scared that Nana's not going to make it."

She purses her lips. "I know. Me too."

"All of it, combined, it's . . . it's just wrecking me. I can't stand it."

"Yeah." We sit in silence, rocking slowly. "This is a lot to be with right now. Have you talked with your mom at all?"

I let out an audible sigh. "Yeah. I called earlier today to check in. But you know her—she just doesn't talk the language of emotions. There was a lot of awkward silence. And besides, she's struggling right now with her own physical pain. I listened to the play-by-play of her doctor's visits, all the details about various experimental drugs she might be able to try—you know, her medical reality. I haven't told her about any of what's going on with Reece—just shared updates on Lia."

"Hmm." She nods slowly and doesn't say anything for a while. Unlike with my mom, silences with Dora and Nana aren't awkward. They feel natural, meaningful even. "Have you been painting? Swimming? Letting it all move through you?"

"I went swimming. I've also been . . ." I stop and bite my lip.

She shakes her head at me. "This is a no-judgment zone, remember? Tell me. What are your vices? We all have 'em. You're not going to shock me."

I scrunch up my face. "American Spirit cigarettes. And, well, it was red wine at Mel's. And good ol' whiskey at Nana's."

"Ah, yes. The smoking-and-drinking combo. I know that one well." A half smile works its way across her lips. "The key to vices . . ."

"Yeah?"

"Is remembering they can serve a purpose at times. They're a welcome respite from the intensity of the pain and emotional turmoil. But at some point, you gotta face that turmoil to make it through to the other side. You skip over that stuff and guess what? You just repeat that madness and make more messes. You know how I know this?"

"Three husbands." I've heard a version of this talk about vices—and repeating messes—over the years. And I've heard about the mistakes she's made with all three of them. Somehow, she's kept trying, kept having the courage to let people in.

"Exactly. So, enjoy those smokes in the short term. And . . ." She perks up and looks at me, eyes glinting from the white twinkling lights hanging above us. "You know what it sounds like you could use?"

Immediately I know what she's thinking. "The Wall?"

She wags a pointed finger in my direction. "Yes, exactly!"

The heavy weight on my chest lightens a bit. Dora was the one who created The Wall for me. The summer Pops died, I was overwhelmed with grief. Nana suggested I see an art therapist, Elise, who introduced me to process painting. When I told Nana and Dora about my experiences in Elise's office, how she encouraged me to express my emotions through the paint and onto the canvas without any consideration of the end result, Dora nodded. But she had a plotting look. Then the following week, she invited Nana and me up to her house and introduced us to what we began calling The Wall: a ten-by-twenty-foot section on the outside of her barn covered with wallboard. It was the biggest canvas I'd ever seen, and it was all for me. I was speechless.

"I still remember what you told me back then," I murmur.

She squeezes my hand. "That you have big emotions that deserve a bigger canvas and the chance to be expressed anytime you feel like it, not just during therapy." I nod. "Well, it still stands true. Some good old-fashioned do-it-yourself therapy could be just what you need again. When was the last time you let yourself have it all out like that?"

I stare down at my feet. "It's been way too long, Dora."

"Well, everything is where it used to be. You're welcome anytime." She releases my hand. "I'll be here at the gallery for a few more hours, so you'll have the place to yourself."

"Dora, thanks. I could really use that." My hands curl into fists again. We sit in silence. Although her presence has alleviated my initial wave of physical revulsion, a storm is still raging inside. Pushing it down is not the answer. I've been doing that, and it's only giving me nightmares. I need to try something different. "Will you tell Mel and James that I left? I want to go to The Wall. Now."

10

I HANG NANA'S SHAWL OVER MY BEDROOM DOOR, PULL off my black clothes, and dig around in the closet. After a few minutes I find what I'm looking for: my paint-stained denim overalls. I poke around some more and come up with a faded pink tank top. Slipping into both, I take a deep breath, feeling like I just put on a life jacket. I'm a bit more equipped for navigating the big waves inside of me.

I jump in my car and head up to Bonny Doon, a community about twelve miles north of Santa Cruz, nestled in the redwoods. The way to Dora's is so familiar that I slip into autopilot as I navigate first the straight, open stretch of Highway 1 and then the dark, twisty roads into the mountains.

About twenty minutes later, I pull into Dora's long driveway, pass the house, and park next to the old barn. When I step out of the car, I'm greeted by the sound of crickets. The night air is cool on my skin. My hands tingle, and there's a buzzing inside my torso, like a swarm of bees begging to be let out. I head straight inside the barn to the shelves in the back. Dora was right: everything is where I left it the last time I painted here, which was years ago, before I met Reece.

I throw some big brushes and the drop cloth in a bucket and grab a few cans of paint. Out on the deck, after setting the supplies down, I flip a switch and the row of gooseneck barn lights illuminate The Wall. Red and orange explosions of paint leap out at me. Splashes of yellow and blue overlap, making lightning bolts of green. Blue and black stripes crisscross each other, fading away toward the upper corner, where I could never reach with a brush. Purple handprints pop out like polka dots over mud-colored layers.

My lips tremble as I take it all in. The world seems to spin for a moment as memories of what prompted these chaotic expressions run through my mind. When Pops died. When my parents separated. When Graham disappeared. When Marco cheated on me.

"They all leave. All the men. First you, Pops. I forgive you; you died. But then Dad left. Repeatedly. Then Graham left. Then Marco left, also repeatedly. Then Reece left. They. All. Leave."

I throw the drop cloth down next to a spot on The Wall that I had whitewashed years ago, covering over a previous DIY therapy session in anticipation of a moment like tonight. I fill the bucket with water from the back tap and pry the tops off of the cans of high-gloss, water-based housepaint. Thankfully, they're not dried out. I dip a four-inch brush into red paint and run it across The Wall in a jagged back-and-forth movement. "Fuck you, Reece." I do it again. "Fuck you, Reece." This time the words seem to erupt from my belly.

Still holding the first brush in my right hand, I grab another and dip it in the black paint. I slap The Wall with the bristles, again and again and again. "Fuck you. Fuck you. Fuck you." The paint lands in splotches, sprays in drops. Then I hold both brushes next to each other and swipe The Wall with them, from right to left, then left to right, up and then back down, overlapping—red on black on red, becoming its own dark-blood color.

My chest burns. An image of Reece taunts me. His dark chocolate-brown eyes gleaming, his wide lips curling up at the edges as he leans in for a kiss. "Shugga, give me some sweetness to tide me over till I see you again," he used to say before leaving the house, even if he was just going to the nearby store for cream for my coffee or wine for our dinner. But then the image shatters like glass and is replaced with one of him kissing Fiona.

"Ugh! Fuck you. Aaaaaarghhhhhhh!" The buzzing inside grows louder. I throw off my sweatshirt. Look around behind me. It's all dark. The closest neighbor is at least a mile away. I growl again, this time louder, "Aaaaaaaaaaaarrgggghhh!" I dip the brushes into the cans again—still red and black. These are the only colors I want right now, the only ones that can express this turmoil. I raise my hands over my head and whack the paintbrushes against The Wall, both at the same time, again and again, letting out a yell each time I make contact. "I hate you I hate you I hate you I hate you! Fuck off fuck off fuck off fuck off!"

"And you! Fiona. Homewrecker. You are a horrible, horrible person." I drop the black brush and slash over what I've just painted with more red. I imagine I'm ripping Fiona apart with each smack of the brush. "Fuck you fuck you fuck you, you hateful, mean bitch." I fill the brush again and slap red up and down, back and forth, up and down, back and forth, over and over and over again.

I stumble and stand back, swiping my arm across the snot on my face. Words push through the knot clogging my throat. "Oh, Nana. Nana, Nana, Nana. Please don't leave me yet. Not yet." I throw the red-coated brush down and pick up another brush. Dip it in yellow. On a mud-colored spot nearby I paint circles, looping one over the other. "Nana, Nana, Nana." I turn some of the overlapping loops into a flower with a yellow stem. "For you, Nana," I whisper. Then I smear a strip of yellow over the loops. And another. I hear Elise's voice telling me so many years ago, "It's not about making anything pretty. It's about letting it all come out. However it wants to."

Shivering, I set the brush down and pull my sweatshirt back on. I notice the swarm of bees is no longer buzzing inside. They're quiet—or gone. The burning in my chest has subsided. The knot around my throat has dissolved. The skin on my cheeks feels tight from dried tears.

Moving slowly, I rinse the paint off my hands in the bucket of water and use a corner of the drop cloth to dry them off. Too tired to deal with cleaning the brushes, I drop them in the bucket of water to soak. As I put the lids back on the cans of paint, I consider driving home, but I don't want to leave The Wall. It's like we just started a conversation again after years of silence and I can't tear myself away.

I grab a blanket from the back of a chair and wrap it around me, breathing in the smell of a bonfire drifting over from a neighboring house. I turn the lights off, lie down on the wicker couch near the picnic table, and peer up at the stars. How many times did I lie out here with Dora and Nana and Pops? "There it is!" I used to point out the Big Dipper to them. One of them would inevitably say, "Open up! It's pouring stardust into your heart so that you remember your magic!" I could use some of that stardust right about now.

11

WAVES CRASH AGAINST THE ROCKS NEAR WHERE I STAND. An airy voice hums a wordless melody. I look around, but I see no one else on this craggy coastline. The song morphs into words and seems to be coming from the waves.

Come see us.

I take a step forward, toward the water.

"Bina?"

The singing stops. "Don't stop," I mumble, reaching my hand out. I take a step into the water.

"Hey, Bina Bell." This is a different voice—a distinctly human one, and it's very close to my ear.

I moan and open my eyes to the morning light. I don't see any waves or rocks, just Dora standing with two mugs in her hands. "Dora? What time is it?" I rub my hands over my face.

"It's a little after eight. I'm sorry to wake you. I was hoping to spend a little time with you before I head into town." She offers me a mug.

"Mmm . . . It's okay." The singing. Was that in my dream? The waves. The waves! They weren't menacing. They weren't part of a nightmare. Something has shifted. I sit up quickly, pulling the blanket with me. "I wasn't really planning on spending the night here last night but . . . hi." I reach for the familiar mug. It has an owl's face on it with the words "Woo-wooo loves you?" coming out of its mouth. I take a sip of what Reece always referred to as my milk chocolate, given how much cream I use in my coffee. I push away thoughts of his morning voice—the sexy, scratchy sound that so often made me reach for him before he slipped out to the studio. "Thanks, Dora."

"My pleasure." She slides a chair over and sits down next to me while scanning the newest additions to The Wall. "Looks like you let yourself have at it."

I lean back on the wicker couch and take a look at what emerged last night. The colors, the textures . . . there's a strange beauty to seeing my emotions like this, outside of my body. It's not pretty. But it's not ugly either. "I was surprised how much poured out of me and how fast it did." The stark black reminds me of the abyss I felt like I was in when Reece told me he slept with Fiona. The red carries with it the energy of a stop sign, an alarm, saying, *This is not okay.* The red and black merge in some places to create shadows that could hide secrets, and in other places they create what look like streaks of dried blood. The bumpy texture where I slapped and sprayed the paint makes me think of a carcass. Like the remains of an imploded marriage, I suppose. "I . . . I lay down to stargaze for a few minutes afterward and then, well . . . here we are."

"Yeah. It can take a lot of energy to hold back those tidal waves of emotions. And when you finally let them go . . . well. It can zonk you out."

"Tidal waves. That's what it felt like, Dora." I take another drink of coffee, the caffeine a welcome boost. "I've had nightmares lately. A lot of them. With menacing waves that seem like they want to drown me." I shudder. "But, last night, no nightmares. Instead, this morning, I heard some kind of singing coming from the waves. But maybe that was just you calling my name." I shrug. "Either way, this is so much better."

"Hmm." She doesn't look at me as she takes a sip of coffee.

I look over at her. "I know what you're thinking." Dora raises an eyebrow. "Selkies."

She shrugs. "Hey, I didn't say it. You did."

"Well, how could I be your goddaughter and not consider that option?" I remember the conversation with James about my nightmares, how he thinks something is trying to get my attention. "You know, you and Nana always encouraged me to ask the Selkies for help. To call upon their shape-shifting magic. To listen for and trust their guidance. And, well, I'm getting the sense they're inviting me into a deeper conversation, just like The Wall is—a conversation I've been neglecting."

"A conversation with yourself?"

I nod. "Yeah."

"Sometimes it takes life falling apart for us to wake up to that most important conversation." She fixes me with a look. "I'm glad you're not neglecting it—yourself—anymore."

"Yeah. Me too." We're silent for a few moments, listening to the birds singing their little hearts out. "Any word on Nana this morning?"

"No. But I'm planning on visiting her during the lunchtime hour, as usual." Given Dr. Patel's strict orders about visiting,

Ruth and Roo have been splitting up the first hour, then Dora has taken the lunch hour, and I've been visiting at 1:00 p.m. and staying until he comes in and glares at me.

"I wonder how long it will be till she . . ." Comes home? Dies? I grit my teeth. "It's bonkers that the doctor won't let us be in there with her all the time."

"I know. We want to be with her—like we can keep her here with our presence. But I know she hates being the patient, and I also sense . . . well, it's a very intimate conversation for someone to be in with their maker." She purses her lips. "Your Nana, she . . . she might be engaged in that conversation right now in ways we can't fathom since it's not close to our time."

"Oh, Dora. I don't want to be the one keeping her here if it's her time to go." The thought of doing that makes me cringe. "And yet, she always is one to do things on her own, isn't she? She's so brave."

"Well, that's where you get it from." Dora sets her mug down and pulls her silver hair off her back and into her hands, combing through it with her fingers. I watch as she starts to braid it, a ritual she has probably engaged in for most of her seventy-five years.

Last night I didn't feel so brave when I ran in the opposite direction of Reece and Fiona, and I mention this to Dora. She points toward the barn with her chin as her hands continue to braid her hair. "Doing what you did last night, coming up here and letting it out on The Wall rather than continuing to try and push down all the waves—being with yourself, letting those emotions move through you—that took courage. That's an intimate conversation with yourself too." She pulls an elastic band out of her pocket and wraps it around the end of her braid.

"I guess so." I pull my knees up and wrap my arms around them. "Although it kinda feels like I just had a major temper tantrum . . . like I was three again and not getting my way."

"Bina Bell. Don't you dare do that." I look at her, startled by her sharp tone. "Don't you minimize something that's cathartic and healing. Sure, it's like a temper tantrum. A meltdown. But it's a healthy one. Process painting is a release of all the emotions building up in you. And there are a lot of them. Let's look at your situation for a moment, shall we?" Her tone softens, yet her fierce brown eyes remain locked on mine. "Your husband is having an affair and has basically left your marriage for this other woman." She leans forward in her chair and holds up a finger. "Your favorite person in the world is in a hospital room teetering between this life and the next." She holds up a second finger, then waves them at me for emphasis. "These are two big things to be with. Of course you have feelings. Of course! And letting them *explode out of you* onto The Wall or a canvas instead of *imploding you*, as they would if you tried to swallow or suppress them—which you can never really do—is a sign of maturity and bravery." Only when I nod slightly, acknowledging her words, does she sit back in her chair and take a drink of coffee. "Okay. Strong talk complete for now. But you needed that."

I reach for a tendril of hair that's fallen out of my messy bun and twist it in my fingers. "I . . . thank you, Dora. I did need that." I feel a cramping in my belly. The coffee has done its job. "I suddenly have to go to the bathroom."

"I'll walk over with you." As we get up, she puts an arm

around me and guides me toward the house. "Bina Bell, remember, you don't have to go through all of this alone. If and when you want to talk with me more about any of this, or use The Wall—*mi casa es su casa.*"

"Thanks, Dora." We say our goodbyes, and I watch as she gets into her car and pulls out of the driveway. Before heading into the house, I glance over at the barn and, for just a moment, I feel like I can hear the voice again, crooning that breathy, wordless melody. "I'm listening," I declare. "I'm finally listening."

12

THE CELL PHONE ON THE PASSENGER SEAT BUZZES AS I'M driving back to town. My finger pauses over the green button, and my heart thumps when I see the name on the screen. I wish he'd called ten minutes ago when I would have been out of range. But I press the button, noticing the dried yellow paint on my fingernail as I do. "Hi, Dad."

"Hi, Sabina. How are you holding up?" His voice is curt, like I'm just another call he has to make before another important business meeting.

"Um, I'm . . ." The truth is I'm not holding up. But I don't want to admit this to him. "It's hard to see Nana this way." Not the full truth, but true.

"Oh, Pip. I know how close you are with your Nana." His tone is sympathetic, at least. "It is hard to see her in that hospital bed. This is difficult for me too."

Yeah, right, I want to groan. *So difficult you keep going about your life instead of making an effort to be here?*

"Mm-hmm," is all I say.

"What's the latest?"

"I'll know more this afternoon when I go in to see her."

"Good. Then you can call and give me an update from the hospital." This isn't a question or a request. This is Dad's way of communicating—in expectations. How can he not want to be here with her, knowing she could go anytime? He kept his distance after Pops died too. He was at the wake, of course. But before and after, he expected me to give him updates. I can picture him checking his watch or looking up at his assistant as he talks, motioning to let her know he'll be done soon. "Are you and Reece staying at the house?"

I grip the steering wheel and force myself to take a breath before answering. "No. I mean. *I* am. Reece isn't with me."

"Why not?" His tone has shifted to an accusatory one.

Why aren't you here? I want to ask. Stopping at a red light I decide to let it all out, just like I did on The Wall last night. I answer through gritted teeth. "He's not here, Dad, because he's having an affair with another woman."

"Hmm." He clears his throat. "Well, Sabina. We both know you have a temper. Did you do something to push him away?"

The light turns green and I press hard on the gas, flying by the Jeep on my right. The dog in the back is a blur of black and white. "Dad, are you kidding me?"

"Reece is a good man. He's also a reasonable man. I'm sure you two can work things out. He might take you back. Just consider it."

His words feel like a slap on the cheek. *What—like Mom took you back, repeatedly?* I want to yell. But at the last minute, I stop the words from spewing forth. I realize I don't want to explode on him like I did on The Wall. I don't have to; I have other outlets. And I know what will happen: I'll bump up against his defensiveness. By this point in life, I've learned that he lashes out when he feels judged in any way, like a cornered wolverine. It makes me nauseous every time. "I have to go. I'll talk with you later. Bye." I jab the red button on my phone, disconnecting our call. At the next intersection, I make a U-turn and head back up to Dora's.

Fifteen minutes later, I stand in front of The Wall again. After surveying what erupted from my inner volcano last night one more time, I whip off my sweatshirt and stare at the pile of supplies I'd carried back out to the deck. Then I let my hands take over and do as I'm guided. I pour red paint into a plastic tray. Grab a nine-inch roller brush. Dip it in the water bucket. Press it into the pool of color, wheeling it up and down till it's coated red.

"See if he'll take me back? What the hell are you thinking, Dad?"

I strike The Wall with the roller brush, hitting the wood right at the edge of yesterday's explosion. Then, I roll the brush up and down, back and forth, as high and as far as I can reach. I press harder. Stretch farther. Each stripe of paint spews forth the fury broiling in my belly. "*I* have a temper? Maybe *I* pushed him away? Oh, Dad. That's classic." I hit The Wall again and again. Drops spray all over it, all over me.

My other hand aches to get involved. I set the brush down, pry open a can, and pour some of its brown paint into another tray. I grab a second roller, dunk it in the water, then tug it through the paint, shifting it into my left hand so I can pick up the first brush with my right. With my hands together and the rollers side by side, I pull color across The Wall in zigzag motions for several feet. "Yeah I have a temper. I'll show you temper. Arrrrgghhhhhh! Fuck you!"

My arms drop to my side then lift up again. This time, I let them move haphazardly in jagged lines. As the brushes stretch up and down, left and right, faster and faster, I'm barraged with memories. Dad telling me to knock it off when I gave him a hard time about missing the award ceremony during my freshman year of high school—the one where I'd received special recognition from my art teacher. Dad flirting with my coach when he'd finally bothered to show up for my swim meet. Dad and I yelling at each other when he insisted I get an internship at his company rather than spend my senior year in Italy for an art program. Dad demanding that I major in business in college. Dad declaring he'd only pay for grad school if I got my MBA, not a master of fine arts. "It's a waste of time, Pip. You can't live on your painting. The phrase 'starving artist' is a reality for too many idealistic dreamers. Get a real job. Like me."

With a staccato beat, I slap both brushes against The Wall in quick, short bursts. "Talk about a waste of time. I've completely wasted my life. I let you bully me into a business career path and then let Reece become my biggest priority. And what do I have to show for it? Nothing. Absolutely nothing. Aarghhhhhh!"

I toss the brown roller behind me and immerse the other one in the paint. Then, I grip the handle and smear the brush up and down, up and down. The red mixes with the brown to create a deep burgundy color. "So, Dad, you're saying it's my fault Reece cheated on me? Left our marriage? Like that's *my fault*? That I pushed him away? Yeah, okay. My fault I fell in love with a guy who was a cheater. My fault I didn't see him for who he really is. My fault I stopped painting to support him in his dream of becoming a successful rock star. My fault I said I didn't know what I wanted and stopped paying attention to my dream. My fault my fault my fault. *Aghhhhh!*" I throw the roller at The Wall. It hits with a splash of paint and falls on the drop cloth with a thud. As I step backward, my foot slips on the other roller brush, and I come crashing down, knocking over the bucket of water in the process.

A sound pierces the quiet morning air. A loud howl. Like an animal in pain.

It takes me a second to realize that the sound is coming from my own mouth. Then I feel a river streaming down my face. I twist over onto my side and hug my knees. A grenade of doubt blows up in my chest: Maybe it is my fault. Oh shit. Maybe Dad is right.

Maybe I have pushed Reece away with my resentment. Blaming him for not trusting what I want, for not pursuing what I want. That's not his fault. That's my fault. That makes me passive aggressive, doesn't it? Oh, God . . . me and my stupid passive aggressiveness ruined our marriage. Great. Of course he's exasperated with me. Of course he's turning to someone else.

Suddenly I feel like I'm falling and there's nothing to hold on to. I hug my knees tighter to my chest. This is all my fault.

What if you didn't blame yourself, Sabina?

The voice is familiar. It's the same voice I heard in my dream this morning. The same voice from the art gallery. I lift my head up from my knees, but nobody else is here. "Who is that?" I ask, feeling foolish but continuing anyway. "Are you suggesting I blame Reece?" My fingers itch for a cigarette. I could blame him for all of this, for some of this. That's what I have been doing. And it's probably justified. But it doesn't change anything. He's still with her. And I'm still a big hot mess.

What if you didn't blame anyone?

The voice is louder, closer. If I didn't blame anyone I'd just . . . what? Probably drown in sadness. Unless the fire of my anger burned me up first. My heart contracts sharply, like someone is squeezing it hard. The pressure doesn't let up. It continues, even worse, like someone is stepping on my chest. Damn it. I won't be played with. "I wish you'd stop speaking in riddles," I grunt through gritted teeth. "Just tell me what you want to say already."

I push myself up to standing and turn the bucket back over. The water just spilled onto the deck and through the cracks in the wood. It'll dry in the afternoon sun. I wish my emotional turmoil could evaporate as easily.

I pry open another can, pick up a regular four-inch brush, and dip it in the blue paint. Then I crouch down and pull the brush up in a large arc, next to the burgundy mayhem. I stand up, then repeat that motion in reverse, slowly squatting down to make another large arc just beneath the first. I continue this process, making wave after wave after wave. After I've covered the whole left side of The Wall, I grab another brush with my left hand and dip it into the can of green. I paint figure eights by swinging my arms wide, then curving them up. Then I pull the brushes down into overlapping loops in front of me—over and over again. My arms move up, drawing arcs that slide away from each other, then cross in front of me, completing another circle. As I stretch higher and bend a little lower with each round of shapes, the pressure on my chest eases up. I've already forgotten the annoyance I felt toward the mysterious voice. "I love you like the ocean loves the shore," I whisper. As I paint, the infinity loops seem to draw me in like they've formed a tunnel. I smell the rank decay of death mixed with the sharp, fresh bite of water teeming with life. Taste salt on my lips. Hear the thunder of the ocean.

Through the sound of the waves I pick up another melody. It's the voice again.

Sabina. The tone is soothing. *What if you didn't blame?*

"I don't know." I hear myself whining. "Why can't you just tell me? Who are you? The Sphinx of the ocean?"

A laugh like tinkling bells tickles my ears. The blue-green arcs of the infinity loops on The Wall shimmer in the sunlight. *Perhaps.* Another flitter of laughter moves through the air around me. *What if you did know?*

My arms move of their own volition, creating blue-green waves, carrying me deeper into the water. "Why does it matter?"

The voice responds a moment later from farther away. *Why, Sabina, it's the key that can set you free.*

13

I TAKE A BIG BREATH AND DIVE INTO AN ONCOMING WAVE. Then, I pop up and start to swim, one arm over the other, twenty paces out. Once I get there, I turn to continue parallel to the shore, falling into a rhythm with my steady, reliable overarm crawl.

It was Nana who taught me how to swim in the ocean with confidence, how to listen to and have a healthy respect for her ever-changing moods and currents. Today, the water is calm and cool. The sun, peeking out from behind some fleecy clouds, is warm on the back of my head. I can't believe I was afraid of the waves in my nightmares. These waters—they're home.

Just like Nana is.

I turn my head, exhale, and then inhale deeply before putting my face back into the water. Behind closed eyes I see an image of Nana in her hospital bed—one from my visit earlier this afternoon. The sight of her—so frail, so immobile—had made it impossible to breathe for a moment.

My hand plunges down through a nest of slippery strands. I lift my face out of the water and see that it's not just a floating piece of dislodged kelp; I'm on the edge of a big bed of *Macrocystis*, giant kelp. Nana encouraged me to learn a couple of Latin names for the most common residents of this place, and this was one I chose. I use both arms to press the familiar brownish-yellow seaweed to the side and swim away from it to go around the bed. As I pull myself forward, I think about a morning after Reece and I had therapy with Brian. We were in bed, just waking up. Reece had pulled me close to him, like he used to do in the early days of our marriage, and whispered in my ear, "Let's find our way back to each other again, Shug." I'd turned around to face him and we'd made love. We'd been slow and tender with each other. Afterward, we'd showered together, also something we hadn't done in a while, and headed out to Millie's Café, where we had lots of French roast coffee and our favorite dishes.

But something had felt off. Making love had been like putting a Band-Aid on something that required so much more. I still felt distant. I didn't know if it was because I resented having prioritized him and his music over my own art or the fact that I still wasn't sure if I trusted him when it came to other women. Regardless, I had been at a loss for how to heal the divide between us, so I never said anything about it. I guess I thought that if I ignored it, it would take care of itself.

I inhale, almost choking on water for a moment, and tread water to catch my breath. The chasm between us seems insurmountable now. Even if Reece changed his mind and said he wanted to work on us, would I take him back? Could we ever recover from this? I run through all the scenarios in my mind yet again, like I've done countless times over the last several days.

There seem to be only two options: continue to wait on the sidelines and do nothing while he has his affair and see if it blows up when the lust wears off, or initiate a divorce. Both ideas make me want to throw up. But I push myself to explore the second option a bit further. If we got a divorce, if I asked for it, would I be the one to leave the house? I don't know where I'd go. Or what I'd do if I'd no longer be helping him with the band. And the band. I'd lose them. They've become like a second family. Other than Mel and Miguel, everyone I know in LA is connected to Reece in some way or another. It's a tangled mess, all intertwined like the kelp strands I was just trying to pull myself through.

On my drive up to Santa Cruz, I'd called and left messages for Toni, the band's longtime manager, and Skyler, the tour manager, letting them know I was going to be out of contact for a few days. I never do that, so they both texted me back immediately, asking if I was okay. But I hadn't responded. I didn't want to mention anything about Reece or Nana.

I pull a strand of giant kelp from my leg and start swimming again, toward the lighthouse. Reece's last concert at Troubadour pops into my head. I see myself backstage, watching the crowd roar as he and Jaxon strut onstage to play "Chasing Ashes" for their encore.

Do I wait around for an encore? Or is this my chance to get off the sidelines? To stop watching him from the wings and get onstage myself? Whatever my stage is. My long-neglected studio at Nana's replaces the image of Troubadour. The old mural study. The Selkies. The dream I'd left behind. Who abandoned whom first?

The sound of a nearby boat alerts me to how far I've drifted from shore—further than I generally like to be. I swim ten strokes back toward the beach and reorient myself. Was I abandoning myself when I quit nude modeling for life drawing classes because Reece didn't like it? Or was that just a compromise, something you're expected to do in relationships to appease the other person? Or was it both? I had felt so free modeling; I loved turning the tables and being a muse and inspiration for others. But Reece had been relentless. He didn't mind when other guys flirted with me, but his jealousy really came out at the idea of other men seeing me naked. So I finally gave in.

But it didn't seem to work the same way when I asked Reece not to do something. I remember standing in the bedroom of his apartment shortly after I'd quit the modeling gig, watching him change his clothes after a rehearsal. I confessed my jealousy of the musical partnership he had with another woman—not Fiona, but a gorgeous and super-talented violinist. They were working on a song together for her next concert, and he was fired up about how good they sounded together, how fun it was to play with her, how gifted she was as a songwriter. But I didn't want him sharing so much of himself—his passion, his turn-on—with another woman. It wasn't actual sex they were sharing together but it sure felt like that.

"I don't want you collaborating with her," I'd told him. I had my arms across my chest and a burning sensation in my belly. He had paused, hands frozen in the air above the buttons on his shirt. His lip had curled up and his eyes had gone cold and flat—an expression of disgust that covered up what I now know was fear . . . fear that he wouldn't be free, that I might hold him back from creating whatever he wanted with whomever he wanted. At the time I felt crappy for putting him in that position. I hated feeling jealous and controlling. But I didn't know what else to do. If he wasn't going to support me in being wild and free and doing what I loved, I certainly didn't want to support him being wild and free either. Not very mature, I know. But I guess that's the point I'd gotten to, after giving so much of myself away.

I kick harder, move my arms faster, pushing the memory out of my mind with each breath. Eventually, my thoughts settle. Near the lighthouse, I flip over and float on my back, feeling my rapid heartbeat. A long line of pelicans glides by, first sweeping low to the water then rising back up. They are so graceful, so in sync with each other. One, two, three . . . there are eleven this time.

I feel lost without Reece. "Adrift" is the word, maybe. Maybe I want to be needed. Maybe that's why I followed him—to have something to hold on to. Or to clutch, like the giant kelp I sometimes want to grab when a big wave is coming. Of course, it's slippery. And grabbing on to Reece is probably the same. It's not the kelp's job to keep me steady. Maybe it's not Reece's either. As I roll over and tread water, scanning around for a seal or dolphin, I hear the voice again: *If he's no longer your center stage, what is?*

Without thinking, a single word pops out of me. "Painting."

Ah, yes. Painting.

I gaze around, watching the sun sparkling on the shifting surface of the water. *It's the key that can set you free,* the voice at The Wall had said.

"Are you a Selkie?" I hear bells tinkling, but they're not really a sound so much as a movement, a sensation rippling through me.

A conversation I had with Graham ages ago washes over me. "The magic and mystery of the wild—that I believe in," I'd told him when he'd asked if I thought the Selkies were real. Graham. His showing up again after all this time is so surreal. It's like he knows I'm drowning in another big wave. I flip over and float on my back again. Whenever I was around Graham, or even when I just thought about him, my heart raced like a thoroughbred and my legs got all noodley, like my knees were missing. He was the first guy I felt that way with. Yet I was also surprisingly relaxed in his presence. We talked about everything: photography and painting, life after high school and college, how he wanted to start a nonprofit to protect the wildlife in Alaska—he hated the trophy hunters. We even talked about how I wanted to make art full-time, but my dad had other ideas for me. Graham had encouraged me to "be like a barnacle" and never let go of what I loved doing.

So much for that. I splash my hand in the water, noticing the pink polish on one of my fingers. "Barefoot in Barcelona," the color is called. I'd polished Nana's nails earlier today with it. That's always been a ritual of ours. I'd pick the color for her and she'd pick the one for me. I'd started polishing my nails today, too, when Dr. Patel showed up with an update. He assured me that Nana's fatigue is a common effect of a stroke. Of course, he followed that up quickly with, "All the more reason to give her time alone to rest."

"Nana," I spin around in the water.

Suddenly, an idea hits me. Nana's always been such a passionate person, yet, now, she lies practically immobile in a hospital bed. What if I can inspire her and, in some way, give her fuel to hang in there, by pursuing my own passions again? What if, rather than taking me away from her, painting somehow allows me to give back to her? "You'd be in full support of me claiming my own center stage and making painting my priority again. I just know it." Saying this out loud sends a current of energy up my spine—as if voicing this brings me one step closer to actually painting again. "Is this the key that will set me free, oh Sphinx of the ocean?"

The sound of laughter grows nearer. I wish I knew what was so funny, because my life sure doesn't seem that entertaining to me. I peer up at the lighthouse, as if it holds answers for me. But nothing comes. I turn around and pull myself through the water with a renewed sense of purpose. It's time to dig out my paints.

14

I LOOK UP FROM MY SKETCH PAD TO SEE TWO FAMILIAR figures—one tall and elegant with a gray bun perched on top of her head, one shorter and wiry, her cropped dark hair streaked with white. They're holding hands and moving toward me. "Is that Sabina?" Ruth's familiar alto voice plucks a chord in my chest. "Oh, Roo, look at this. It's our dear Sabina."

Ruth and Roo have been together for as long as I've known them. It hadn't really been a surprise to the Library Ladies decades ago when Roo divorced her husband to be with Ruth. Roo—short for Ruolan—told me when I was in college that her marriage had pretty much been arranged. Her desire to not disappoint her parents had kept her in that relationship for years, until she met Ruth. I've always been inspired by how well these two get along and support each other. They give each other space to indulge in their passions—cooking for Ruth and gardening for Roo—while connecting over their love of books and community service. Ruth reads to the prekindergarten kids at the library once a week and Roo volunteers at the circulation desk, helping visitors find what they're looking for.

I stand up and lean right into their waiting arms. When I pull away, I see the wrinkles in Ruth's forehead deepen. "Dora said you're having marriage problems. And on top of that, all that's going on with Cordelia. How are you doing?"

"Hanging in there." I tell them briefly about my visits to The Wall and going swimming, how both are helping to keep me from drowning in overwhelm.

Roo reaches out and holds my hand, registering the black charcoal on my fingers. I look down and see dirt on hers. "Art always was your channel," she says at the same time I say, "You've been in the garden." We smile at each other.

"Well, a woman's gotta have her outlet," Roo says, letting go of my hand. "We can pray for a miracle that Lia makes it through this. But we also have to be willing to look death in the eye and acknowledge it could be her time soon."

"That's why it drives me crazy that the doctor won't let me stay with her all the time." I bite back tears for what feels like the tenth time today.

"We know. Believe me, we know," Ruth says as they draw me into a hug again.

After we talk about Lia's visitation schedule, Roo changes the subject. "Sabina, we have a favor to ask."

I tilt my head and Ruth smiles at me, picking up where Roo left off. "We Library Ladies are putting on a fundraiser for a local nonprofit called Mariposa. Isn't that such a beautiful word? It means "butterfly" in Spanish." She pauses, and I smile. I knew that, but I love how she has a way of appreciating small things. "Anyway, they provide after-school services—art and music and other creative classes—for adolescent girls. They're dedicated to building leadership skills and confidence, helping the girls face the difficult situations they're in. Helping them find their wings, so to speak."

"We have twelve women artists," Roo says, "contributing pieces to the fundraiser." She goes on to explain that the artists get 40 percent of the proceeds, with the other 60 percent going to Mariposa rather than the gallery owner—which in this case is Dora. "Plus, you'll be written up in the local newspaper for certain, and maybe even in the *San Francisco Chronicle*," she adds.

"One of the artists had to pull out." Ruth twists her hands together. "We need a twelfth artist to complete the show. That's where you come in!"

"Oh, Ruth, Roo, I . . . I'd love to support you, but . . ." To be in a show after not painting for years? No way.

"But you're so talented!" Roo's voice is pleading. They'd bought a couple of my paintings over the years at the Fourth Friday gatherings. I'd love to know if they're still hanging in their house or if they're shoved in a closet somewhere. "I'm sure you could create something in time. And besides, you said you were going crazy."

"I think this is a fabulous idea," Dora says as she walks into the waiting room and loops her arm through mine. "One of the best ways to heal is to share your heartbreak and be seen in community."

"Dora!" I want to stick my tongue out at her like I did when I was younger.

"What?" She shrugs innocently. "It's an obvious win-win situation. Or maybe a win-win-win, since I get to have something of yours in my gallery."

"The theme of the show is freedom, since it takes place on the Fourth of July weekend. And all you have to do is create three paintings," Ruth says quickly.

"Three?" My stomach clenches. "That's a lot." I think about what I found in my studio yesterday after swimming. Although all the tubes of paint were in the cupboard where I left them, they were all cracked and dried out. Dead from neglect. "And I don't even have any paint."

"Well, we do have an art store," Dora retorts. "A place you used to love to visit, if I remember correctly."

I scowl and continue with my excuses. "But I don't want to spend all my time painting; I want to be with Nana."

"This was her idea," Roo says with a sly smile.

"What?" My initial surprise quickly fades. Of course this was Nana's idea.

"Really, it was." The bun on top of Ruth's head tilts back and forth as she explains. "She didn't want you to use her as an excuse not to do it either. She thinks this would be a great project for you to focus on right now."

"But . . . the studio is full of books."

"Oh, right!" Roo pokes Ruth's arm gently. "That's where they are. Those were donations we didn't have room for in the library storage. We'll send someone to pick them up. We're almost ready for them anyway."

My mind races. Sure, I did just commit yesterday to making painting my center stage—in part with Nana in mind. But that was just for me, for now. Not for an art show, let alone a fundraiser. Nobody wants to buy my process paintings. "Three paintings? By Fourth of July weekend? That's less than two weeks from now. What if they're not done by then? What if they're not fundraiser-worthy?"

"If they're not ready, we could call your series *Still in Process*," Ruth says encouragingly. "Your art has always been the way you work through your emotions. This would be so inspiring for the girls to see. And everyone else. It would be a great reminder too that art's not about being perfect. It's about expressing yourself."

Dora nods her head forcefully. "Great idea, Ruth. It's true. You have a gift for this, Bina Bell—allowing all the messy hub-bub of your heart to come out in powerful ways."

I run my hands through my hair. "I've just been throwing up on The Wall. Nobody would want to buy any of that emotional debris."

Dora clucks her tongue. "Once the throwing up is done, something else is emerging. It's quite . . . something . . . for lack of a better word."

Roo smirks at me. "Any more excuses in there?"

I try to swallow but my mouth is dry. I take a deep breath.

"So, you'll do it, Sabina?" Ruth asks, shuffling side to side.

I look from face to face, taking in the three sets of eyes tracking me. I don't want to say yes just to please them—like I did with Reece all the time. I close my eyes and only then notice that my fingers are tingling. They want to paint. *I* want to paint. This isn't how I thought it would look right away, when I committed to making painting my center stage. But I know by now the Selkies work in mysterious ways.

I open my eyes and smile. "Yes," I assert with more confidence than I feel. I may be signing on for just another kind of crazy, but at least this way, I'm doing something I love. And it's for a great cause.

There's a fluttering in my chest, and then I'm sandwiched in hugs. Saying yes to the Library Ladies feels different. This time, I'm also saying yes to myself.

15

THE WOMAN AT THE ART STORE'S COUNTER GREETS ME WITH a smile. "Hi. Can I help you find something?"

"It's okay. I know where to go." I head to the back corner where all the canvases are. My hands tingle. Just as I start to think about what sizes might set me up for a project I can actually complete, a vision pops up in front of me like a flash from an old-school camera. And just like a flash, it imprints on my eyelids. Three large canvases. Three women. All looking at me. All looking *like* me only . . . exaggerated. One is huddled on the floor in the shadows. One has her hands over her head as if she's throwing something. One is standing at the edge of the sea.

I feel a quiver of excitement and a shudder of fear—all in the span of a second or two. Then the questions come: Who are these women? What if Nana dies while I'm painting? What am I getting into? Then, I remember Nana's clear directive to me as I sat next to her in the hospital a little while ago. "I love you. Now go. Paint."

I pull out a few different-sized canvases from the shelves, holding them up in front of me. Delight in this small ritual bubbles through me like carbonation, tickling the grief and fear that have been occupying my body lately. The familiarity of this—the possibility of a blank canvas—is soothing.

"A woman's gotta have her outlet." I hear Roo's wisdom echoing through me.

After a few moments, I select three thirty-by-forty-inch canvases and can't resist stroking their plastic-covered surfaces. "Okay, women," I murmur quietly, feeling silly yet excited, "Now, show me what else I need to bring you to life."

I set aside my stack of canvases and head toward aisle eleven, where there's a sea of color. Row after row of paints. I walk next to the row of tubes, running my fingers along them like I might the keys on a piano, with one long stroke. Yet instead of hearing music evoked by my touch, I see a melody of visual possibilities.

As I contemplate my options, I think about Ms. Vera, one of my college professors who taught a year-long studio class on Friday afternoons. Her main intention was to help us unlearn all that we thought art should be to discover what it could be, so she gave us permission to paint anything we wanted, in any style we wanted. She'd amble around the room, her jet-black hair held in a bun with chopsticks or an office clip. She'd tap her long, ring-covered fingers on our shoulders or the edge of our easels, saying, "More. Give yourself to the painting, more. Don't hold anything back. Get naked on the canvas."

One month I painted a self-portrait—a whimsical rendition of myself, reminiscent of the Pippi nickname I'd had as a girl. Ms. Vera tapped her chin several times before turning to me. "So, this is how you see yourself?" Without waiting for an explanation, she'd said, "Go deeper. Look beneath the surface. Look beyond how others see you. Find yourself." Then she walked away, leaving me with my mouth open and a drop of sap-green paint dripping onto my sneaker. A few weeks later, I'd unveiled the final version of my self-portrait to her. In the new version, I'd attempted to show the anger and sadness about my relationship with Marco that I'd been pushing away. My skin was tinged a deep maroon. One eye had tears streaming from it. The other eye had a yelling face reflected in it—the yell that I hadn't allowed myself to let out. Ms. Vera examined it for several painfully long moments without saying anything. Then she turned to me and said, "You did it, Sabina. You showed us something real that we don't see on the surface. Well done."

If only I'd listened more closely to Ms. Vera. She had been the one who suggested I get my master of fine arts. She seemed sad when I told her I was getting an MBA instead, though she didn't actually say anything discouraging.

I take a deep breath and refocus my attention on the paints before me. My hands know what they want. Titanium white, Mars black, cadmium red, Naples yellow—in the basket they go. Along with ultramarine. And burnt sienna. Burnt umber. Cerulean blue. Red oxide. Cadmium yellow, viridian green, gold, bronze, yellow ocher. I feel like I'm gathering old friends together for a reunion.

The women imprinted on my eyes waver in and out of view, like a mirage. Part of me feels like I should stop and sketch them before they disappear, but another part trusts that they will linger and show themselves when they need to.

I don't know what condition my brushes are in or what tools I still have at Nana's, so I decide to get some of each. The brushes are in the next aisle over. I pick out over a dozen long-handled brushes right away. Is that too many? No. Not when you're starting over from scratch. With that thought, I take them all—stiff brushes and soft-bristled brushes, brushes of all sizes—flat, round, filbert, and fan. They are all coming home with me today. My hand reaches out and grabs a rake brush and a few different palette knives too. I love using these not just to mix paints but also to create interesting textures and patterns in the painting itself.

As I head toward the front of the store to check out, I'm suddenly grateful that Reece and I never fully merged our finances. I still have my own credit card that goes to an account he doesn't see. Despite the cost of this tool kit replenishment, when I go to sign the credit card receipt, I feel almost proud. I'm investing in me, in my creative process, for a change.

Back at Nana's, I carefully remove the three large canvases from my trunk and deposit them in the studio. As I round the house again to get my bag of art supplies from the car, I hear my cell phone ringing. By the time I dig my phone out of my purse, I've missed James's call. My heart starts racing as I click through to voicemail and listen to his message:

> Hey, Beans. How ya doing? I was gonna invite you to dinner at Charlie Hong Kong tonight but they need me to pick up a double shift at the hospital. Sorry! Also, umm, I hate to be the bearer of bad news but . . . thought you'd want to know there's been another Reece

> sighting. Outside Verve this morning. Saw him on my way in to get a coffee. And he wasn't alone. Sorry I'm telling you this in a message. I tried to call. Went to voicemail. My next shift starts in just a few minutes, so I gotta go. But, Beans. I know this sucks. I'm reaching through the phone with a hug.

I feel like a rock has busted through the fabric of my newly rising sails. What the hell is Reece still doing here in Santa Cruz? With her? I kick my tire, then notice I'm still driving around on the spare. Shit. At least that's a simple fix. It just requires me to take it to Lloyd's. But my marriage? If only it could be fixed with a trip to the mechanic. If I even want it to be fixed.

I walk into the studio and set the bag of art supplies on a pile of books. Then I slump down onto the stool. All of a sudden, I have no energy—not even for the mindless work of toning the canvases so they're prepped and ready for painting. Why bother? What's the point? Painting is not going to solve my Reece problem. It's not going to save Nana. Sure, it might raise some money for a nonprofit. But really, who is going to buy my art? Art that comes from a sad, lonely, pissed-off place?

I rest my head back against the wall. The image of one of the women I envisioned while at the art store hovers behind my closed eyelids. She, too, has collapsed into herself and is sitting on the floor surrounded by shadows.

My chest heaves. If I don't fix things with Reece, if we can't heal this, I'm not just going to lose my marriage. I'm going to lose my home, my job, and the future that I thought we were going to build together too. After that, what's left? A woman on the floor surrounded by shadows, I guess. Not a pretty picture. Not what I imagined for myself when I started down this path.

My body starts shaking with long, racking sobs. I cough, choking on snot and tears and an image of Reece and Fiona in bed together. Is he bringing her to our house? Are they fucking in our bed? I drag myself out of the studio and into the house to blow my nose. I squint at myself in the bathroom mirror. My eyes are all puffy, and the fluorescent light makes me look half-dead. That seems about right, given how I feel. I collapse onto the toilet seat and sit there with my head in my hands for a long time.

At some point, I realize that I've cried all the moisture out of myself and my tongue is sticking to the roof of my mouth. I pick myself up to wash my face and make some tea, and somehow these small actions get me to walk back toward the studio. I grab the old sketch pad and tin of charcoal I'd taken with me to the hospital. I flip open to a blank page, close my eyes, and call up the vision of the woman in the shadows I'd seen at the art store. Then, with my eyes open, I touch the charcoal to the page, and something or someone else takes over. My muse. The woman herself. A black stroke becomes the curve of her back. Another few strokes reveal her bent over on the floor. A line here and there creates the room she's in. Her face emerges with the next few smaller strokes. As I darken the pool of shadows she sits in, I become her, or she becomes me. It doesn't matter which. We are both sitting on the floor, caved in, and crushed by the weight of having been abandoned.

Ironically, with each mark I add to the page and each detail that makes her more vivid and lifelike, that heaviness inside me lifts just a bit. As my sketch fills in, my body empties out. I sense that if I continue, there will be nothing left inside me but spaciousness.

I keep moving my hand over the page as though my life depends on it.

16

THE RICH SCENT OF GARLIC, GINGER, GREEN ONIONS, and soy sauce greets me as I open the door to Charlie Hong Kong. Nana and I used to get takeout from here all the time, and it's still my favorite restaurant in Santa Cruz. It's strange to walk in here without her. But after visiting Nana and then spending a couple of hours prepping my canvases, I'm in need of some comfort food.

After placing my order, I turn around and see a leather jacket on someone standing near the door. No one wears leather in Santa Cruz. And Reece has that jacket. I take a step and then another small step, attempting to get a look at him without him seeing me—which is absurd, as the place is so small. An old instinct kicks in. The Selkies. I send out a silent plea. *Help me, please. Shape-shift this moment, will you? Let this be just some other guy doing the leather rock star thing. Not Reece. Or if it's him, get me out of this. Send me someone, something. Anything. Please.*

Just then, the guy turns around. It is Reece. I swallow hard.

Everything seems to move in slow motion as Fiona walks in the door. She links her arm in his at the same time he registers my presence. His eyebrows shoot up. Drops of perspiration prickle my upper lip. "What are you doing here?" I blurt out.

"Sabina! Wh-what are you doing here?" Reece's eyes dart back and forth between Fiona and me.

I cast a scorching look at Fiona and another back at him. There's a metallic taste in my mouth. Reece shifts from side to side. Can he feel the fire of my anger? I wish it could burn him. Make him feel the pain he's putting me through. I strike out with my words. "Nana had a stroke. She's in the hospital."

His brow wrinkles. "Is she okay?"

I grit my teeth. Exhale loudly through my nose. "You lost every right to that information the moment you started sleeping with her." I jerk my chin toward Fiona. She tightens her arm around Reece's. His eyes widen, and he opens his mouth, but no words come out. I glare at him. "Is this your idea of fun? Coming here hoping I would be here so you could rub my nose in your affair?"

"Of course not," he says briskly, but his voice wavers. "I . . . I didn't know you were here. I . . . we're . . ." He swallows, looking over at Fiona. "The Pinks played at The Catalyst last night . . ." His voice trails off and his eyes drift up and behind me.

"Sabina?" I know that voice. After not hearing it for sixteen years, now I'm hearing it for the second time in just a few days? What a crazy coincidence. Unless . . . shit. Unless it's not a coincidence. I did just ask the Selkies for support.

I register a light touch on my lower back and then it's gone. Still, the contact pulls me further into my body, momentarily calming the volcano inside me. Graham scans my face, then looks over at Reece and gives him a nod. Then he returns his attention to me. "I have a table. Shall we?" He motions toward the back of the restaurant.

I quickly assess my options: head back with him, or push through Reece and Fiona to exit through the front door. I go with Graham, but Reece stops me. "Who are you?" He glowers at Graham.

All kinds of potential retorts pile up in my mouth: my bodyguard, my date, my first love, a ghost from my past. But Graham beats me to it. "I'm Graham," he says, simply. *Well done*, I think. It'll kill Reece not to know more. He'll think the worst.

Without looking at Reece, I spin around and say to Graham, "Let's go." I head toward the back of the restaurant, passing people holding chopsticks at tables covered in brightly colored cloths. I spot a table with a bowl of food, a glass of what I recognize as the house ginger lemonade, and a fleece thrown over a chair. But I don't sit down. My hands are curled into fists, and I feel like I might explode all over the little eat-in area, sending bits and pieces of me flying out like shrapnel that hit the other diners. I have to keep moving.

"Hey," Graham says gently, "you want to get out of here? I can get a carton for my food."

I turn slightly toward him, not wanting to see Reece and Fiona up front, if they're still even here. "I, yeah . . . I mean, I'm . . . you don't have to go."

"Tell ya what." He attempts to make eye contact with me but I can't look at him. His kindness is almost too much. I don't want to cry here. I won't cry here. So I focus on the birds decorating the tablecloth under his stir-fry. "My Jeep's out back. How 'bout you meet me there? I'll get my food packed up and grab yours. Green curry chicken, extra sauce?"

"Yeah." He remembers. And he's shown up at the right place at the right time. Again. I'm grateful and annoyed. I don't need rescuing. But I did call out for help. So maybe I do. Ugh. "You know, I think I'm just going to walk home."

"You sure?" He sounds like he's talking to a frightened animal who might lash out. "You look like you could use a friend to talk to." I look up at him then and notice his eyes crinkling at the edges. "The Jeep is open. If you want."

I hand him my now-wrinkled order slip and stride out the back door just as a tidal wave of emotion moves through me. *Fuck!* This is madness. Any shred of hope that Reece might fight for my forgiveness is gone. Obliterated. Hope is deader than dead. Reece obviously wants to be with *her* and doesn't care at all about me and the years I gave to him and his career. And I guess I still care enough about him that this hurts like hell.

"Woof!" A bark interrupts my downward spiral. I look around and see a black-and-white dog standing in the back of the only Jeep in the lot. "Woof!"

I walk over and put my hand out, palm up. He licks it, and I move closer to rub my hand through his soft fur. His muzzle is gray, as if he's getting up there in years, but his bright blue eyes are clear and look right into mine, as though he can see my heartbreak. "Hey, you." I get a sloppy face lick, and then the tears come as I bury my face in his furry neck.

~~~
~~~

I'M TRANSPORTED back to a moment with Graham on the Santa Cruz wharf, about a week after we started hanging out. We were sitting out at the end, where the sea lions congregate, with our legs dangling over the water and ice cream cones in hand. "What do you love about your romance novels so much?" he asked before taking a bite of his cone.

"There's always a happily-ever-after. They always work it out and end up together."

He frowned. "You know it doesn't always happen that way in real life, don't you?"

"Well, yeah. Duh. That's why I like the fantasy of romance. It's better than the real thing. The real thing always seems so hard."

"Yeah. I know what you mean."

"You do?" I looked at him.

He paused, as if deciding whether or not he wanted to talk. Then he opened his mouth and said, "Well, my dad, he's . . . he hasn't been around much. And when he does come around, he's always in some kind of trouble. My mom still loves him though. I don't know why. He causes us all more heartbreak than anything else." He turned and looked at me. "What about you?"

I knew all about heartbreak too. My parents had recently separated, and Dad was living with this woman named Donna. I hadn't even met her. I was secretly relieved to not be at home anymore, where I'd had to witness my mom's broken heart every day after school, when I'd come home to find her curled up in the maroon brocade armchair close to the window. She'd stop staring out at the back gardens long enough to say, "Hi, Pip, how was your day?" I never said much because I knew she wasn't listening to the answer. I felt helpless, unable to say or do anything to help her feel better or make Dad come back. And I missed him too. Not the new version of him that just walked away from us, but the other version. But I didn't know how to tell Graham all of this without crying or yelling, so I gazed out at the ocean in silence. Just then, I saw a blue-gray dorsal fin emerge from the water. "Graham!" I stuck my arm out, pointing.

He looked just in time to see the bottlenose dolphin leap out of the water. "Oh, wow!" Then another one jumped nearby as their Latin name popped into my head: *Tursiops truncatus*. Graham reached out and grabbed my arm. "What?! Amazing!" Although neither of them jumped again, we watched their dorsal fins arc up and down as they traveled eastward. Graham turned to me, his eyes wide, his mouth open, his cone held loosely in his other hand. "Bella. That was amazing!"

"It was. You know what Nana and Dora would say right now, don't you?"

"'All good things are wild and free,'" we said together.

The smile slid off my face. With my heart cracked open by the dolphins, I told him about my mom and dad. About how I just didn't understand it. "'All good things are wild and free' doesn't justify what my father is doing though. It isn't about . . . hurting someone else. He's hurting her. Me. Both of us." Graham put his arm around me and I leaned into him. He said some kind words, but what meant the most to me was that he was holding me. I felt heard and like I had space to, well, feel.

"I SEE you've met Bodhi." Graham's deep voice pulls me out of the past. Bodhi barks a greeting at the sound of his name.

"Yeah." I let go of the dog to wipe my face. "He's beautiful. Husky, yeah?"

"Yep. Siberian husky. He's a great dog." Graham reaches a hand out to his companion. "I was going to take him for a walk after I ate. Actually, I was going to let him off leash so he can just run. This ol' man's got a lot of energy to let loose."

I can relate, I think, as I turn to face him. "I know how much you like to be the knight in shining armor, Graham, but I don't need to be rescued. I'm not a damsel in distress."

"Sabina, this is no rescue mission." He shakes his head and his eyebrows scrunch together. "I saw you when you came in, and then I saw your shoulders rise up a few inches when that couple came in. That's when I felt a tug to come check in with you. That's all." He fiddles with the Jeep's tailgate handle. "I wasn't trying to rescue you. I know you don't need rescuing. And now, well, I'm being absolutely 100 percent selfish. Now I get to spend time with you and we can eat dinner together. That is, at least, if you want to."

Heat courses through me and I can't tell if it's anger at Reece or attraction to Graham or both. I look away to catch my breath then meet his eyes again. "That guy in there—that couple?" I thrust my chin toward the restaurant.

"It's okay. You don't have to explain anything."

I nod but continue. "He's my husband. He cheated on me with her. Well, more accurately, he's choosing her over our marriage."

He exhales loudly, then raises the hand holding the bag of

food and points toward the restaurant. "Do you want me to go back in there and punch him? 'Cause I will. You just say the word."

"Graham! No more hero nonsense, remember?"

"I'm sorry." He shakes his head and lowers his arm but then raises it again. "Actually, I'm not sorry, not really. Besides, I think I could take him." He squints and cocks his head to the side and it's like he's seventeen all over again and we're talking about Zach at the surf break.

I burst out laughing. "I admit. I've definitely had moments of wanting to punch him—and her too. But before either of us does that, let's get out of here."

"You got it. You okay with holding the food?" He holds it up to me. "If I put it in the back, I can't trust Bodhi to stay out of it. He's good, but, you know, why tease him like that?"

As we head out of the lot and pull onto Soquel Avenue, the late evening sun is peeking from behind a stack of clouds. I rest my head back. With one hand, I stroke Bodhi, who has moved up to stick his face between us. My other hand is dangling out the window, feeling the movement of air. The food creates a hot spot on my lap, and the smell of curry calms me.

"You okay with a little bit of a drive? I found this great spot up off of Highway 1 where I can let Bodhi off leash to run. We could eat there."

"Yeah." I have a sense Reece might stop by Nana's house to . . . what? Check on me? Talk to me? Dare to ask me what I'm doing with Graham? Whatever. I have no energy for any more contact with him tonight. Better that he arrives at an empty house.

We drive through town in silence. I close my eyes and slip back to that summer again.

WE WERE in Wilder Ranch State Park. I was up in an oak tree with my sketch pad. Graham was off nearby taking photos.

"Bella!" I looked down and there he was, stepping out from behind a large redwood. I waved at him and packed up my pastels, tossing them into my backpack along with my sketch pad. As I dropped to the ground, I heard him say, "I'll show you mine if you show me yours." I turned around to see his barely contained grin and sparkling eyes.

My cheeks flushed. "What are you talking about?"

"Our art, of course." He lifted his camera.

"It's not fair for you to get to see mine now when I have to wait for you to develop yours."

"Oh, come on." He let out a dramatic moan. "Don't make me wait till Fourth Friday."

At the mention of Fourth Friday, butterflies stirred in my belly. Usually it was just the Library Ladies at my unofficial art exhibits. This would be the first time Graham was there. He'd seen some of my art over the past few weeks but not everything.

"Come on, Bella . . ." He came closer, and I held my backpack behind me. "Just a peek?" I shook my head, barely able to contain my own grin. He kept moving closer and I stepped back till I was pressed up against the oak tree. Then his face was right in front of mine. "Then if not a peek, a peck?"

"You're such a cheeseball," I teased, as the butterflies created a racket in my chest.

He shrugged and took a tiny step closer. I couldn't stand the anticipation, so I lifted my face to his. And then his lips were on mine. I dropped my backpack and wrapped my arms around his waist. He pulled me closer to him, cradling my head with one hand, his other hand still holding his camera.

"I'M IN a bit of a time warp seeing you." Graham's voice in real time pulls me out of my nostalgia yet again.

I open my eyes and squirm in my seat. "Yeah, me too."

He clears his throat. "We had a really special time together that summer."

I look out my window and take in the tall eucalyptus trees, their bark peeling in long strips. As I look over at him, I can see the ocean glimmering behind him. "We did."

"I'm so sorry for the way I left, Sabina, without saying goodbye. That was really awful. I'd like to explain."

I put my hand up. "Let's not go there right now, okay? It's been . . . rough . . . these past few days and, well, I could use a breather. I don't want to dredge up the past any more than it's already here. I'd like to just enjoy the ocean and the sunset and some food and . . . Bodhi," I reach out and stroke the dog. "And let it all be. At least for now."

He looks as though he's going to protest but says, "Okay."

Why him, why now, after all this time? I can picture Nana poking me and saying, "The Selkies work in mysterious ways."

17

WE REACH AN OVERLOOK AND PARK. GRAHAM GIVES Bodhi a signal, and the dog jumps out of the Jeep and runs down the path to the beach. "I'm not quite hungry yet," I say. "In fact, I could use a walk before eating. You know how you said Bodhi has a lot of energy to let loose? I feel like that too."

"Sure." Graham sets down the bag then turns to face me. "Race ya down?"

I slip off my flip-flops and toss them into the Jeep. "You're on!" I turn and take off, flying down the sloping path after Bodhi. Graham's laughter, close behind, propels me forward. Once I reach the beach, I keep running, heading toward the water. Face up, eyes closed, I breathe in the fishy, intoxicating scent of the ocean. My chest swells. I'm not sure if I want to cry, laugh, scream, or all three, all at once. I feel like flinging myself into the water but then think about how cold I'll be for the rest of the night. Instead, since I'm wearing cutoffs, I go in up to my knees. My eyes fly open. "Ahhhh!" It feels so good to put sound to all that is moving through me.

I whirl around and see Graham standing several feet away,

watching me. "I guess I still got it!" I say as I thrust my arms up in a gesture of success.

"You sure do, Bella." He gives me a big grin.

Walking back onto the shore, I ask, "Graham, are you flirting with me?"

"Just calling it like it is."

"Listen." I put my hands on my hips. "You know how I said I've been having a rough few days?" He nods. "Well, between finding out my husband is cheating on me and Nana having a stroke . . ."

"Oh, Bella, is she . . . ?"

"She's still alive. But she's in the hospital, and it's uncertain how it will go. So, between being angry at Reece," I wave one hand back up toward the cliff, "and broken up about her, I don't have the heart strength for anything else right now. If you really meant what you said back there, about being a friend I can talk with, well, great. But none of this." I wave my hand in the space between us. "None of this not-quite-flirting-but-flirting-innuendo thing. It's just . . . I can't do it." For a moment I feel naked, exposed by all I shared and by the way he's watching me. And yet, I feel relieved rather than uncomfortable.

"Sorry." He puts his hands up. "I can be a friend."

I slip my hands off my hips and into my pockets. "All right. Friends it is."

He looks down the beach. I follow his gaze and see Bodhi sniffing some driftwood up ahead.

We look back at each other, and he smiles. "'All good things are wild and free.'"

I can't help but break into a smile as well. "You remember that?"

"Yeah. I got the tattoo to remind me every day."

I gasp. "You did? I wanna see it."

He tugs on the sleeve of his T-shirt and holds up his arm. And there it is, on the inside of his tan, muscular bicep—the art I'd drawn for him that summer: a wolf standing on the words "All good things are wild and free" as though they're the ground beneath him. I reach my hand out toward his arm. "Can I?" He nods. As I move closer, I'm aware of that riptide again, pulling me in. My fingers tremble as I touch his inked skin. I drop my hand but trace the loops of the words with my eyes, taking in the details of the wolf—from his piercing blue-green eyes to the hundreds of tiny spirals that make up his dark gray fur. "So you really did it. Even though . . ."

"Yeah, I did. I told you I was going to." He pulls his sleeve back down.

"It's really powerful." I step back, looking up at him. "It's one thing to see it on my sketch pad, another thing to see it on you. He looks like he's ready to run off your arm and join Bodhi on the beach."

"I know. The tattoo artist did a great job. He really admired your artwork. Said if you had more to send it his way." He shrugs. "But that was . . . well, another time ago."

"I didn't want to draw that design for you at first." I had feared it wouldn't be good enough. I also feared that if I did do it, he'd regret it.

"But you did." He rubs his hand over my art. "What changed your mind? You never did tell me."

"It was something Nana said to me." I spot Bodhi farther down the beach and nod in the dog's direction. Graham and I fall into step next to each other, walking in silence for a few moments. I set a quick pace.

The tide is low, and the sand is firm and cool. This cove is similar to the one I've been swimming in, with cliffs on the north side. But there are a lot more rocky outcroppings, and the beach itself is longer and narrower. I don't think I've been here before. Farther down the beach in the other direction are some people around a bonfire. Its scent reminds me that I haven't had a cigarette today or yesterday, not since I started swimming again.

"When I was debating whether or not to make the design for you, Nana gave me Thoreau's book *Walking*. The one that 'All good things are wild and free' comes from. She explained that, for her, the phrase isn't just about being free in the wild, free to do whatever we choose. It's also about letting go of judging ourselves and honoring our inherent worth. Only then, she said, can we be free to be our true selves, without apology." I look out at the ocean, imagining a group of Selkies out there, swimming under the surface, being their true selves. "That conversation with her helped me let go of feeling like my art wasn't good enough for you or your body."

He places his hand on his tattoo and frowns. "I never knew that's what you were concerned about. I thought . . . I thought I wasn't worthy of wearing your art."

I jerk my head up to look at him. "Really?"

"Really."

My hand automatically reaches for the waistband of my

cut-offs. No, I don't want to do this. Or do I? "I got mine too."

His eyebrows shoot up. "What? Show me! I mean, it's only fair. I showed you mine."

I pause. We've been hanging out together for less than an hour and already we're lifting our clothing for a show-and-tell? But I want to show him. I want him to know that our dare meant something to me too. So I pull up my tank a little and fold the top of my shorts down to show him the mermaid tattoo on my left hip. She's sitting on the same line of text.

He bends down to take a look. His breath is warm on my skin. "She's beautiful. The blue and purple scales. Her red hair, so much like yours. There's even a sparkle in her green eyes. Super cool."

"Thanks." We smile at each other. I pull up my shorts and lower my tank.

"When did you get yours?"

"After . . ." *you left*, I finish quietly to myself. I, too, had gotten the tattoo to remind myself of our summer together. "At the end of that summer."

"Hmm." He tucks his hands in his pockets. "Well, I guess since we both followed through on the dare, we don't owe each other anything." I blush, remembering our bet: if one of us didn't go through with getting a tattoo, we had to run down the beach naked while there were other people around. Now, that dare doesn't scare me. But back then, at fifteen, the idea was mortifying.

A holler from the bonfire gets our attention. We turn to see a couple of guys in bathing suits running into the water. Graham chuckles and I wrap my arms around myself, knowing what the ocean feels like without a wetsuit.

When we turn back around, Graham asks about Nana, and I tell him what I know about her condition. "She wants to see you, by the way." Her face had lit up at the mention of his name and the news that he was in town again.

"She does?" He stops and turns to face me. "I'd love to see her. Could I go with you, next time you visit?"

I think about Dr. Patel's orders. But I really want to witness Nana's reaction when she sees him again after all these years. "I visit her every day at 1:00 p.m. I'll be going there tomorrow."

"Shoot. I can't tomorrow. How about the following day?"

I'm curious what he's doing tomorrow. Didn't he say family and work brought him to town? Who is this family? But I don't want to ask. All I say is, "Okay."

We continue walking down the beach. As I move here, between the ocean and Graham, I notice how I no longer want to explode, like I did earlier at Reece, nor do I want to break down and cry. My breath comes more easily, and my pace slows. Graham adjusts his stride to match mine.

Striated clouds cover the sky, stretching to the horizon. My hands tingle. I'd love to recreate this scene on canvas, to capture the contrast of the warm clouds and the cool sky. I'd use a palette knife to produce the choppy grooves of the cloud formations. I try to take a mental picture, hoping I can hold on to it for some other time.

I suddenly remember Graham's photo, *Her Power*, and ask him about it. He tells me he took it on a beach near Esalen in Big Sur, explaining how lucky he'd felt to be alone on the beach that morning with those fierce waves. "I swear, it was my muse who dragged me out of bed early, while it was still dark outside, knowing what awaited me if I just listened and went." He goes on to tell me how the picture ended up in Santa Cruz through Tom and Dianne, the family friends he stayed with the summer we were teenagers, who have some of his photos in their gallery down in Carmel. Another gallery owner from Santa Cruz saw his work and requested some for his place. *Her Power* was all that was available for First Friday.

I tell him that photo was part of what inspired me to start painting again after years of not picking up a brush. He cocks his head at me, his eyebrows raised. "How did you let that happen?"

His words are like the stingers of five hundred bees pressing against my skin. "Are you judging me?" I blurt out. Only then do I take in his furrowed brows, which look more perplexed than judgy. Shit.

"No. Maybe. I don't think so." He shakes his head and laughs, that deep rumbling sound. "It's just that . . . that doesn't make any sense to me. You, not painting? That's like a Selkie without her skin. Really, how did you let that happen?"

I bite my lip. How can he, after all this time, see this so clearly—something that Reece never saw? Something that I ignored? "I'm sorry. I accused you of something I've been doing: judging myself. I let other priorities get in the way." And other *people's* priorities, or, more specifically, *one* other person's priorities. But I stop myself. He doesn't need to know the details. "What matters is that I'm back at it now. Or at least, trying to be. What really baffles me is that out here on the beach, I get an intense desire to paint. But, inside the studio, well, so far, no such luck. It's only been a couple of days but . . ." I think about the vision I saw in the art store of the three women just yesterday. "Even though I can see what it is I want to paint, I can't yet bring myself to paint it."

"What tends to be the catalyst when it comes easily for you?" Graham whistles for Bodhi to come, and we all head back down the beach toward where the Jeep is parked.

"Anger," I reply, surprising myself. But it's true. Look how much erupted out of me at The Wall without me even thinking about it.

"It's usually that I'm pissed about something," I add. "Or heartbroken."

"Yeah. You know all about how anger fueled my start with photography." I do. Shortly after we first met he had told me how he would get so angry with his dad—both his absence and his showing up out of the blue, sometimes drunk—that he started disappearing into the forest with his camera. Then his anger found a new target. He hated seeing trophy hunters come to Alaska and leave with beautiful, majestic animals—wolves, wolverines, coyotes, foxes, lynxes, grizzlies—just for their hides. He started taking different kinds of "shots" of animals as a way to bring awareness to the issue and stop the killing of animals for sport.

"It's also . . . when I'm at The Wall—remember my DIY therapy?" He nods. "When I'm there or just painting for myself, there's no performance. I'm just expressing myself, for me." I can't help but think about Reece. It's like he was born for the stage, for all of that attention. He seeks it out and has a way of commanding it from his audience and from anyone who is around him, on and offstage. Me, not so much.

"In other words, when you're being wild and free on the canvas?" I can hear the smile in his deep voice.

My shoulders drop, and I let out a long breath. "Exactly."

The sun slowly drops below the horizon as we continue talking about the creative process. When we reach the Jeep and decide to head back into town instead of staying here to eat our food, I realize this is the nourishment I've been hungry for. These conversations about art have been missing from my life for so long. I've talked with Graham more about my painting tonight than I have with Reece in the last few years. I feel bolstered, remembering that this issue with my muse, with performance anxiety—it's not just me. It's part of the journey. I guess I just need to keep trying and believing that it is possible to resurrect my relationship with my muse. And it sure would help if I could do this in time for the upcoming show.

18

THE NEXT MORNING, AFTER A LONG SWIM AND A HOT shower, I decide to get it over with and check the messages that Reece left after our Charlie Hong Kong run-in. I set my phone on the kitchen counter and press play on the first of three messages:

> Sabina, I . . . I know I don't have any right to expect you not to be hanging out with another guy right now, but seeing you with someone, well, we need to talk about what's going on. Please call me.

He's using his conciliatory tone. He's trying to get what he wants from me. I'm very familiar with this play of his, and it pisses me off. "You're the one destroying our marriage with your affair. And now seeing me with another man has you, what—reconsidering? Wanting to have both of us? Sorry, Reece. It doesn't work that way." I delete the message and listen to the next one.

> Sabina, why aren't you calling me back? I saw you drive off with that guy. Graham, is it? What's going on between you two? Are you screwing him? Just because you're pissed at me? That's not cool. Call me.

I shake my head. "Fuck you, Reece." Let him think the worst. Get a taste of what that feels like. I press delete and listen to the last message:

> I just wanted to let you know I'm back in LA, back in the house. Call me, will you? It's . . . it's not the same here without you. And Kia, she, well, has some questions about the contract with the recording studio. We had to make some changes, and, well—

I stop the message without listening to the rest of it. Of course he's missing me now that he needs my support and wants something for the business. "You fucker!" I yell into the empty kitchen.

My hands are tingling. I lift them up and stare at my fingers. "You want to paint this out, don't you?" I consider going to The Wall, but isn't this why I got all the painting supplies—to get this stuff down on some real canvases? Remembering the stash of old clothes I'd stumbled upon the other day when looking for my overalls, I run upstairs and throw on a pair of jean shorts and a paint-splattered T-shirt. Printed across it in big black letters are the words MAKE ART. CHANGE THE WORLD. I haven't seen this thing in ages. I used to call it my "get after it" shirt. On my way out the door to the studio I grab one of Mel's juices from the fridge.

In the studio, I move some of the boxes of books around to have access to the small sink and space around my easel—enough for me and my old three-tiered rolling cart, which holds a very dusty glass palette. Unwrapping my new brushes prompts a flashback to the night on the beach when I smoked my first cigarette in a while. This feels like a ritual, too, but a much healthier one. The air around me seems to pulse with electricity as I set one of the large, thirty-by-forty-inch canvases on the easel. The layer of underpaint I applied yesterday is dry. An image of a woman, one of the three that came to me in the art store, wavers in front of me. *Red. Lots of red*, I hear as I fill a jar with water. So I pile cadmium red, red oxide, and burnt sienna onto the palette. I grab one of the stiff bristle brushes, dunk it in the water a few times, then dip it into the paint. I pause, then draw the brush up and down, back and forth, in long strokes across the center of the canvas. I soon trade out the brush for a palette knife, load it up with paint, and slap thick layers on the canvas in shapes that resemble flames.

"Enough, enough." I'm spitting out the words. To whom, I don't know, but they just keep coming out of my mouth. A staccato beat reverberates with each strike of paint on the canvas.

"Enough." A red blaze.

"Enough." Another one.

"Enough!" And another. There are three rough curves on the middle of the canvas now. All fiery flames making up the core of this woman.

"You left me, Reece." *Thwack.*

My arm moves without my prompting. "You left *me*. You betrayed my trust. You betrayed me."

Even as I'm allowing all of the anger to pour out of me, I can perceive the woman's presence, waiting to push through the paint and show herself. It's as though the more I release my anger, the more fuel there is on the canvas, the more she can come to life.

Keep going, I hear. *Let it all out. Let him have it.*

"And now you miss me. You want to talk. You want my help! You arrogant ass. Why would I support you with your business ever again?" Images of our home in LA, our bedroom, our bed, churn through me. "Enough!"

More images surge forward—this time of his studio, his album, our office. "Arrgh!" We didn't just have a life together, a marriage; we had a business together. For him! For his music. I set the palette knife down and clench my hands into fists. I want to punch something. Instead, I march out into the yard, punching the air. "Enough. Enough. Enough!" I'm not even trying to make sense of it. I'm doing what Nana always encouraged me to do: let go. "Aaaaaagh!"

As I head back into the studio, the golden wedding band on my finger catches my attention. The ring meant to bind us together for life. Now, it feels like a handcuff to something dead. "Enough!" I yank it off, resisting the temptation to throw it across the room. But where to put it? I consider sliding it onto a nail where we used to hang Pops's tools, but I don't want to have to see it. A broken birdhouse sits in the back corner of the work counter, as though Pops will come in and fix it one of these days. I stuff the ring inside it. "We're broken, Reece, just like this thing that's been sitting here for who knows how long. We're done. There's no fixing us."

I turn my attention to the canvas. I pick up a flat brush, dip it into the paint, and stroke the canvas with curves that outline the form of the woman emerging through the red layers. Oval head. Round breasts. Soft belly. Powerful thighs.

Words that Mom once used to describe my dad hover in front of me like dust motes. "Fidelity isn't his forte." I freeze, my brush poised in midair above the canvas. "Oh, fuck. Did I recreate your marriage in mine?"

Reece's and Dad's faces blink like strobe lights. They're both charismatic flirts who love to be the center of attention. "No more!" I yell. I slap more red onto the canvas, giving shape to her arms. The right one swings forward, above her head. "No more of this madness!" Her other arm, also overhead, swings back, behind her. She looks like she's about to throw or strike something. "Whatever it takes. I'm not ever repeating this awfulness again. I'm done. Whatever I have to do. This . . . whatever this is. Damaging dynamic. Destructive cycle. No more. Enough."

This is what's beyond blame.

It's that same voice again. "What's beyond blame?" I ask out loud, no longer feeling the need to know who it is I'm actually asking. I stop painting and stand stock-still.

This is the key to your liberation.

"The key to my liberation," I repeat out loud.

Yes.

With sudden insight, words bubble up from my belly. "Taking responsibility for my part in all of this, you mean."

Yes.

"Being willing to change this dysfunctional pattern."

Yes.

"Acknowledging I was the one who abandoned myself . . . before Reece ever left me."

There is a long silence, then . . . *Yes.*

I throw my head back and look up at the ceiling. Fuck. How could I have left myself? My belly churns. Who am I *really* angry with?

I squeeze a pile of Mars black paint onto an empty corner of the palette. Then I pick up another palette knife, load it up, and slide it onto the canvas in choppy waves, again and again, so the paint is fanning out around the woman's head to form an uncontrollable mane of hair.

I sense the fire woman staring at me, even though she doesn't yet have eyes. What does fire do? Burn it all down. Destroy. And the color black evokes a sense of death. Loss. Emptiness. My hands continue to move from palette to canvas and back. The intensity I'd been feeling, the fire of fury, has softened, yet it still burns.

Finally, I set down my palette knife, after I don't know how long—maybe an hour? Maybe two? I grab the bottle of juice and step back to study the painting. She's a powerful, dreamlike figure. Naked. Wild. Raging.

I take a few gulps of the orangey concoction and think back to my conversations with Ms. Vera. She'd say that the technical description for this type of painting is "figurative expressionism." Two big words to basically convey that this woman is a realistic representation of my internal emotional terrain.

Setting the juice aside, I take note of what else the painting needs. It's asking for something—some contrasting color, some surprising subject matter. A sea of green, maybe? Once this layer dries, perhaps I'll blend some yellow ocher and cerulean blue together to create it. Her face still requires some detail work. And I see another image of her black flaming hair unfurling, becoming cawing crows at its edges.

I finally take a deep breath, exhaling fully into the studio space—a space that feels like it has just been reclaimed after many years of abandonment. I like what I see on the canvas. It's not done, and it's not perfect, but it's a strong start. It's the kind of art I always wanted to be doing, the kind I want to do now. "Thank you for coming to me today. For helping me express all of this . . . anger. Confusion. Stuff." I tilt my head. "Do you have a name?" Although I don't hear anything, something stirs in my body, right above my belly. I put both of my hands on top of the stirring and bow to the woman. "I'll return again soon. I promise."

After cleaning off my brushes and palette in the little stainless steel sink, I walk outside and lift my face to the sun. It's time to go see Nana. But before I go, I find my phone in the kitchen and text Reece.

> Reece, you've made your decision. To be with Fiona. So I've made my decision. I've taken my ring off. We're officially separated.

I hesitate. Do I really want to draw this line in the sand? Is it just encouraging him to cavort around town with her even more? Do I care? "I'm doing this for me," I say out loud. My words seem to hang in the space around me, spitting sparks just for a moment before fading away.

> Toni can help Kia with the contract changes. I need to focus on Nana right now. I'll reach out again when I'm ready to discuss more details. Until then, no more messages. Please give me space.

I stare at the text, sucking on one of my curls. I consider telling him that Graham is an old friend. That nothing is going on between us. But if Reece and I are now separated, I no longer have to answer to him or explain myself. There's a fluttery sensation in my belly as I press send. I close my eyes for a moment. It feels like the immense waves from my dreams are holding me.

19

I PUT THE PLUMS I BOUGHT AT THE FARMERS MARKET in the fridge. Then I grab an old vase from above the sink for the dahlias and fill it with some water before stepping out on the back deck. My stomach is all topsy-turvy. I tug the elastic band from my hair and shake it out, combing through it with my fingers.

"Bella?" The sound of Graham's voice is so close it startles me, even though I knew he was planning to come by. I ran into him at the market and met his very pregnant sister, Sam. Turns out she's the family he's been referring to. He'd asked if he could come by and see me after dropping her off at her house, saying there was something he wanted to talk to me about. And here he is, in the yard, with his hands tucked into his back pockets. I catch myself admiring the way his T-shirt is pulled tight across his muscular chest, then promptly pull my gaze up to look at his face. "Hey."

"Hey." He flashes a smile. "I knocked on the front door, but . . ." He shrugs. "Hope it was okay to come around back?"

"Yeah. Of course." He steps up on the deck and his woodsy

scent fills my nostrils. "How about some lemonade? It's not Nana's lavender lemonade, but it's what I've got."

He nods, and I slip inside and grab a couple bottles from the fridge. Before opening the sliding glass door again, I watch Graham pacing on the deck. Seeing his nervousness somehow settles my own nerves. I take a deep breath. Whatever it is he wants to tell me . . . I can be a friend. I can listen.

Outside, the air around us suddenly seems heavier, like a storm front is moving in. But there are only a few wispy clouds in the sky, and it rarely rains in Santa Cruz in the summer. I hand him a bottle and sit down in one of the Adirondack chairs. He sits down next to me and guzzles about half of his lemonade in one go. In response to my raised eyebrows, he says, "What can I say? My mouth was parched."

The sound of a squirrel's chattering catches our attention. We watch as it runs up the back wooden fence and disappears over the other side.

"So, that was fun," he finally says. "You meeting Sam. Grabbing a bite to eat together."

"Yeah, it was. She's hilarious." I'd almost peed my pants a couple of times listening to her stories about being pregnant. "And I can't believe she's the executive director of Mariposa! Such a synchronicity."

"It is. But I didn't come over tonight to talk about that. Sorry. That sounded abrupt. It's just, well, I'd actually like to tell you why I left that summer. If that's okay?"

"Oh." As I rearrange my legs underneath me, I get glimpses of our last night together—back when we were teenagers.

~~~

WE WERE locking our bikes up behind Nana's garage late at night. Graham was telling me about the northern lights, how I would love their otherworldly waves of color dancing in the sky. I took his face in my hands, and, before I could stop myself, I said, "Graham Gray, I love you."

I'm not sure which one of us was more surprised. A look moved across his face that I couldn't quite decipher—shock? Delight? And then there was a glimmer of a smile on his lips. But he didn't say anything. Unable to bear the tension, I leaned up and kissed him, feathery soft. I blurted, "See you tomorrow!" and then I turned and ran inside, my cheeks warm, my heart pounding. And that was it. I never saw or heard from him again. I just got to think about how I said the wrong thing for months—or maybe years.

BIRDSONG PULLS me back into the present, where thirty-three-year-old Graham is watching me, waiting for me to answer his question. Although I didn't want to talk about the past the other night, on the car ride to the beach, now, well, it seems important for me to know. And important for him to get to tell me. Maybe there's something in his story that will shed light on my relationship dynamic with men.

I sit up straighter. "Yeah. I'd like to hear that."

He bites his lip, then jumps in. "So, there was an accident. A car wreck." He fidgets with the bottle cap. "I didn't think this would be so tough. Telling you this." He lets out a breath. "Being here, with you, at Lia's, makes it all seem so . . . fresh. As though
~~~

it happened yesterday." He takes another gulp of lemonade, screws the top back on, and sets it down beside him. He rubs his hands on his jeans a few times, from his thighs to his knees. When he glances over at me, there's a flicker of . . . shame? anger? in his eyes.

"Remember me telling you my dad was a drunk?" I nod. "How he left us when I was ten but showed up from time to time?" I nod again. "Sometimes, he'd show up and say he'd gotten cleaned up and would apologize and bring flowers. My mom, well, my mom . . ." There's a tenderness in his voice, tinged with a hard edge.

Graham looks up and then back down at the deck. "My mom, she was always so good to us. She believed in us, Sam and me. She taught us to be strong, to never settle for anything less than our dreams and what was important to us." The words come out of him in a gush. "When it came to my dad, well. He was the love of her life, even though he was unreliable. He wasn't that way in the early years. And he never hit us." He looks at me then and shakes his head. "It's just . . . he was always, well, as my mom told me, he had his own demons he was wrestling with—or running from—or giving in to. She'd kick him out when he showed up drunk, but when he showed up clean, she let him in. She had compassion for him. And she wanted us to be able to know him, have a relationship with him. She couldn't bring herself to keep him from seeing us, as long as he was sober." He exhales loudly.

"The night—the last night I saw you, the phone rang. Late. Tom and Dianne were already in bed. My mom was at the hospital in Anchorage in critical care. They said to come right away." He leans back in his chair, then leans forward again. "When I heard the news that she might not make it, I tore through the house, planning on jumping into my Jeep and driving up there. I obviously wasn't thinking clearly. Tom got me to slow down. Got us tickets to fly to Anchorage. Drove us to the airport in my Jeep. They—he and Dianne—flew with me."

He takes a breath but then jumps right back in, like if he doesn't get it all out quickly, he'll never get it out. "I got the story from Sam, later, at the hospital. Dad had come to visit. He was sober when he showed up. He'd restored a '67 Mustang and was so proud. He'd brought a picnic for them and wanted to take my mom to see the fireweed fields. They were her favorite wildflowers, and they were in bloom." His eyes are on the hydrangea bushes, but I sense he's seeing Alaska's bright pink-purple stalks. "I got the rest of the story from the cops who showed up at the scene. They'd found a shattered bottle of champagne in the wreckage." He takes a deep breath. "He took a corner too fast. The car flipped. My mom," he stops and swallows, "went through the windshield."

"Oh, Graham." The words slip out.

"My mom was alive when they took her to the hospital. When they called me. And then when I got there . . ." He pauses. When he continues, his voice is deeper, huskier. "When I got there, she was gone."

I gasp. I can't imagine experiencing this kind of devastating loss at seventeen. I can barely handle the thought of Nana leaving me now at thirty-one.

"It still gets me. Remembering walking into that room and . . ." His voice trails off.

I reach out and put a hand on his arm. "That must've been impossible."

He meets my eyes for a moment then looks away. "It . . . yeah. It was the worst moment of my life. Made worse because I felt responsible for her death."

His words, though spoken softly, carry a charge as if shot out of a gun—bullets that have already inflicted their damage on the shooter. After a moment of silence, I ask quietly, "Why did you feel responsible?"

"I should've been there to stop it. Instead, I was here, with you, having the best summer of my life."

I'm stunned into silence for what seems like a minute. The words "best summer of my life" pull on my attention. But his anguish pulls even harder. The pain is visible in his face, still. Looking at him, I realize that he's been beating himself up for sixteen years. "But how could you have stopped her or the accident? I don't understand."

He stands up, and my hand slips from his arm. He walks to the picnic table and leans against it. "I know it sounds crazy and totally irrational. But I was the one, before I left home to spend the summer here, I was the one who was always there, always keeping her, well, keeping him, really—my dad—from doing more harm than he had already done. And I wasn't there. And look what happened." His eyes drift down. He crosses his arms over his chest and folds his hands under his armpits. I can see in his stance the impact of the burden he carries.

I fold my legs up and wrap my arms around my knees. His life was completely upended. His reality totally shifted. But it still doesn't make sense. Why did he sever our connection so thoroughly? Why didn't he call to tell me what was going on? I could have helped, maybe.

There's a storm in the ocean of his eyes. "Seeing my mom broke me. I exploded. I was so angry. I wanted to kill my dad. Fortunately, he'd left the hospital before I arrived—somehow, he got off with a few cuts and bruises. I was not myself and I was definitely not the . . . the carefree, happy teenager you knew. And then there was Sam. She was devastated. She had been arguing with Mom before our dad showed up, wanting to see some boy. She was only thirteen at the time, and my mother wouldn't allow it. 'I hate you' were the last words Sam said to her."

"That must've wrecked her." I'm picturing the bubbly, fun woman I met this afternoon, wondering how she navigated her grief.

"It did." He sits back down in the chair. "We were drowning, both of us. And with my mom gone and my dad MIA, I had to step up and take care of Sam. Tom and Dianne were like life preservers. They stayed for a month—put everything in their life on hold. Made all the funeral arrangements. Took care of the paperwork to have me become Sam's legal guardian. Since I turned eighteen a few days after . . . well, it was the right thing to do." He stares off at the back fence.

"I couldn't call you," he continues. "I knew if I did, you'd come—you and Lia and Dora. I just couldn't bring you into that. I didn't want to—pollute—what we'd shared." His eyes lock on mine. "That summer changed me, Bella. It gave me a taste of something I hadn't experienced. There was so much light and joy and . . . magic, I guess. But after my mom died, well, you and all of that felt completely lost to me. I felt like I would never be able to have anything good again." He looks away. "I was convinced anything good would be taken away."

I remember how I bawled on Nana's shoulder for weeks after he disappeared. I know now that my own pain paled in comparison to what he'd been going through. But I still don't get it. Why, after those first few months, didn't he just call?

He rubs his hands over his face. "I felt awful about leaving without saying goodbye, without telling you what had happened. I reached for the phone so many times, thinking about what a relief it would be to talk to you. But I didn't pick it up. And the more time went by, the guiltier I felt." He looks down at his hands. When he glances up at me again there are two creases between his eyebrows. "I guess I didn't want you to see who I'd become. I was angry and just holding it together enough for Sam. I put off my plans to go to college. Got a job—some lame retail thing at a sporting-goods store. I hated it. I was turning into one of those people that just goes through the motions. Tom encouraged me to keep doing photography, which I did. It was the only thing that saved me. That and Bodhi."

He stands up and starts pacing again. "Bodhi showed up about a year later. A friend of Sam's—her dog had a litter. I didn't want yet one more thing to take care of. But something about him, when I looked into his eyes . . . it felt like my mom was throwing us a lifeline through him. That guy gave us something—someone—to love. And I swear, from day one, it was like he knew his job was to look after us. He kept us afloat."

He stops and rakes his hands through his hair. "Then Sam was getting ready for college, and I was afraid it might do more harm than good to reach out to you after so much time had passed. I figured you'd probably hated me for a while and then gotten over it and wouldn't want to hear from me. I didn't want to cause you any more hurt than I already had." He moves as though to reach out a hand to me but crosses his arms again instead. "So when Sam—can you believe she ended up moving here with her husband?"

"No and yes. You know what Nana always says."

"True." There's a whisper of a smile on his face. "When Sam called me from the hospital last week, after she fell, and asked me to come, and then I ran into you on the beach, well, it felt like my mom was throwing me a lifeline again. Like she was encouraging me to see you and see if you would . . ." He clears his throat. "If you could forgive me?"

Warmth floods my chest. "Graham." I unfold my legs to get up and stand in front of him. This is easy. "I forgive you."

He's still looking down and doesn't seem to register my words. "I'm so, so sorry, Bella. I never meant to hurt you."

I squeeze his arms and shake him a little until he meets my eyes. "Graham, I forgive you. It's okay. I forgive you."

He pulls me close and holds me tight, his head buried in my hair. My body is on fire with the heat of our closeness. His confession. His raw vulnerability. We let each other go at the same time and I step back and retreat to the chair. The space between us is filled with a current that doesn't know which way to go.

He takes a deep breath and hooks his thumbs in his front pockets. "Thank you, Bella."

"Of course." I pause. "Have you forgiven yourself?"

He exhales loudly. "I'd be lying if I said yes. Haven't been able to forgive my dad, either."

I fold my legs up in front of me. "Remind me of your mom's name?"

"Sarah," he says softly.

I tilt my head and give him a small smile. "What's with you and all these women with names starting with *S*?"

"You're all strong women." He says matter-of-factly.

"Mmm. Well, from everything you've told me about your mom, about Sarah, I can't imagine that she would want you to blame and not forgive yourself."

As I hear my own encouragement, a thought springs to mind: perhaps I need to forgive myself, too, before I can forgive Reece. I hug myself tighter. Can I forgive myself for leaving myself?

Graham shrugs. "You know, I never understood how she was able to forgive my dad. When he was sober, he was funny and charming and smart. But when he was drunk, he could be a real ass. I asked my mom about this. How could she keep opening the door to him after everything?"

I wonder the same thing about my mom. I'd asked her repeatedly why she stayed. Why she put up with dad's infidelity. Why they didn't go to couples counseling. When she saw that I wasn't going to let these questions go, she'd finally confessed that at some point, it had just become easier to accept him for who he was rather than attempt to change him or leave him and start over. I'd been infuriated with her resignation—that she just chose the "easier" path and didn't want more for herself. That she let him have what he wanted and didn't stake out her own ground.

"Know what she told me, when I asked her?" He doesn't wait for a response. "She told me that we should forgive each other our demons because we all had them." He shakes his head. "Some were more harmful and intense than others, she said. But it was the people that struggled the most that actually deserved, no—she said 'required'—forgiveness because they were the ones that had such a hard time giving it to themselves. She said it was our job, if we could, to give them extra doses of forgiveness with the hopes that eventually that might spill over into their world and show them what forgiveness could feel like."

I brush away the tears in my eyes. "She sounds like a saint."

"Well, I guess that makes you a saint too." He gives me a crooked smile. "You just said you forgive me."

"And you hope my forgiveness might spill over and help you find some for yourself?"

He nods. "Something like that."

20

I TURN MY SKETCH PAD THIS WAY AND THAT, VIEWING the different compositions I've been playing with all morning. I'm not sure if this painting will be horizontal, like the woman in shadow, or vertical, like the red woman.

What I do know, what I remember from that first flash at the art store, is that this final woman is on the beach. There are dense clouds above her, but I'm seeing a soft, apricot-pink light along the horizon, which runs midway across the entire background. She stands on the sand in front of the water about a third of the way from the left side. But what's unclear is who she is and what direction she's facing. Is she a Selkie? Is she me?

"Which is it?" I whisper. "Horizontal or vertical? Show me, please?"

I get a nudge to move my body, so I do as I'm guided, just like when I paint. I set the pad down, stand up from the stool, and stretch my arms overhead, bending left and right. Ms. Vera always encouraged us to dance, do yoga, or move our bodies however they wanted to move before and during a work session. "If you try to create from the neck up, your painting will never fully inhabit the canvas," she said. She believed that taking time to enjoy our bodies and feel them in action—our hearts beating, our breath flowing, our hips swaying—was critical to bringing a painting to life.

As I rock from side to side, I hear Graham's voice from last night: *Best summer of my life. Changed me. Drowning in guilt. Demons. Didn't want to pollute what we had.* And my voice: *I forgive you.* I release my arms and bend over, letting my upper body hang like a rag doll. What if the story I have that all men leave is true but also false? I step my feet out a bit wider and swing my torso back and forth gently, my head almost touching the ground. I've made the story—the one that all men leave—mean something. I've made it mean there must be something wrong with me. Ugh.

What if that's the false part? I hear. It's her voice again. The Selkie-Sphinx.

I rise up to standing again, slowly, so as not to get a head rush, and begin to swirl my hips. I put my attention on my breath as I inhale through my nose and exhale out my mouth. Graham left, but not because I did anything to push him away and not because he wanted to leave. He wasn't trying to hurt me. He wasn't rejecting me or rejecting intimacy with me. He had his own reality going on—his own incredibly painful reality that had nothing to do with me.

And what about Dad?

I exhale loudly and shift into a standing lunge. I turn my torso to the right and stretch my arms out to either side of me: warrior pose. Dad left for business. He also left to be with other women. I often felt like Dad left even when he was still in the house. He'd retreat to his office. When I knocked on the door, he'd say, "Come in," but his tone said, *Leave me alone.* I remember the pit I'd feel in my stomach. It made me reluctant to visit his hideout after that. I'd wanted a different kind of relationship with him, one in which we enjoyed each other's company and sought each other out—and I'd had that with him in my younger years. But as I got older, we grew apart. I always resented him for that. Of course, now I know he had his own reality too, and I suspect it had its challenges. Maybe there was something about life with Mom that he had to escape, or something else painful there that I don't know anything about—something that had nothing to do with me.

And Reece. I drop my arms and shake them. This loose, uncontained movement feels so good that I start to shake my entire body from head to toe. Reece is different. He did leave. He left me. And not to be on his own. To be with another woman. I wonder, now, if he left us—me, our marriage—before Fiona. Were there other women?

I stop shaking and clench and unclench my hands as a rush of heat rises into my face. My eyes are drawn back to the canvas with the red woman, which is leaning against a pile of boxes by the studio door. Would I dare ask him if he's been with other women besides Fiona? I don't know if he'd be honest with me. And do I really want to know? Images of us sitting on the couch, sitting across from each other at our kitchen counter, sitting in the car together all pile into my view. Moments when he was there physically but not mentally or emotionally. He could be distant and aloof—impossible to reach even if there was only a foot or two of space between us.

Just like Dad.

My jaw aches. I realize I've been clenching it for a while now, as I have been a lot lately.

But he wasn't the only one who left, I hear.

I swing around and look at the seven-year-old study of the Selkies. I'd propped it up on the counter behind me. "That's true." Suddenly, I can't bear to look at my old work. I squeeze my eyes shut. I'm the one who walked away from that opportunity to paint a mural. I'm the one who left my dream of creating art for a living.

I hear her voice again: *Can you forgive yourself?*

I rub my chest and frown. Can I? I'm not sure. But I do know it takes being willing to face my past. I open my eyes and contemplate the dancing figures on the small canvas. "I'd like to," I say out loud, to them, to myself, and to the voice. "I just don't know how to." I've never done it before.

There's a ding on my phone. I've been carrying it everywhere, just in case there's news about Nana. I pull it from my pocket and see that the text is from James.

> Beans. Graham Gray? Hellllllooooo! HOT! He's here with Lia. Dr. Patel is at a conference which means visiting rules are lifted for the day. Party!! You coming or what?

Shit. It's 1:12 p.m. I told Graham I'd meet him at the hospital at one o'clock. I quickly text James back to let him know I'm on my way. Then I flip my sketch pad closed and tuck it under my arm. Before walking out, I take one last look at the Selkies.

"What do you know about forgiveness?" I ask. "Perhaps you'll show me?" I pause at the door of the studio. "I'm not leaving for long. I'll be back. I promise."

21

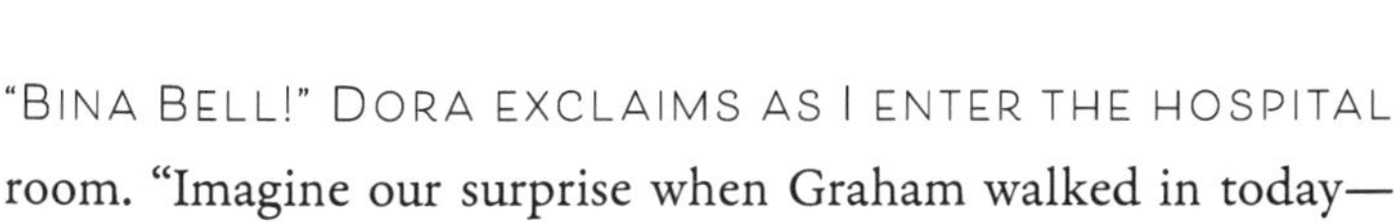

"BINA BELL!" DORA EXCLAIMS AS I ENTER THE HOSPITAL room. "Imagine our surprise when Graham walked in today—after all this time." She shakes her head and slides a chair up next to hers for me to sit in. "Come on over. We've been having a catch-up."

"Hey, Bella." Graham's sitting on the other side of Nana's bed. For a moment, I see his seventeen-year-old self superimposed on his thirty-three-year-old face. For a moment, I imagine it's just like old times, and instead of meeting up at the hospital we're gathering for a picnic on the beach. But the incessant beeping of the machines next to the bed pulls my attention out of pretend-land and into Nana's eyes, where there's no denying that things are very different now.

I look back at him. "Hey, Graham. I'm sorry I'm late." I bend over to kiss Nana on the cheek. "Hey, Nana." As I sit down, I put a hand on Dora's shoulder. "I thought it would be fun to let it be a surprise."

"It was." She smiles. "It is."

"I told them what I told you last night, about what happened that summer," Graham says, his voice deep but not as rough as the other night. I imagine it's helping him to share his story with us, even after all this time.

Nana looks at me. "It's good to talk about these things," she slurs.

"It is," Dora agrees. "Life, death, the unexpected departure of loved ones. Not always easy but important."

I try to take a deep breath but all I can manage is a shallow gasp for air. I don't know what to say. The grief is like a rogue wave, coming out of nowhere and wedging itself in my throat. I don't want to talk about death. I want Nana to stay. I can't imagine life without her. And Reece? I'm going to have to figure out life without him. And what about Graham's losses? His mom so young. His childhood. The best summer of his life. Mine too. It feels so selfish to think about it right now, but it's in there, too—the loss of what might have happened between us had he not left. The unfairness of it all suddenly grips me. I can't move or talk. All I can do is stare at the light cotton bedspread and notice the circles of little yellow flowers on it, a pattern that just repeats itself over and over and never really goes anywhere.

Dora slides a photo onto my lap. "Bina, look."

It takes a moment for the image to come into focus. When the haze of tears fades, the picture of Nana, Dora, and me catapults me into another time. The light of sunset shines around us, making us appear as if we're glowing. Nana has an arm over my shoulder, and Dora is reaching out, tickling me. We're all laughing. Only Nana is looking at the photographer, her smile including him in the moment.

"It's so beautiful," is all I can say.

"It is," Nana says. "I remember that day."

"It was one of those ordinary-extraordinary magical days." I can feel Dora's hand warm on my knee.

"But . . ." I look up at Graham.

"It was on the roll of film in my camera when I left."

We're all silent, as though we've all slipped through time to that night on the beach with our picnic and campfire—dancing, roasting marshmallows, caught up in the joy of what seemed like an eternal summer. None of us had any clue that it would be our last evening together.

"There are moments like these when I sense my mom nearby, smiling. I think she would have really connected with you all. And I think you would have enjoyed her company too."

"Graham, it would have been an honor to have known your mom. Of course we would have adored her," Dora assures him. "We adore you."

"Maybe I'll meet her when I go," Nana says.

I flinch at her words. I want to clutch her hands in mine, but I can't seem to move. "You know, the myth of happily-ever-after is that it lasts forever." My voice is choppy and strained. "But nothing really lasts forever, does it?"

"That's why we must love as much as we can while we can." Nana's words thrum in my chest. Love her as much as I can while I can? Absolutely. But what about Graham? I told him I loved him, and then he vanished. Now I know why, but still. That love didn't last forever. I twist the edge of the bedspread between my fingers. And what about Reece? I vowed to love him for better and for worse, till death do us part. But I'm not sure I do now. What we had . . . well, it looks like it didn't last forever either.

I glance up at Graham, who's tracking me in his observant way. How can I still feel attracted to him after all this time? I mean, who he is now, really? We've had a few conversations; so what. Yet I do feel like I know him—who he is—at his core. But is that just romance-novel fantasy? An escape from the difficult reality I'm facing? I shake my head. I should be focused on Nana right now. But everything I'm feeling is all mixed-up—all of the love, all of the pain—like a jumble of washed-up kelp on the beach. I can't seem to separate it out into its different elements, its different strands.

"Tell us something about your mom." Dora's gentleness catches my attention. I look over and see her holding Nana's hand.

"Her name was Sarah. She . . ." Graham's eyes roam around the room for a moment. "She could tell what time it was based on the light—the way it came in through the windows, the shadow it cast. When half the year you're bathed in darkness, like you are in Alaska, you know, the light can become an obsession, a kind of . . . lover. She'd often make remarks about the light. She had different names for it even." His face brightens as he says this. "Like, her favorite was the early morning light. It always triumphed over darkness and brought with it the chance for a new beginning. She called it the 'breath of life.'"

I lift the picture I still hold in my hands. "I can see where your gift for light came from."

He nods his head. "Yeah. She invited me to see light—and, really, life as well—as something to be awed by."

"That's a legacy." Nana gives him her half-mermaid-tail smile.

"You know, Lia, I never considered that before, but you're right. She did leave a legacy in that way."

"And it is a gift," Dora looks down at the photo in my hands. "You captured not only the light of sunset but that special light in each of us." I hold the photo up so Nana can see it again. We're silent again for several moments.

Graham leans forward. "Lia, would it be okay if I asked you a question?" Nana nods. "What do you believe happens when you die?" His question seems to come from his seventeen-year-old self. I sense he's lived with it for a long time.

"Mmm . . . like a Selkie putting on her fur and sliding into the ocean, returning home. Only, I'll let go of my skin. Not gone. Just different." She speaks slowly yet confidently. "I'm not afraid to die. But . . ." She looks over at me and Dora, her eyes sparkling with tears. "I will miss this. You. Both." She looks at Graham. "You too."

My chest aches. I press my lips together and breathe in through my nose, attempting to ward off the storm threatening to overtake me. I imagine Nana in a different form. Shape-shifting like the Selkies. It's a beautiful idea. And yet it still makes me desperately sad. I can't help wanting her to stay in this form—the one that allows me to be with her. How will I get by without her wisdom, her advice, her encouragement?

"Dora, tell them. Grand Reset," Nana implores.

Dora pats Nana's hand. "Okay, sure." She pauses, looking like she has to dredge a story up from the depths of the past. "When Patrick, Lia's husband, died—the year before we met you, Graham—Lia missed him something terrible. For years, she grieved him. Yet, that summer before you showed up, she decided she was going to allow his life—the life he had lived so richly—to be a gift to her even more by allowing his death to spark a 'Grand Reset.' That's what she told us Library Ladies. That she would have a Grand Reset. Rather than living a lesser life for missing him, she said she would live an even fuller life to acknowledge the gift that it is."

"That's when all the fundraisers started, wasn't it?" I ask. Nana half smiles and nods. We've had plenty of conversations about all the fundraisers she's started and gotten involved with over the years, like the quarterly used-book sales at the library. The countless car washes for the local schools. She and Dora even designed a scavenger hunt one year to raise money for a local nonprofit dedicated to cleaning the beaches.

"And the Wednesday-night Just Because dinners that always started with a cocktail hour. Remember those, Bina?" Dora asks.

"How could I forget? You made mocktails for me until I turned twenty-one and could drink the real thing. And there was always music."

"I remember a couple of those too," Graham says.

"Rainbows, Sabina." Nana raises an eyebrow at me.

"Rainbows?" Graham asks.

"Yeah. Remember?" I press my fingers to my mouth, picturing the crystals hanging in the window back at Nana's. I take a deep breath before continuing. I want to be strong for her, so she knows *I know* I'll be okay. "Wherever sun and rain meet there are rainbows. It's our job to look for them. Nana always told us that." I place my hand on Nana's blanket-covered leg. "So, Nana, you're encouraging us to have our own Grand Reset and look for the rainbows after you . . . go?"

She takes a labored breath before answering. "Yes."

I drop my head into my hands. How can I even think about looking for rainbows and starting all over when I don't want to live in a world that doesn't have Nana in it?

22

THE FUNDRAISER IS THIS WEEKEND ALREADY. IT'S BEEN almost two weeks since I left LA. Two weeks since Nana's stroke. Only two weeks, and yet my life is completely unrecognizable from what it was before that conversation with Reece. Before that call from Dora.

Nana's had less energy. The doctor said she's not getting worse, but she's also not getting better. Knowing that every moment I spend with her could be our last is surreal. I have this sense of urgency, like I need to notice every detail about Nana now, before she's gone. Like the way she looks at me in moments of alertness, like she sees something in me I'll never see in a mirror. Her long fingers with their knobby knuckles. The brown age spots on the backs of her hands that we jokingly refer to as "constellations."

And yet, as I lie next to her, listening to her breathing, my thoughts drift to Graham. He's been in Esalen for the past few days teaching his workshop. He said he'd come by when he got back into town to get all the boxes of books out of the studio and take them to the library. Dora insisted that I had painting to do, so she asked him for this favor. I'm looking forward to seeing him again, and I'm not sure that's a good thing.

I bring my attention back to the room. "Nana? How was it for you to see Graham again the other day?"

She ponders my question for a moment with eyes closed. "Like finding a . . . a . . . missing puzzle piece." I'm glad for both of their sakes that he showed up when he did. That she got to find this missing puzzle piece before it was too late. And that he gets to know he's forgiven, by all of us. "You two," she adds, after a pause. "Something sp-special."

"Yeah, we did share something special back then. I . . ." I hesitate but, then, Nana always has been the one person I can share everything with. "I can't help but wonder what might've happened between us, and in our life trajectory, if that accident hadn't occurred. If he hadn't left that summer."

She places her left hand on mine. She still hasn't regained her strength or ability to do much with the right one. "Well, there are what-ifs and what-nows."

My eyes widen. "Nana, are you encouraging me to explore something with Graham? Even though I'm not officially divorced?"

"Mmm. More that . . . look for the rainbow."

"Oh, Nana." I flip my hand over slowly to hold hers. She's right; Graham being here now, showing up after all this time, is a rainbow for certain. And her saying that makes me realize that she and the Selkie-Sphinx sound awfully similar sometimes. I haven't told her about the voice I've been hearing, even though she's the only one I've been able to talk with before about these kinds of things—the parts of myself that are weird and confusing and otherworldly. So I fill her in, admitting that there are moments when I feel like I'm going crazy.

"Sabina. Remember. Not weird-bad. Just weird-different." There's a glimmer in Nana's eyes, something I haven't seen lately. "Wisdom is coming up from your depths."

"My depths?" I shake my head. "But it seems like it exists outside of me, like it's coming from a distance."

She slowly lifts her hand out of mine and taps my heart. "This, Sabina."

"My heart? My wisdom?" I rest my hand on hers. She nods and closes her eyes.

We lie in silence together for a while. The sounds of hospital activity outside her room feel faraway. I hope Dr. Patel doesn't come anytime soon.

"Sabina?" She's still pronouncing her "b" as a "w."

"I'm right here, Nana."

"The fundraiser. It's soon."

"Yeah, it is. I'm nervous, Nana. I don't feel ready." I pause to take a deep breath. She's been so happy about the fact that I'm painting again. Each day we swap progress reports: I tell her what's emerging on the canvas and she shares what happened in therapy. Her progress continues to be slow. She's able to lift a spoon from the tray, even though she's not able to get it all the way to her mouth. But we're focusing on the small wins. "I still have to write my artist's statement. And finish the third canvas. I did get the sketch I showed you, the one of the woman in shadows, turned into a painting. Finally." I grunt and roll over on my side, careful not to hit her in the process. "But even if I had everything done, I don't think I'd feel ready. It feels really vulnerable to share my paintings with the public. Who will want to buy them? And almost worse, how can I part with them? They've been such an integral part of my process. What if they sell and I don't want to let them go?"

She squeezes her lips together, then releases them. "Butterflies."

"Yeah. These butterflies feel like they have rough edges though. It's not fun to feel so many of them in my belly. I also . . ." I'm not sure if I want to admit this next part to her as I know what she'll say. But I say it anyway. "I feel guilty spending time painting and preparing for this event when all I want to do is be here with you." I hesitate. The truth I've been wrestling with for these past two weeks pours out of my mouth: "You . . . you could go at any time Nana. I . . . I just don't know how to be with that."

"Oh, little mermaid." Hearing her familiar term of affection for me makes tears prick at the backs of my eyes. "I will always be with you, even after I die."

"How will I know you're with me?" I feel like a desperate little girl as I ask this question.

"You'll know." I listen to her breathe till she speaks again. "We can't control death. You staying here can't . . . can't stop death."

I suddenly feel dizzy and close my eyes. I'm reminded of the conversation I had with Dora up at The Wall—about how we both think that we can keep Nana here with our presence, how we think we can stop death from happening by being with her as much as we can. That's trying to control death.

I think then about being on tour with Reece and his band.

If I was on the road with them, he'd come back to the room with me, not anyone else. Did I travel with them in order to control him? To ensure he didn't stray? I gasp at this. Did I give up what was most important to me—my painting, my dream of becoming an artist—to babysit my husband? My hands curl up into fists and then release. Then I clench and release again, and again—as though I can discharge the pain of this realization through this pointless action.

"Let go of trying to . . . to control," Nana whispers. "We can't all be . . ." I watch her mouth start to move again, but it takes a moment for her to form the words. "Waiting for death. There is so much life to live." She closes her eyes and we sit quietly for a minute, maybe two. Then she starts talking again, very softly. "I have some things to tell you . . ."

"What things?"

But before she can say another word, a nurse comes in to check Nana's vitals and do whatever else they do every hour. By the time she leaves, Nana looks wiped out. "Nana, you were going to tell me some things. But it can wait, yeah?"

The sound of Dr. Patel clearing his throat pulls my attention to the doorway. What is it about this guy that reminds me of Dad? "Hello, Cordelia. Sabina." He steps to the foot of Nana's bed. "Although visiting hours ended ten minutes ago," he says as he casts his eyes over at me and taps the gold watch on his wrist, "I will allow you to stay for a bit longer so I can fill you in on the important details about your grandmother's status."

I sit up straighter in the chair as he tells us about her latest scans and the potential risks Nana still faces—a pulmonary embolism, something called deep vein thrombosis, and even pneumonia. Any of these could be fatal. I blink hard, trying to keep up with all of this information. "Rest is the number one most important thing for Cordelia right now, which is why I'm enforcing the visiting hours. It's the best way you can help her get better."

A mixture of annoyance and guilt moves through me as I stand up and prepare to say goodbye till tomorrow. Instead of leaving to give us privacy, Dr. Patel remains at the foot of the bed, flipping through Nana's chart. "Nana," I whisper in her ear. "I want to hear the things you wanted to share with me. Tomorrow?" She nods her head and I kiss her cheek. "I love you like the ocean loves the shore."

"I love you, Sabina. Like the shore loves the ocean."

23

"GIANT DIPPER?" GRAHAM ASKS.

"You're on." I'd felt guilty on the walk here for doing something so carefree while Nana is in the hospital. But my hesitation begins to disintegrate like a mouthful of cotton candy as we make our way through the bustling crowd. Being at the boardwalk again brings back so many memories. Pops and Nana and I used to come here once a week for the saltwater taffy, family rides, and arcade games. Pops and I had a long-standing contest to see who could get the highest cumulative score on Pac-Man, and Nana and I had counted how many times we could toss a ring in the clown's mouth from the carousel. Our highest score was a whopping two.

And then there was my summer with Graham. We'd both had season passes, and we came here at least once a week. His favorite ride was the Double Shot, the one that drops riders from a 125-foot tower—not once but twice. I always made us go on the Cyclone, the large disk that spins so quickly that riders are pinned in place where they stand, pressed against the back wall. We held hands, screamed, laughed, and kissed for hours. We often started off on the Giant Dipper and jokingly referred to it as our warm-up—or, in our more daring moments, "foreplay."

On this cool July afternoon, the sounds of the boardwalk combine to create a symphony: people chattering, kids laughing, a toddler having a meltdown, music blaring from speakers, whistles and bells from the rides and games, teenagers screaming. And the smells—waffle cones, french fries, hot dogs, funnel cakes, and countless other deep-fried things—swirl together in an intoxicating ambrosia.

"Graham, I have to admit," I tell him as we wait in line for the roller coaster. "You were so right about coming here. We haven't even been on a ride yet and the boardwalk is already working its magic."

When he'd come by the house earlier to pick up the boxes of books, I'd been struggling to write my artist's statement. He suggested I get out and have fun, saying that, for him, words describing his work and process come more easily when he's relaxed and inspired, not desperate. So, when he mentioned the boardwalk, I hesitated for only a split second. *It's okay for us to hang out*, I reassured myself. *We're just friends.*

The line starts moving. We stick our wristbands under the scanner at the entrance gate, then walk up to the empty train to find seats near the front. I giggle as the bar comes down over my lap and the train lurches forward. As soon as we get moving, we're plunged into darkness. I scream along with the other riders as we drop and turn, even though I knew the tunnel was coming. Graham's laughter echoes in the darkness next to me. Once we're out of the tunnel, we start climbing up the largest pitch. The clackity-clack of the old cog system pulling the cars upward is as nerve-racking as I remember. It's like they've designed the sound to convince you that the thing is too old to support another round of riders. I know better, but my stomach still contracts. To my right, the ocean sparkles in the late afternoon sun. I wipe my sweaty palms on my shorts and grip the bar as we near the top.

"I dare you, Bella!" Graham shouts. "Eyes wide open. Arms up!"

For a split second we're poised at the top of the rise looking down the steep track. With a sideways glance at Graham, I let go of the bar and lift my arms into the air. And then we're falling—fast. "Oh my Gooooooood!" I holler as the coaster plummets. Air rushes up in my face. My belly jumps into my throat.

We rise and fall again, and with every turn, we're thrown against each other and the side of the train car we're in. Every time I start to lower a hand to the bar, Graham nudges me gently and laughs, daring me to raise it again.

After the two-minute ride is up and the train slows to a stop, I stand up and instantly stumble into him. "That was amazing!" I gush. Heat soaks through my skin, drenching me in desire. I pull away.

"Yeah, it was!" He grins.

I bump into the person in front of me who's stopped to look at the photos taken during the ride. I've never actually bought one of these overpriced pictures, but I always check them out to see what kind of crazy expression I was caught making.

"Bella!" Graham points at the top corner of the screen where the pictures are. The photo captures us mid-plunge during one of the big drops. My mouth is wide open and my hair is streaming all around me, kind of like the red woman on the canvas. Only my body is coursing with adrenaline, not anger. "Oh wow. I look kinda wild!"

"Yeah, and very much free of writer's block." Graham laughs.

"Let's go." I tug on his arm, ready for more. "How about the Typhoon? Remember that one?"

"The tall one that spins us upside down? Hell yeah!"

For the next hour, we ride almost everything—the Shockwave, the WipeOut, and the Undertow, in addition to the ones that used to be our old favorites. Several times, one of us reaches out a hand to the other and then, just as quickly, drops it, remembering we're *just friends*. But as we take our spots on the Fireball, we both reach out at the same time, catching each other's eyes as our fingers intertwine.

"Eyes wide open, remember?" He squeezes my hand. "It makes it even better."

I grip his hand. There's an ocean of movement between my thighs. My heart pounds.

Even after a few more rides and some of the boardwalk's famous funnel cakes, I'm not quite ready to call it a night. "How about one more ride? A mild one this time, given my full belly." I rub my stomach. "How about the Sky Glider?"

He gives me a thumbs-up and we toss our empty plates and dirty napkins into a nearby garbage bin. On the way to the ride, we walk closely without touching. And then we're sitting next to each other in one of the two-seater swings, dangling over the park. The ocean stretches out beside us. I can even see the lighthouse way over on Seabright Beach from up here.

We talk quietly about his workshop and what we'd each be

taking pictures of if we had cameras. For me, it's the sunlight reflecting on the ever-shifting surface of the water. He asks what colors I'd use if I turned this image into a painting. I smile at the question and explain how I see it requiring combinations of several different colors, like Prussian blue, veridian, cadmium yellow, and alizarin crimson, to capture the unique light and shadow in each ripple in this seascape.

He's drawn to the people riding on the Sea Swings below us. He shares how much he enjoys seeing the raw realness of some-one's face when they don't know they're being observed.

"Would you be taking my photo too?" I ask boldly.

He looks at me, and for a moment, I feel seen in a way that makes me feel naked. My heart thuds. I don't look away.

"If I were," he says slowly, holding up an imaginary camera, "I'd see how the setting sun sparkles in your hair, picking up the copper strands among the darker strawberry waves. How your eyes widen when you talk about painting, revealing shades of sea moss and evergreen forest in their depths."

I swallow and try to find my breath. A strong desire to flee overtakes me. But since we're hanging from a cable in midair, I pull on one of my curls and ask him the first question that comes to mind. "Have you ever been married?"

His eyebrows squish together. "That was abrupt."

"I know." I hesitate, but since I've already redirected his focus, I might as well keep going. "I just, well, you know about my relationship status, but I don't know anything about yours. I don't see a ring. Have you ever been married? Any significant relationships, current or past?"

"Okay," he says. "Different topic. Got it." He lowers his

hands, the imaginary camera forgotten. He searches my eyes as if hoping to find the reason for my sudden interest in his relationship history. "I haven't ever been married. I grew up fast after my mom died, taking responsibility for Sam, making sure she finished high school and got into a good college." He scratches his jaw that has a scruffy—and sexy—five-o'clock shadow on it. "Once Sam was off to school and it was time to focus on my life, I put everything into my photography business. I had a few relationships, but nothing that ever lasted long." He rubs his bicep. "I guess you could say I never found someone I could be my real wild and free with."

I bite my lip and glance out at the ocean. I'm happy to hear this, though it makes me feel horrible to admit it. I shouldn't be happy that there haven't been more women in his life. That there's not someone currently. That he's touching his arm where my art is imprinted on his skin. But I am.

He clears his throat. I look back at him. "As I think I mentioned to you before, I've carried around this fear that nothing good can last. That anything, anyone, I really care about will eventually be taken away."

"You did mention that." I keep twisting my curl around my fingers. "Interesting how your fear or belief is that they'll be taken away. And mine is that they'll leave." I suck in a quick breath. "Do you remember that last night we hung out together?"

"Of course. I've replayed it in my mind a million times."

Hearing this sends the butterflies dancing over my skin. "Do you remember what I said to you?"

He lifts a shoulder and gives me a small smile. "How could I forget?"

"Well, at the time, I thought you might have disappeared the next day because I'd told you that."

He scrubs a hand over his face. "Oh, Sabina. I'm sorry. That must have been even more heartbreaking. To think that I'd run out of—what? Fear?"

I nod. "And, well, you didn't say it back." I'm practically whispering.

He closes his eyes, as if to recall that night. Does it come to him as vividly as it did to me the other day? Us making out on the beach, stargazing, riding our bikes back home, the words spoken behind Nana's garage? Then he looks at me and takes a deep breath. "I didn't want you to think I was saying it just to say it back. I wanted to say it at another time so you would know it was true, that I really meant it. Because, well, I'd been wanting to tell you that for a while."

"Really?" I press my fingers against my lips. My legs swing back and forth. I'd always been afraid I was the one who'd fallen harder.

"Yes, really. You were braver than I was. And I regretted that, you know. That I never told you how I felt."

We stare at each other, caught in the murky space of past and present colliding and transforming into something else entirely—the unanswerable question of how our lives might have been different had the events outside of our control not happened.

He reaches over to where my hand is resting on the seat and links his pinkie with mine. "I fell in love with you that summer, Bella. And if I hadn't gotten the call that I did about my mom, I was planning on telling you the next day."

His words are a salve on an old scar. My fifteen-year-old self is finally getting to hear him say what she wanted to hear from him so long ago. And, despite the chasm of time that separates these moments, it still feels good.

"I know that was a long time ago. We were just teenagers. And yet, if things were different now, I'd be curious to explore this . . ." He lifts our pinkies up and moves our hands slightly back and forth. "Between us."

I stare at him. Even though the Sky Glider is a tame ride, I suddenly feel like we're plunging down a track of the Giant Dipper. My heart's beating fast and I want to hold on to something tightly.

He shakes his head as if sensing my disturbance. "But since things are as they are, just friends." He lowers our hands to the seat and squeezes my pinkie before letting it go. "I just couldn't not say it anymore."

We're silent as the ride comes to an end and delivers us back on the ground. My pinkie finger aches for his touch again.

24

THE THIRD CANVAS RESTS ON MY EASEL. ITS HORIZONTAL orientation was clear to me when I woke up this morning. Now, several hours later, I've sketched out the majority of the scene with a water-soluble pencil. I've even painted a first layer of the sky with white-gray clouds covering the top quarter of the canvas, and I've started on the ruffled surface of the ocean, which spans the majority of the lower half. I might add thicker layers to the tips of the waves with a palette knife, creating an effect that's known as "impasto"—where the paint rises a bit off the canvas. But that can wait. First, I want to get to know the woman who is going to be the focal point of this painting.

So far, there is a blank spot in the foreground where she will stand. I know she's going to be looking at me. But what is she leaving and what is she moving toward? What is her mood, her aura?

As I step over to the sink to clean off my palette, I glance over at the broken birdhouse in the corner. Graham noticed that I wasn't wearing my wedding ring the other night. He'd asked about it, but I hadn't felt like talking about my marriage with him.

Now, I can't not think about it.

When Pops and I used to fix broken birdhouses that fell during a storm, we'd pick up the pieces. Take them to the shed. Pound in some nails. Maybe replace a chunk of wood that was too bashed up to salvage. We made those birdhouses good as new—and sometimes even better. They were always fixable. But my marriage doesn't seem fixable. We can't just nail it together again and hope another storm doesn't blow it off the tree. It feels like there's something wrong with the construction or the materials—something more foundational. Besides, it takes two people to fix a relationship, and right now, well, neither of us is showing up for that.

I set the palette down on the cart and resist the urge to bite my fingernail. That damn question our therapist used to always ask us—ask me—flicks on and off like a neon light in my head: *What do you want?* I know I need to answer this question for myself. But how?

I inhale deeply through my nose and plant my bare feet in a wide stance, all the while gazing at the canvas, waiting for the third woman to reveal herself to me. With the other paintings, the women seemed to reflect what was already consciously moving through me—the emotion and anguish. With this woman, it's like she's reaching inside of me and trying to pull something out . . . some truth, maybe. But, so far, whatever it is has been hanging out just beneath the surface, like a treasure buried in the sand. I know it's there, but I just don't fully see it yet.

"Who are you?" I ask the canvas. "What do you wish to show me?"

The imaginary ebb and flow of the sea on the canvas tugs at me. My hips sway. This conversation that occurs at the always-shifting threshold between the sea and the shore mesmerizes me. The dance of overlapping and pulling away, overlapping and pulling away. They are always in constant conversation, constant relationship. *I love you like the ocean loves the shore. I love you like the shore loves the ocean.*

When is the pulling away a natural movement of intimacy? When is it separation? Is there a difference?

I always perceived pulling away from Reece as a separation. If I tried to be less invested in his music, his band, or the business and more invested in my art, I upset the balance of things. He wanted my support, but not in a healthy way. Not in a way where we contributed to each other. He wanted the "make me your number one priority at the expense of yourself" kind of support. And I gave him that. Which stopped me from having an intimacy with myself, a closeness that I've only just been rediscovering lately.

I wiggle my body and take another deep breath. I guess I really separated from myself to have what I thought was intimacy with Reece. But how could I have had intimacy with him when I wasn't being intimate—or honest—with myself? If I was separating from who I truly was, and am, and wanted to become, in order to be something for him, what was that, exactly?

I pull out the paints I need to make the woman's skin tone: titanium white, cadmium yellow, alizarin crimson, burnt umber, and ultramarine blue. Maybe she's just waiting for me to be ready to paint her. Maybe I just need to start doing something. I squeeze dollops of each color onto my palette, then flip my left palm up and hold it next to them. I might as well use my own flesh to guide my mixing process.

"The joy of mixing," Dr. Vera used to say, "Comes when you remember it is an art and a science. It can be as playful, passionate—even as erotic—as painting itself."

My other hand moves fluidly, using a palette knife to blend a bit of the yellow with the red. That's too yellow, so I add in a bit of the burnt umber. The tingle in my fingers runs up my arms as I continue, finally adding white to lighten the mixture. But it becomes too saturated, too intense. So I add in some blue, then a bit more white. "There," I say out loud. "Got it."

I pluck my angled brush from the water jar, dip it into the creamy paint, and close my eyes. What do I want? Do I want Reece to reach out and ask for forgiveness, to tell me he wants to work on our marriage? What would I need to hear from him to consider going back? I don't know what he could possibly say or do to show me that he's changed, that he could be trusted to not betray us again. We'd have to seriously reconsider whether or not I should be involved in the business end of the band. And I'd have to be sure I could learn how to be with him without leaving myself again. "Hmm." The noise escapes my lips. I open my eyes, set the brush down, and shake my arms loose at my side.

Is Reece capable of being the kind of man who would support me with my dream? Does that kind of partner even exist, or is that a fantasy too?

Graham seems like he could be supportive in that way, based on what he said to me in the Sky Glider the other night. If—and this is a huge if—we ever decided to let go of the "just friends" thing, what kind of relationship could we have?

Ugh! Reece. Graham. Graham, Reece. Men, always. I spin around in circles, my body mirroring the madness in my mind. "Why is it always about men? When did this start? And how can I make it stop?"

After a few minutes, I return to stillness and stand in front of the canvas, staring at the blank spot. The term "tabula rasa" floats into my awareness. "Blank slate." These two words remind me of Nana's Grand Reset. What do *I* want for *my* life going forward? And is a romantic relationship at the center—or part—of it?

I think about all the boxes of books that were in here, including, as it turned out, many of my old Harlequin romances. The story of the happily-ever-after, the woman ending up with the man, has been ingrained in me. Sure, a lot of that came from the culture around me, but a lot was a result of my choices. I reached for those stories. I devoured piles of them as a teen. Even through my twenties, I kept reading them. And I watched more rom-coms than anything else on the big screen. Although Nana taught me that my happily-ever-after was my responsibility, whenever it came time to make a big life choice, like what to do after college or after my MBA, a man always factored into my decision-making. Going along with the man's opinion, invitation, or request seemed like the "safe" path. A path I could count on. A path that would support me.

But that's not how it's worked out.

What do you want? I hear.

"To stop thinking I need a man to survive and complete me." There. I said it. Out loud. Goosebumps pop up on my arms. Truth bumps, as Mel calls them. "To stop making the dream of happily-ever-after all about a man. Just like Nana's been telling me for forever."

As soon as the words are out of my mouth, a vision of the woman appears before me. Her feet are planted in the sand. Her back is to me. Hmm, I guess she won't be looking at the viewer? And then I see it: the long, dark brown fur draped over her shoulder. "You're a Selkie," I whisper. "You're returning to the sea, to your true home."

A warm sensation floods my belly. I couldn't ask for a clearer confirmation.

My hips sway back and forth.

What do I want? To stop looking for "the one" . . . the one who will be my forever man.

What do I want? To let go of thinking I need a man to define me, to give me purpose, to take care of me.

What do I want? To prioritize what's important to me.

What do I want? To be wild and free, wherever I choose to be, in the sea or on land.

But what does this mean? And can I have it?

I grab my water-soluble pencil and prepare to sketch the outline of her body as I think about how, in *The Little Mermaid*, one of my favorite childhood movies, Ariel traded in her voice for legs so she could walk on land and be with the prince. She had to give up something. I was happy for her on some level, but it always bothered me that she made what felt to me like a huge sacrifice. What would it be like to have a happily-ever-after where the mermaid doesn't give up anything—where the man gives up something to be in the water with her? Or what about stories where neither one of them sacrifices anything, and each walks their own path? Each one gets to be wild and free, true to their creative inspirations and muses. They could come together and overlap—just like the shore and sea do—in ways that contribute to each other's growth and happiness but never with a promise to each other of forever.

What kind of relationship would that be? It would definitely be more than the empty shell I'd created with Reece. Each person would be starting from a real, intimate relationship with themselves—not leaving what's important to them to be something or someone the other person wants. Both would be sure to come home to themselves first. Or better yet, they'd never leave in the first place.

The woman guides me to give shape to her with soft yet sure strokes. An oval for her head. The points of her shoulders. The flare of her hips. The curve of her calves. She stands about twelve inches tall—approximately the same size as the woman in the shadows. The red woman is the largest of the three, taking up the majority of her canvas. Yet this woman will still be striking. Given that she's a Selkie, it seems right that the sea takes up so much space in this composition.

Lines continue to flow from the pencil to outline her fur. It hangs over her right shoulder and extends down to cover her back, buttock, and upper thigh. I can already picture its shiny wetness. I'll add more burnt umber and some bronze to the flesh-colored mix to make it and apply the topmost layer with my rake brush to provide texture.

But there's something about her head that I'm missing. The women on the other two canvases are both looking at me. I can't decide if she is or not. "What are you inviting me to see?" I ask her. I stand still, listening. When I notice I'm biting the pencil, I put it down. I gaze at her back. She's pausing here, before putting on her fur, before entering the water. What is she waiting for?

The Selkies aren't afraid of the depths of the ocean because they're made to inhabit them. They aren't afraid of their own big emotions because they're just like the waves of the ocean. They are wild at heart, even when a man takes their fur. And they eventually find their way home. They eventually find their way to freedom.

For a split second, I feel her reach inside of me and pull up the woman who was collapsed in the shadows. "Ohhh . . ." Sudden recognition hits me. If I'm the woman in the shadows, and if I'm the red woman, then I'm also the Selkie woman. At least, I can be, if I choose to be.

In a flash, it becomes clear: Her body faces the sea, but her head is turned back over her right shoulder. Her eyes, green and bright, stare into mine, as though she's asking, "Well? Are you coming?"

I suck in a breath. What would it be like to return home to myself and be mine . . . forever? And, rather than look for a forever man, be a forever woman for myself?

25

A WAVING HAND CATCHES MY ATTENTION, AND I SEE Mel moving through the crowd toward me. “Sabina!” She wraps me in her arms. “Congratulations on your first show!” Miguel joins in with one of his bear hugs.

“Mel, Miguel, you made it!” Knowing they drove all the way up from LA for tonight makes me hug them even tighter.

“Of course,” Miguel says. “We wouldn’t miss this for anything.”

Someone lets out a whistle—James, of course. “You look smoking hot, Beans.”

I twirl, feeling a new buoyancy. The ruching on my dress isn’t something I’d usually choose—Reece would hate it—but it feels just right now. When I went to see Nana before coming here, she said that I looked like a mermaid in it. I thought so, too, which is why I’d bought it.

Mel puts her arm through mine. “Now show us your art. You’ve been so mysterious about it!”

“Yeah, Beans, end the suspense,” James adds.

“All right.” I laugh. “Follow me.” My belly churns as I lead them to the other side of the gallery. Yet, as we reach the wall where my paintings hang, I feel taller. My arms hang long and loose at my sides. "I introduce you to *The Abandoned Woman*, *The Angry Woman*, and *The Forever Woman*."

The names of each woman, and each painting, had emerged the night before I brought them to the gallery to hang. They were so obvious once I heard them. All three are unframed. Their raw edges seem fitting for these primal expressions of emotion.

The Abandoned Woman, from the charcoal drawing I'd turned into a painting, reflects my lowest low over these past few weeks. She's a dark figure in black and white, sitting in a heap on the floor, surrounded by cerulean blue shadows. One arm reaches out toward the viewer. Gazing at her now, I'm almost tempted to reach my hand out and touch hers, to tell her she's not as alone anymore as she once thought she was. I haven't abandoned her. Well, I did—but that's changing.

The Angry Woman is red and naked, with blazing eyes. She has thick black hair that's flying wildly all around her, lifted at the ends by crows moving up and out of the canvas. A smile stretches across my face as I look again at the small golden rays that emanate from her hands. They remind me of the burst of energy I felt when I took off my wedding ring on the day I painted her—the day I declared to Reece that I considered us officially separated. Truth bumps pop out on my arms as I hear, *Fire doesn't just destroy, it also transforms.*

Then there's the Forever Woman. She stands where the sea and shore overlap, with her Selkie fur draped over her shoulder. As she looks at me, I am reminded that I am her, and she is me.

The waves she is about to step into are immense yet inviting. I can almost hear her whisper: *Keep going. Don't be afraid. You have your fur now. You're at home in these waters.*

"Wow, Bina." Mel is the first to speak. "These are intense."

"So powerful," Miguel says.

"Beans, this is your process, isn't it?" James asks. I lift my eyebrows and nod.

"It's like . . ." Mel drags her eyes away from the Forever Woman to look at me. "It's as though they could walk off these canvases into the night with us. Their energy . . . it's so palpable."

I take in a deep breath. "Thank you."

"Wow!" exclaims a woman behind us. "Are you the artist?"

"I am. Hi." I turn around to shake her hand. "I'm Sabina Bell."

"Of course your name is Sabina!" The woman with her says. She has a beaded hoop nose ring that catches the light. "My goddess. This woman on the canvas, the Angry Woman? Reminds me of the Sabine women. Pissed at being seen as property that could just be taken."

I lift my chin slightly, pleased that she makes the connection. "I'm actually named after them."

"Well, then, you have a powerful name. And these are powerful women." She glances at me then back at the paintings. "That last one, she looks determined, on a mission."

"It's called *The Forever Woman*," Mel says. "And, hey, it comes with a poem. You all want to hear it?" The response—a chorus of yeses—surprises me. I've been so focused on my paintings that I hadn't noticed how many folks are in this corner of the room. An especially loud "yes" comes from Graham. I'm glad he's here. We share a smile. As I turn away, I catch his sister Sam's eyes. She gives me two thumbs-ups before turning her attention to Mel.

"'The Forever Woman,' by Sabina Bell." Mel gracefully extends her hand to point me out. Then she reads the poem that's posted next to the painting on a sheet of Nana's cream-colored stationery. Unlike my artist's statement, which I'd struggled with at first, the words for this piece tumbled out of me several mornings ago after a swim, after I'd been in the studio, hanging out with these three women and attempting to make peace with letting them go.

Frustrated and exhausted from walking in
their world,
their way,
she leaves it all behind.
No more, she says to herself.
No more shaping my life around men.
She prepares to slip on her fur,
her key to her wild self,
but pauses to make a promise:
I am no longer looking or waiting for the Forever Man,
the fantasy of The One
who will take care of me.
I do not need to be taken care of.
I am the Forever Woman.
Forever my own ally.
Responsible for my own
happily-ever-after.

Nobody says anything for a moment. But when the enthusiastic applause hits my ears, the breath I'd been holding releases in a gush. There's a flash of light that makes me blink. A woman with a bright red-and-orange head wrap peeks out from behind her fancy-looking camera and gives me a quick smile. As I smile in return, she takes a few more shots.

Another woman asks if she can get a copy of the poem. I see others nodding their heads, looking at me hopefully. For a moment, I freeze. This is a lot to respond to all at once. Is all of this for me—for my work?

Dora swoops in and puts an arm around my waist. "Isn't Sabina's art provocative?" I hear clapping all around me. "I'm proud to introduce you all to Sabina Bell." The sparkle in her eyes tells me she thinks I can handle this—or, maybe more importantly, that I deserve it. "All of her art is for sale. Plus, there are photos of her paintings and this powerful piece on the gallery website. Feel free to share the poem with all of your friends too. Perhaps this will be the beginning of the Forever Woman movement!"

As people swirl around us, Dora says, "There's someone I want you to meet." Then she guides me over to the woman with the camera. "Hey, Zuri?"

It turns out that Zuri is a journalist for the *San Francisco Chronicle*. "I think your message really resonates with women—I mean, it sure does with me," she says excitedly. "You're giving us permission to feel and express feelings that are usually deemed unacceptable. Would it be okay if I asked you a few questions about you and your art?"

"This is how artists are made, Sabina," Dora whispers. Then she releases me with a little nudge.

For a moment I feel a bit lightheaded and want to reach out to Dora or Mel. But then I catch myself. This is what I want—to be my own woman, to speak for myself, to embrace new challenges. I take a deep breath and focus my attention on Zuri.

"So, Sabina," she says, holding her phone out to record our conversation, "can you comment on *The Forever Woman* and the inspiration for this piece?"

I tell her about the Selkies and use their myth as a metaphor to describe how I'd given up my own fur, thinking that was the only way to survive, and what I've learned about the messages our culture sends to women. "What I'm coming to discover is that true freedom lies in committing to myself." I tap my hand on my heart for emphasis. "And promising never to leave myself again."

Zuri nods her head. "Right on." She asks me a few more questions about my painting process before shaking my hand. "Thanks, Sabina. I'll let you go. Looks like you have some fans waiting to talk with you." As she walks away I turn to see what she's talking about.

A middle-aged woman wearing a pink tunic steps up to me, her eyes shimmering with tears. "Sabina, thank you for putting into words, and on the canvas, what has been eating me alive for so long. These," she waves her hand at the paintings, "well, they give me permission to feel what I've been feeling. They give me permission to let it out." She grasps my hand. "Thank you."

As she walks away, Sam appears and embraces me. "Oh, Sabina. Your art. So powerful! These women? Wow. I told my husband I've never seen anything like them."

"Thanks, Sam." My cheeks burn and my face scrunches into what I hope looks like a smile. "That means a lot to me."

"And thank you, again, for contributing to Mariposa with your art. We're all really grateful." She releases my hand. "To be continued, soon, I hope."

The night unfurls like a river, carrying me in its current. I lose track of time, and of Mel and the others, as more women approach me, each with their own abbreviated story of feeling abandoned, angry, betrayed, desolate. They also share, each in their own way, how the Forever Woman feels like a lighthouse, her powerful beam pointing to somewhere beyond where they've been.

By the time Mel comes up to me, the crowd has thinned out. "Hey, Bina!" She gives me a hug. "I'd say your first show has been a wild success! So many women came up to talk with you. We want to hear everything, but we figured we'd let your fans have you here." She elbows me gently, a grin on her face. "We'll have you all to ourselves soon enough. Are you exhausted? Or . . ."

"Are you kidding? I'm wired." I rock back and forth on my toes.

"Awesome. The guys just left a little while ago for Surf City Billiards. Graham too. He seems pretty cool. And pretty hot." She laughs. "Anyway, we were hoping you'd be up for a celebratory drink."

"I'd love that! Oh, but I wanted to go see Nana too." The moment I say the words, I know they're not realistic. Visiting hours are over. Yet still, Nana is the one I most want to debrief this night with.

"Honey, your Nana is most likely sleeping right now." Dora appears at my side and kisses my cheek. "Go. Have fun. Celebrate!"

"And look, Bina," Mel exclaims. "All of your paintings sold!"

It's only then that I notice a red dot on each of the placards. I spin around toward Dora. "Dora, who bought them?"

"Well, if it wasn't the darndest thing," she says, a smile spreading across her face. "Someone bought all three and asked that they be donated to Mariposa. They thought that the paintings should hang in their office, near the activity rooms. You know, to inspire the girls."

I put my hands on my hips. "Wait, what? Who did that?"

"I'm sworn to secrecy." She pulls her fingers along her lips to mimic zipping them up.

"Well that's cool," Mel says. "Congratulations, Bina!"

I don't respond. My mouth is suddenly dry. I turn to look at my paintings. I can't believe they won't be coming home with me. But I also can't believe they'll stay with Mariposa, and all together. I could even visit them if I wanted to. A sudden desire to salute or bow to the women overtakes me. I stand up taller, taking a moment to look into the eyes of each one. Then I bow, giving thanks for the gifts they've given me. As I do, I hear, *It's time to let go and move on.*

26

"To Sabina!"

The whiskey goes down smooth, and I close my eyes to enjoy the warm path it blazes through my chest. The sounds of pool balls cracking against each other, people chattering, and 1980s music on the jukebox all wash over me. I let out a long breath and open my eyes, taking in the sight of Mel and Miguel, James and his boyfriend, Caleb—who we're all just meeting tonight—and Graham. I marvel at how effortlessly Graham mixes with my friend group, how natural it seems for him to be here.

"Beans, holy shit, woman." James clinks his glass with mine. "Your process, your paintings, those women . . . we want to hear everything."

I answer their questions about my art and the conversations I had. I feel like I'm floating as I tell them about Sam's friend who invited me to come talk to her women's studies class and the woman who asked me to teach a process-painting workshop for her book club. This sense of pride is a new feeling. While it's similar to what I experienced at Reece's album-release party, it's also very different. This is all mine.

"So, Beans," James says after all of this, "I love your independence and you being your own forever woman. But don't shut us all out, 'kay? Just because you don't need men doesn't mean we're not fun to have around."

"James," Mel calls out before I can respond. "It's not about you. It's about her. Sometimes, well, a woman needs to know she can make it on her own. It's not against men. It's just her being for her." Mel looks over at me, and I feel a sudden urge to both laugh and cry. She gets it. Just like all the women I spoke with tonight. "And check this out," Mel says, pausing to get everyone's attention. "Guess who sold all her art tonight?"

"Congratulations!" Miguel exclaims. "Do you know who bought them?"

I tell them what Dora told me about the anonymous buyer and the donation. I suddenly get a sneaking suspicion and point at Graham. "Do you happen to know anything about this?"

"No." He genuinely looks surprised. "I think it's a brilliant idea though. I actually wish I'd thought of it myself."

"Well, whoever it is, you know what this means, Beans?" James raises his glass. "Not only have you had your first show, you've sold your first paintings as an adult—as a professional artist. *Salud!*"

After another round of toasts, I start to feel uncomfortable with all the attention and am tempted to bite my nails. Instead, I ask about the other art at the show. They take turns answering my questions as we watch Miguel lose a game to Graham after pocketing the eight ball prematurely.

"Premature eight-jaculation," James sings out. "That'll teach you for being cocky." There's a burst of laughter. "Rack the balls, babe!" he calls out to Caleb.

After the next game is underway, I excuse myself to go to the restroom. James's words reverberate through me as I cross to the other side of the bar: *Don't shut us all out, 'kay? Just because you don't need men . . .* As I weave through a tight cluster of people, I trip over someone's foot and stumble, almost falling into a couple of guys sitting at the bar.

"Well, hello, beautiful," one of them says.

"You can sit in my lap anytime," says the other guy, who I notice has a very long beard.

Before I can say a word, there's an arm around me. "She will do no such thing," Graham says as he guides me toward the restrooms.

As soon as we reach the hallway, I shake off his arm. The need to pee has faded, but in its place a different kind of tension is rising, annoyance flushed with heat. "Graham, what are you doing? Were you following me?"

"No. Yes. Maybe. What?" He shrugs. "You looked like you might be unsteady on your feet when you walked away from the pool table."

"Unsteady?" I plant my feet more firmly on the sticky floor as if to prove him wrong. "I can take care of myself, you know." The words come out more sharply than I intend them to.

"Yeah, I know. You've made it clear you don't need to be taken care of." He scowls at me playfully, but there's something in his eyes that I can't decipher.

I blink a few times, wishing the alcohol hadn't made everything so soft and fluid. "Are you . . . are you mocking me? And my art?"

"No. No, Bella." He shakes his head. "Not at all. I'm sorry. I saw you fall, and then those guys—"

"You just think you have to be the hero, don't you?" Yet again, my words are cutting. But, like a steamroller, I keep going. "Like when we first met, pulling me out of the water. Then whisking me away from Reece at Charlie Hong Kong. And now this." I jut my chin toward the guys at the bar.

"Hey." He lifts both hands, palms up, in a shrug, perhaps even an apology. "I admit. This time I was doing the overprotective thing. I know you could've handled it yourself. I just didn't like the way they were looking at you." He glances back at the bar and scowls again. I shake my head. *The way they were looking at me? Like I'm his property or something?* "But those other times?" He pauses. "Have you ever stopped to consider that none of that was me rescuing you? That I'm not being the hero and you're not the weak one? You're the one that's powerful, Bella, calling me to you. You told me back then, when we were teenagers, that you called out for help when you fell off your surfboard, right before I showed up."

It takes a moment to retrieve that memory from so long ago; it's like I'm dragging it up from the bottom of the sea. "Yes," I say slowly. "That's true. I did call out to the Selkies for help."

"And, at the restaurant, did you call out for help silently? Asking for some Selkie magic to make them disappear or something like that?" He cocks his head, lifts an eyebrow.

I think back to that other moment from not so long ago—one that I don't really want to revisit.

He's right. I grant him a small nod.

He smirks then, damn him. "What if your ability to call out and ask for support—what if that's one of your powers?"

I squint at him. "I'm not a damsel in distress!"

"That's exactly what I'm saying!" The deep baritone of his voice sets off a shower of sparks in my pelvis. "You're not a damsel in distress. Ever. Unless you tell yourself you are. So, all those instances when you think you're so powerless, what if that's actually when you're powerful? You asked for support and it showed up. It just happened to be me both those times."

"But every time you offer support, every time you step in and intervene, I feel like you see me as weak, like you think I can't do it on my own."

"That's you saying that, not me. I don't see you as weak. Don't put that on me." He runs his hands through his hair. "Look," he says forcefully. Then he pauses, leans back, and takes a full breath. When he continues again, his voice is softer. "After my mom died and I had to take care of Sam, I was overwhelmed all the time. But I didn't want to let my mom down. I thought I should be able to do everything on my own. What a crock of shit. The truth is, I couldn't. Tom and Dianne and . . . the therapist they ended up paying for . . . they all helped me see it wasn't a weakness to ask for support. We're not islands, Sabina. Life gives us more than we can deal with, and learning how to ask for support is our strength, our power." He pauses and rubs his forehead. "I know you're strong. I know you're capable. And I care about you and want to support you. Not because I see you as powerless. But because I see you as . . ." He trails off and looks away.

Although I hear his words, it's like they have to wade

through whitewater to get to me. Damn whiskey. What he's saying, though—that my calls for help aren't a sign of weakness—there's something to that. I know this when it comes to calling upon the Selkies for support. But whenever he shows up and "rescues" me, I just hate it. I tap my toe, resisting the urge to bite my nails or suck on a curl. My body is buzzing.

He looks back at me with intensity in his eyes. "I noticed the Forever Woman has a Selkie fur over her shoulder." I nod. "Well, I would never be the man that takes your fur."

A rush of heat moves through me. I want to pull him to me and push him away at the same time. "I really want to be angry with you right now."

He exhales sharply out his nose but doesn't say anything. The world as I've known it in relation to men, or at least to this man, is crumbling. I look down, half expecting to see debris floating around me: the flotsam and jetsam of the stories I believed about myself, the plotlines from my old romance novels, and that dang knight-in-shining-armor-and-damsel-in-distress dynamic I resisted for so long. He's not the savior, the rescuer. I'm not weak. I'm strong. I'm powerful. Can I believe this for myself—not just with the Selkies, but when it comes to other people too?

"I admire you. It's an honor to get to support you." Graham speaks to me as if from far away. "I'd do anything for you, Bella."

Something inside me cracks, and I'm no longer able to resist the force of the attraction between us. I reach out and pull him to me. His chest, stomach, hips—all of his weight—presses against me. All of his hard parts on my soft ones. Our lips hover for a moment, a breath away from each other. And then there's no stopping the tidal surge. I brush his mouth with mine, hungry for a taste of him, and open my lips, inviting him in. His tongue is slow and wet and carries a hint of whiskey. His five-o'clock shadow rubs my chin. I want to touch him, feel him, everywhere. I slip a hand up into his hair and moan. His arms tighten around me. "Bella," he whispers roughly and steps forward, moving me backward till I feel wood paneling on my back and there's no more space between us. Our tongues intertwine. He kisses me harder, deeper. I tug on his hair. His responding guttural groan vibrates through my body as one of his hands slips up to hold my neck and the other one slides down to my lower back.

Laughter erupts from behind him. "Well look at you love-birds. That's why he wouldn't let you sit on my lap."

I pull my head back and see the bearded guy from the bar waddling into the men's room. I stare up at Graham, my breath catching in my throat. "Graham."

"Bella." His voice is raw, his eyes questioning.

My cheeks burn. "What have I done?" I whisper, my hand flying to my mouth, aware too late that I spoke the words out loud. That riptide is still there, pulling me toward him, but I can't do this. I can't let this—this heat, this chemistry between us—take over. I stay stuck in place, my back against the wall.

"Bella." His voice is gruff. "You finally let me in through the ten-foot wall you'd surrounded yourself with."

He's right. But I . . . Damn it. I can't do this right now. Drown in lust with him. Not when I'm just learning how to live my life for me. And not when I'm still technically married. It's only been a few weeks since my marriage imploded. This is way too soon. When am I going to learn?

I put my hand on his chest, intending to push him away,

but he misunderstands and bends in for another kiss. I push him, gently but firmly. "Graham, no." He takes a step back. "That wall is there for a reason. This shouldn't have happened. I . . . you . . . we . . . no." I shake my head forcefully. "No. You know my situation."

"I do. But, please, don't put the wall back up." His face is a jumble of emotions—guilt, desire, resignation. They mirror my own.

For a moment I hesitate. My legs wobble. My lips throb.

And then it's as if the Forever Woman is rising up inside of me, her voice too clear to ignore: *This is your time. For you. For us.*

I focus on feeling my feet on the ground. "It's . . . I have to . . ." The words pour out of my mouth, as if each one carries a brick that will rebuild the wall between us. "I've proven that I don't know how to stay connected to myself and be involved with a man. I want to change that. I want to have both. But to do that I have to learn how to be with me, for me, first. I don't mean to shut you out . . ."

He jams his hands into his front pockets. "But that's what you're doing."

"I don't know any other way right now—I'm sorry—but—"

"You don't have to apologize." He shakes his head. "Just . . . don't."

"I . . ." I catch my breath. "That shouldn't have happened. I, I just. This night. So many emotions." I'm not even sure what I'm saying but I can't stop. "And damn it. There's this riptide between us and every time you come close I get pulled in. I can't seem to . . . feel me. I just, I don't, I can't . . . I can't keep doing this with you, Graham."

Two creases appear between his eyebrows. "What are you saying, Sabina?"

"This time is for me, my art, my Forever Woman self." I wrap my arms around my chest, attempting to stop myself from trembling. "I need to feel me. I need to not keep getting pulled toward you. So I think . . . I've gotta go." With one last look into his ocean-eyes, I turn and flee.

I push my way through the crowd and reach the pool table just as Mel and Caleb are giving each other high fives. "Hey," I say, interrupting their chatter. "Thank you all so much for celebrating with me tonight. I'm suddenly really tired. I'm just going to get an Uber home." I wave off James and Mel and practically run out of the bar. I don't stop when I reach the sidewalk. Instead, I slip off my fancy sandals and jog up Pacific Avenue. There's a noisy crowd outside The Catalyst—the nightclub where Fiona's band performed recently. Ugh. I slow down a couple of blocks later, across the street from Rosie McCanns—the pub where Nana had her stroke. Damn, this place is full of emotional landmines. I lean against a streetlamp, close my eyes, and count my breaths like I count pelicans. After about fifty of them, I pull out my phone.

27

PALE MORNING LIGHT PENETRATES THE DENSE FOG. IT'S making everything in Nana's hospital room appear to be coated in a silvery patina. Sounds in the hallway combine to create their own sonic fog of white noise. I feel like we're in a bubble, Nana and I, suspended in between life and death by my inability to let her go.

Tuning in to her, I hear a long, slow, rattling breath and then silence. After several long moments, she breathes again, her chest hardly rising. I watch closely, making sure there is a next breath. I don't want this one, or the next one, or any of them to be her last. While I was out celebrating my show and kissing Graham, Nana was slowly slipping away. I should've been here. I should never have left her side.

It was Dora who had called from the hospital just a little while ago, awakening me from a deep slumber. Dora, who had been at Nana's side since the crack of dawn, tugged by some invisible hand to come be with her. Somehow, she'd eluded Dr. Patel's radar. When Nana slipped into unconsciousness, Dora thought it was just sleep. But it's not. And it's not pneumonia, a pulmonary embolism, or another stroke. "It just might be her time," the nurse had said. Dora's voice had been frayed at the edges as she told me that I'd best come to the hospital right away. When I arrived, she stepped out—ostensibly to get some air but really to give me time alone to say goodbye.

I take a drink of orange juice from the bottle I grabbed on my way out the door, then reach out to hold Nana's hand. It's cool and velvety soft. She doesn't react to my touch at all. "Oh, Nana." I bury my head in our joined hands. "Nana, I know it's time to let you go. To tell you it's okay to go. I know it's selfish of me to want you to stay." I lift my head and stroke her white hair. I will never feel her hands braiding my hair again. That reality forces the air out of my chest. I gasp, and then the crying starts. "You were the one who was always there for me. When everyone else left. Pops, Dad, Graham, Marco, Reece. It's always been you. Here for me. What will I do without you?"

I'm reminded of the nightmares I was having just a few weeks ago. I feel like the same hungry, dark waves are coming to take her from me. I want to squeeze her hand tighter, to keep her from being swept away into the abyss of nothingness. And maybe to keep myself from being swept away, too, as the same fear from my nightmares invades my lungs.

A few minutes or a few hours later, there's a warm hand on my back. "Hey, Bina Bell."

"Hey, Dora." It takes a moment to lift my head to look at her. "I feel awful that I wasn't here sooner."

"Honey, don't beat yourself up. There's nothing you could have done if you'd come last night or earlier this morning." Dora's voice is scratchy. "Dr. Patel said it could be any minute now, or Lia could hang on for a few more hours or even days. So let's be in this vigil together." I nod. "The mean doc apparently has a heart—he loosened his rules for us. We can take turns in here so someone is always with her. And I called your folks. Your dad's on his way. Your mom's still struggling. She can't make the trip."

I stand up slowly and reach for Dora. As she hugs me close, the sob that was stuck in my chest escapes. Quiet footsteps enter the room and I feel Mel's arms around us; I give in to the sensation of being held. Somehow, it's easier to cry when we're all doing it together, getting each other's shoulders and hair wet in the process. I don't even care about the mess because they're tears. Sacred tears, as Nana used to call them.

"These are sacred tears," Dora whispers, and I can't help but snort. "What?" she asks, lifting her head off of my hair.

"That's what I was just thinking about—Nana calling our tears sacred."

We all pull back to breathe but keep a hand or arm on each other. For a moment, I sense the Abandoned Woman, the Angry Woman, and the Forever Woman holding us too.

After we've all wiped our faces and talked about logistics, Mel leaves to find Miguel, and Dora convinces me to go get something to eat. I find James in the cafeteria with a box of pizza in front of him. I drop down next to him and snag a slice of pepperoni from his plate. "Why get pepperoni if you're not going to eat it?"

"Caleb likes it," he says through a mouthful of crust. "He brought it for me when I told him I was sticking around to keep tabs on Lia after my night shift." He waves his hand at the pizza.

"This is breakfast. Or brunch, I guess, given it's almost noon. Caleb was here. We ate together, but he had to go. So now the pepperoni is all yours."

I grab a can of Coke from what remains of the six-pack on the table and flick it open. "She's doing that wheezy-breath thing." Even though we're the only ones in the cafeteria besides the cashier, we talk in hushed voices. He tells me about the "death rattle" and how it's a sign that a person is close to the end. I confess to him that I'm not ready for her to go.

"Of course you're not." He squeezes my knee. "This is the goodbye you never, ever want to say."

Mel pulls up a chair next to me. "She's still with us," she assures me.

James slaps his hand down on the table. "Mel, you're just in time for the big question!" Then he turns to me. "Okay, what really happened between you and Graham last night, Beans? Hmm?"

I slug my Coke. It feels strange to talk with them about last night when Nana could be taking her last breath in the other room. But I feel restless, and talking about something other than death is so appealing right now. So I blurt it out, like a burp. "I kissed him."

"Well, geez, girl. It's about time." James wipes his mouth with a napkin.

"And?" Mel leans forward, her eyebrows raised.

I set my can down. "It shouldn't have happened. This so-called just-friends thing isn't working. The more time we spend with each other, the more I . . . I feel like I lose me." I look back and forth between them. "And I'm not going to do that again, you guys. I'm not going to lose myself to another man."

"So you kissed him and then told him to go away? Huh. I see how you are." James shakes his head, letting out a teasing, "Tsk-tsk."

"I know. The push-pull dynamic. It sucks." Last night's kiss pulses through me like a heat wave. But then I remember the look in Graham's eyes—like I slammed a door in his face. Which I guess I did.

James picks up another slice of pizza and turns to me. "Beans, you painted that portrait called, very powerfully, *The Abandoned Woman*, and here you are talking to us about not wanting to lose yourself while also pushing Graham away. A man who, if he were into men, I'd be all over, by the way. If I were available, which I'm not." He pauses and looks at his pizza. "Did you know, pizza is the only food I like naked? Sans any topping besides cheese?"

"Stay focused, James," Mel says. "You were about to say something brilliant."

He plucks off the dime-sized discs of pepperoni and sets them on the side of his plate. I grab one. James swallows a mouthful of pizza and gives me a piercing look. "Beans, what if you can have a relationship with a man without losing yourself?"

His question presses into me, like a firm hand on my sternum. I fiddle with the tab on top of my Coke can. "I've never been able to do that. I'm not sure if I know how to do that."

A few nurses come into the cafeteria then, and we watch them in silence as they go through the line—first picking out sandwiches and pouring coffee, then checking out with the cashier. They all sit down together at a table on the other side of the room, chatting and unwrapping their food.

"Maybe . . . maybe it's time to update your myth," Mel says slowly.

"Say more," James and I say at the same time. Before I can say anything, he hands me another can of Coke. "Jinx—and already bought you a Coke."

I give him a little smile and set the can down on the table before turning back to Mel. "Update my myth?"

"Well, it seems like in the old story, the Selkie has two choices." She lifts up one hand. "She can live in the sea and be wild and free, alone, or," she lifts her other hand, "she can be on land with the guy but be without her fur, and not be wild and free. What if there is actually a way to do both?" She waves both hands in the air. "You know, if she *did want* to be with the guy, not as a captive but as a partner, whether that guy ends up being Reece . . . or a hot photographer . . . or someone else down the road? That would be an updated version of that story, right?"

"I think she's onto something, Beans." James lifts his naked slice of pizza into the air to salute Mel before taking another bite.

I see a woman with her fur over her shoulder and a gleam in her eye. I hit my forehead gently. "I know, I know. That's exactly the dilemma—or I guess you could say 'possibility'—I was exploring as I painted the Forever Woman. How to have both. And, most of all, not give up my fur to be in a relationship. And not only *not* lose myself but also not make a man the center of my world. But still have love. And support, and companionship. Maybe that's crazy . . . but maybe not."

Mel's tawny eyes light up like little suns. "Looks like your muse is working you. Probably making up for lost time."

I glance over at her sharply. "So true." I lean back in my chair and bite my pinkie nail. James wiggles his eyebrows at me, and I take my finger out of my mouth. "But I think I have to figure out how to be in my own skin first, on my own. I can't be kissing Graham and . . ." My words trail away as I remember the feeling of his warm, full lips on mine. The way we fit together. Just like when we were teenagers. But I'm not a teenager anymore. I can't let lust have its way with me. I want to focus on my painting; I *can* let *that* have its way with me. The show is over, but who knows what else my muse is going to show me if I keep painting?

A sudden urge to be with Nana overtakes me, like a long strand of kelp just slid around my torso, tugging at me to get up. Enough talk about updating my myth. Nana's what matters most right now.

28

DAD'S BEEN UNUSUALLY QUIET SINCE EVERYONE LEFT. I glance over and see him holding Nana's hand. He catches my eye and gives me a small smile. "I'm sorry I couldn't come to your show."

"It's okay, Dad." I had invited him knowing full well he wouldn't come. But something stirs in me. Is it really okay with me? No. So why am I lying? To attempt to assuage any guilt that he *might* feel? Heat courses through my body. "You know, Dad, if I'm being honest, I really would have liked you there. Why didn't you come? Would it take me being on my deathbed for you to come to me?" The moment the words are out of my mouth, I wish I could take them back. This is the last thing I want to do—pick a fight with him while we're keeping vigil for Nana.

"Sabina." He lets go of Nana's hand and sits up straighter, stiffer. "Don't you think you're overreacting? Besides, I didn't think it was that big of a deal. It wasn't like it was a solo show. It was a group fundraiser."

My head pounds. *It's not a solo show. It's a fundraiser. It doesn't really count.* Images of empty chairs pop into my head. The empty chair at the kitchen table. The empty chair next to

Mom at a high school award ceremony. The empty spot in the bleachers during my swim meets. Even when he did make it to events in physical form, he was usually distracted.

Mental snapshots of all the bars, stadiums, and concert halls where I stood backstage pile on top of these memories. Was I giving Reece what I'd never had and always wanted from my father? And even from Reece himself? "You know, I've spent most of my life trying to get—and keep—your attention." My voice is shaky, but I keep going, pushing the words out. "Yours first, then Reece's, thinking if I became what you—what he—wanted me to become—like a business whiz or a number one fan—then maybe, just maybe, you'd stick around, pay attention long enough to actually *see me*." I shake my head. "What a waste of time."

A movement in the hallway catches my attention. A nurse walking by looks in at us, startled by something. Only then do I realize I'd stopped using my quiet bedside voice. I can't bring myself to make eye contact with Dad, so I look down at my hands, which are curled into fists. "She's going to go soon. And I won't have anyone to talk to about all the things I only ever talked to her about. I won't have her here to remind me that I can do it—whatever 'it' is—an art show, a divorce, a reconciliation. I won't have her here to support me through any of it going forward. Not any of it!"

"Sabina." Dad's tone is chastising.

I get up out of the chair, letting the sketch pad and charcoal pencil on my lap fall to the floor. Dora stands in the doorway. I wave her hand away and stagger past her into the hallway. I'm not sure where I'm going. All I know is that, right now, I can't be in the room with my father.

I make my way down the stairs and find myself at the door that leads out to the rose garden. I rest my forehead on the cool glass window. Dad's words come flying back to me—"Don't you think you're overreacting?" I grit my teeth and pace back and forth in the short hallway. Dora caught my eye for a moment before I left the room. I wonder if I looked like some kind of wild animal to her. That's how I feel. Ready to howl at the sky. Hit something. Throw something. Lay down on the earth and disappear into the fog. This in-between place with Nana is agony. The fight with Dad must be some kind of sideways release from the pressure cooker I'm in. I could really use a session at The Wall, but I'm not leaving here.

Not until . . .

My chest tightens. I press my lips together as a well of tears gathers behind my face. Then, I burst open the door and run to the tiny gazebo at the back edge of the garden.

Once I'm beneath the covered space, I brush off all the microdroplets of water from my sweatshirt and flip my hood over my head. I discover I can only take about three strides in one direction before having to turn around, but I have to keep moving. And, for some strange reason, I want to be here, in the gazebo. Just like my hoodie, it's helping me feel somewhat contained—held. So back and forth I pace. "Damn you!" I yell into the fog, unsure of who I'm yelling at. Dad? God? Nana? Reece? The universe?

After several minutes, I sink down onto the cool wooden floor, pull my knees up to my chest, and wrap my arms around them. Then I rock back and forth, taking deep breaths. I close my eyes and rest my head on my knees. What's it like for Nana right now, to be so close to death? Is she afraid? Is she on some kind of carriage ride with Death, like Emily Dickinson talks about? When I arrived earlier today, Dora was reading poetry to Nana. I don't know if she can hear us, but Dora seems to think so.

A buzzing sensation at my hip pulls me back into the gazebo. I reach for my phone. Dora? No. It's Reece. I shove the phone back into my pocket. Did Mel tell him about Nana? I don't think she'd do that. But then why is he calling?

James asked me a little while ago if I'd reached out to either Reece or Graham. I told him no. "Maybe now isn't the time to push all the men away," he'd said. And he's got a point. But if I call Reece . . . no. I just can't face him right now. I don't want to talk about anything related to us. Even if he offered to come up here, to be with me . . . I cringe. No. I just . . . can't. And I don't have it in me to see or talk with Graham right now either.

I shiver in my damp sweatshirt, staring out at the pearly-gray fog that envelops me. I remember something James told me earlier today, in the cafeteria. "When you go, they go." He said he saw this happen all the time when working at an assisted-living home. The family gathered around, and the dying person seemed to rally and hold on for their benefit. It wasn't until the family left the room that they finally let go and died. I wonder if Nana's been sticking around for me. If all she needed all along was space.

Graham's photo, *Her Power*, flashes into my awareness. *Don't fear the waves reaching for her.* The voice is quiet, close, comforting. *They're not menacing. They're welcoming.*

My phone buzzes. It's a text from Dora:

Come back to the room.

29

I'M IN A ROWBOAT. DARK WAVES LOOM OVERHEAD. I scream and duck down, holding on to the gunwales. The waves descend. Cold water swallows me. Suddenly, the boat is gone, and I'm underwater. When I open my mouth to call her name, water floods in. I choke. *Nooooooo.* My yell is silent, futile. "You took her. You can't have her. Give her back. I want her back!" I thrash around, but as my arms and legs flail against the cold liquid, I seem to only sink deeper into it. "You don't get me too." I reach out, try to grab hold of something, and hear a crash.

I roll over and blink. The nightmare fades away as details of the darkened room come into view: the ceiling fan, the closet door that's draped with scarves and shawls.

The duvet cover is wrapped around my legs, and I struggle to release its grip on me. I turn to see the time, but the alarm clock isn't on the bedside table. Right, the crash. I peer down at the floor and see its outline, but there are no numbers blinking back at me. It must have come unplugged.

I stumble out of bed and head downstairs. My mouth tastes like hell. I grab the orange juice from the fridge, take a few swallows, and turn around to lean on the island. The nightmare clings to me. I can't quite shake the fear of being engulfed by something so much larger than me. And yet, now that I'm awake, the desolate emptiness has come back. This feeling threatens to suffocate me.

Nana.

I finally know what I really want, but it doesn't matter. I can't have it.

I want her to not be gone.

30

"HI, SABINA." DAD'S VOICE ON THE OTHER END OF THE phone is kind—gracious even. "How are you?"

"I . . . I'm wrecked." I wasn't able to fall back asleep after the nightmare. I drifted from Nana's bedroom down to the living room couch in the early hours of the morning, and I'm still curled up here, hugging a pillow to my chest. With the fog obscuring the light, even the crystals look dull.

"Yeah." He's quiet for a moment. "I've lost someone too. It's hard."

He's right. It is hard. And although my relationship with Nana was so very different from his, this is still a big deal. He's lost his mom. He no longer has any living parents.

He clears his throat. "I've made arrangements for us to meet with the lawyer tomorrow."

I clutch Nana's pillow even more tightly. "Ed?"

"Yes. Ed. Mr. Townsend. I'll pick you up at 3:00 p.m." He's all businesslike, as though his mom didn't die less than twenty-four hours ago. I know we cope differently, but still.

"But why? What's the rush? Can't it wait till after the wake?" I suck on a curl, glad he can't see me.

He makes an impatient snort. "We talked about this. Don't you remember? I have to leave the day after the wake."

I don't remember talking about this. But of course, as usual, everything has to revolve around him and his important plans. Even this. I pull my hair out of my mouth. "Why do you need me to go with you? I mean, it's not like there's anything new. You'll get the house. Just like Nana and Pops planned way back when. What else is there to deal with?"

"Yes, well, from the sounds of things, that might have changed." He coughs. "Which is why I want to talk with the lawyer right away. Apparently, your Nana had him come see her while she was in the hospital. He wouldn't say what she asked him to do, but he did say he wants you to be there too."

Nana hadn't said anything to me about any of this, which isn't totally surprising. We never did talk about her house or anything else having to do with estates and inheritances and that sort of thing. I guess I never really thought about it. I didn't want to think about there being a time when she wouldn't be here.

I suddenly realize I've been zoning out and he's still talking. "I think she might've made some decisions when she wasn't in her sound mind. We need to make sure that no one's trying to pull the rug out from under us or anything like that."

I close my eyes and pinch the bridge of my nose. Take a deep breath. "Dad, nobody would do that. And besides, the stroke didn't impact Nana that way. She still had her mental capacities up to the very . . . end."

"Well," he says harshly, "you think you know everything

there is to know about your Nana, but you don't. You might be surprised to know she wasn't perfect."

So this is how he's handling his grief? By insulting his own mother? I look at the photos on the wall across from me, seeking out one of Nana and Pops smiling at each other. "Well, she sure seemed perfect to me."

A short, sardonic laugh crackles through the phone. "Why don't you ask Dora? She knows all about my mother's affair. See how that changes the way you view her."

And with that, he hangs up.

31

"IS IT TRUE?" I ASK DORA AS I WALK IN HER FRONT DOOR.

"Is what true, Sabina?" She reaches for the jacket I'm peeling off. After removing the old pair of Uggs I'd found in Nana's closet, I can't seem to get up from the entryway bench. I stare at the boots. Nana's never going to wear them again. She's also never going to set foot in Dora's house again. I look up at Dora. Grief, like one of my charcoal pencils, has etched more shadows and lines on her face overnight. I reach a hand up to my own face, as though I can feel what it's done to mine.

"I just talked with Dad. He told me that Nana . . . that she had an . . . affair?" The words together—"Nana," "affair"—won't combine properly on my tongue. I'm sure Dora will laugh and say it's a misunderstanding.

But she doesn't. She rubs her chest instead. "Oh goodness. So, the ghosts have come out of the closet."

"Skeletons, Dora. Not ghosts," I correct her gently. But with a sad grimace, I realize both work in this case.

"Right. Well then," she finally says. "Come on in. I don't care that it's not even noon; I need a drink for this conversation."

I drag myself off the bench and follow her into the kitchen. "So it's true? And why didn't she ever tell me? Why didn't you?"

"Well, Bina, it was a long time ago." Dora takes two pint glasses from the cupboard and fills them with ice. She grabs a can of ginger ale from the fridge and splits it between the two glasses. Then fills them up the rest of the way with Jameson.

"That's a lot of whiskey, Dora . . ."

She shrugs. "It's what the occasion calls for." I hand her a lime from the fridge, which she slices in half and squeezes into our glasses before stirring them with a long-handled spoon.

"If Nana had an affair yet still stayed married and somehow . . . somehow worked through that . . ." I picture Nana and Pops, the way he'd reach out and stroke her face, the way she'd brush at the raised tuft of hair on his crown with her fingers. "Don't you think that's something I'd want to know? Something that might help me repair my own marriage?"

She hands one of the glasses to me and tucks the bottle of Jameson under her arm. As we head toward the living room, I'm struck by how my own parents' relationship never inspired me to want to repair my marriage.

"That's exactly it, Bina." Dora talks to me over her shoulder. "Lia was concerned if she told you, well, that you might think she was encouraging you to work things out with Reece." She scoots a pile of books aside and sets the bottle and her glass down on the coffee table. "Lia wanted you to be free of any influence so you could choose your path, whatever you decide, to try and work things out or to get divorced."

"Since when did she filter her stories for me?" Nana and I

were always honest with each other. At least, I thought we'd been. She always said she'd told me about all of her many missteps in hopes I could learn from her experiences. "Did she . . . did she not want me to think poorly of her? Was that it?"

"No, not at all." Dora's reply is quick, like she's thought about this before. She settles into her floral-print armchair and nods at me to have a seat on the couch. "She wasn't ashamed. In fact, the whole thing turned out to be quite liberating for her."

"Really? How?" My questions hang in the air, unanswered. Flickering lights catch my attention, and I step over to a sideboard where two large white candles are burning. A framed photo of Nana and Dora rests between them. It's an old one. Nana still has her fire-engine red curls. Dora has a thick fringe of dark bangs. They're smiling at the camera with their arms around each other's waists. I grab the hand-knit blanket hanging over the side of the rocking chair and wrap it around me before settling into the couch. The sunshine pouring through the tall windows feels too bright—harsh, even. I'd prefer a cave or den right about now. A dark place to nurse our heavy hearts.

"How did this come up, Bina?" I fill her in on my phone call. She nods and lifts her glass. "To Lia."

"To Lia." I raise my glass, then take a sip of the bubbly cocktail. I hold it in my mouth for a few moments, welcoming the tickle and burn, inviting it to take the edge off of the heaviness that's penetrated my bones. I remember Nana telling me she had some things she wanted to tell me, but we were interrupted—by the doctor, maybe? I can't recall. I never brought it up again and neither did she. "I wonder if this is the story Nana wanted to tell me before she died."

"She wanted to tell you, Sabina. She did. But now, well, now I guess it's for me to tell you." She takes a deep breath and begins. "Lia was in her early twenties. She'd been married for just a few years. Craig, your dad, was young. Maybe two years old?" She cocks her head. "Anyway, Lia got word that a friend from her youth had died during childbirth. She decided to leave town to go to the funeral. Her mother came to help Patrick with Craig, and off she went, alone." Dora's eyes drift away from me and out the window. "At the wake she ran into Jeffrey, another old friend from childhood. They got to talking. Found out they were both married. Both had a child at home. So, there they were, at the wake of a dear friend who had died too young, caught up in an otherworldly space of grief and nostalgia, facing their own mortality and discussing how they wanted to live their lives more fully in the time they had remaining."

"Sounds kind of like a Grand Reset."

"Yeah. It does, doesn't it?" She shifts in the chair. "Lia, she'd . . . well, she'd been feeling suffocated being a wife and a mother. It was so much more than she'd expected. The responsibilities, the daily drudgery." She holds a hand up. "Don't get me wrong. She loved Patrick and your father. But there were times she wanted something more, something different." She pauses. Sips her drink. "Lia and Jeffrey had shared an attraction to each other when they were teens, but they hadn't ever explored it. That chemistry was still there. Lia's grief mixed with the sense of freedom she felt at being away from home and her responsibilities." Dora takes a large swallow from her glass. "That night, she went to bed with Jeffrey."

I try to picture Nana before she was a grandmother. In her

twenties, married and a mother . . . and feeling suffocated. Attracted to an old friend. Graham's face flickers before my eyes.

"She told me later that being with Jeffrey—they ended up spending a long weekend together—unlocked something inside of her, something she'd been missing. She called it 'her primal' or 'her wild and free.'" Dora stares off into space, both hands wrapped around her glass. I wonder what it's like for her to remember all of this—and if their life mantra came from this experience of Nana's.

Dora shifts in her seat again and turns toward me. "When she returned home, she wasn't sure if she was going to tell Patrick. But that night, when he reached for her, she let it all out. As you can imagine, he was upset. No man wants to know his wife has slept with another man." She looks at me. "Just like no woman wants to know her husband has slept with another woman. Or anyone else, for that matter." I nod my agreement. "Patrick left town that night for several days. He did what he always did—processed his anger and hurt and everything else on his own, in silence." Again, she pauses. "Then he came back and asked her if she loved Jeffrey. If she wanted to see him again. Lia told him that he, Patrick, was the love of her life. That, as it turns out, Jeffrey hadn't unlocked something inside of her; she had. Just like she had been the one to lock up those other parts of herself when she got married.

"She told me she felt like a Selkie discovering her own fur. She'd been hit with the fact that she was the one who had locked it away all along—not her husband, not her son. All the resentment she'd been feeling evaporated. She was grateful to be a wife and a mother and to be alive. And she asked Patrick to forgive her.

"It was rough between them for a while." She stares out the window. When she speaks again, I sense she's far away, in some other time or experience of her own. "When trust is betrayed that way, there's a rip in the fabric of your togetherness." She puts down her glass and rubs her hands together. "It took time and tenderness to reweave that fabric. Patience too. But they ended up being stronger for it. That's a testament to Patrick and his willingness to forgive. And to Lia, too, who became more fully devoted to herself and her relationships. Her time with Jeffrey helped her set herself free."

My head is swimming, and it's not just from the cocktail.

It's not the man who locked her fur away . . . she did.

And she set herself free.

Yet another seismic wave blasts apart my views on men and relationships. I rest my hand on my tattoo like I might hold on to a buoy. *All good things are wild and free. Including me. I get to be wild and free without making sacrifices. I get to set myself free.*

"You could call what she did 'cheating,' Bina Bell, but that sounds so demeaning. She allowed herself to love two men and be changed by both of them. She also chose to stay with her husband and was incredibly thankful that he forgave her."

We're both quiet as we sip our drinks. I think about Pops and what it must've taken for him to forgive Nana.

"If Reece is the love of your life, and you want to try to save your marriage, it will require forgiveness and both of you to work on the repair. But if he's not . . . well, that's something else entirely." She sets her glass on the table then bends forward, toward me, elbows resting on her knees. "Whatever you end up deciding about Reece, your responsibility is to unlock whatever you've locked up inside of you. Have you locked away your inner rock star, for example, and blamed Reece for that?" Her voice becomes more animated, passionate, yet a river of sadness runs through it. "It's common. We're taught to. We're not encouraged as women to have and express all of ourselves. Our sexuality. Our insatiable hunger. Our deep desires. My generation learned to stifle so much of ourselves. And even these days, a woman who is told it's her job to take care of others is committing a personal revolution when she allows herself to receive pleasure and enjoy life for herself."

She rests back into her chair. "I know it's easy to blame Reece for his betrayal because the affair is so obvious and painful. But even if I could take away the pain, I wouldn't. It's this pain that can be a catalyst for your own unlocking." We both look over at the flickering candles. Out of the corner of my eye I see Dora lifting her hands into a position of prayer.

There's so much to take in. I have nothing to say. I just want to be alone. I just need . . . I don't know what I need. Space.

I kiss Dora on the cheek, thank her for sharing all of this with me, and go outside into the midday sun. The Wall beckons me. I cross the yard and walk the length of the barn, tracing my fingers along the boards. Then I close my eyes and focus on the way the paint has dried. There are rough edges, thick patches, and smooth sections. Their textures are a little all over the place—just like the feelings I was expressing. Only after I moved their tumultuousness out of me could I breathe and find my ground.

Now I can't help but wonder what else I've locked away.

32

"WHAT DO YOU MEAN SHE LEFT THE HOUSE TO SABINA?" Dad thunders.

"Craig. There's no need to raise your voice," Ed says from his leather chair.

Dad turns and glares at me. Is he upset with me? As if I had something to do with this! I sit on my hands and keep my focus on Ed's thick mop of white hair and horn-rimmed glasses. I still can't believe all of this is real myself. Am I dreaming?

No. Getting in Dad's car was very real. The drive to Ed's office was very real. The plush mahogany chair I'm sitting in, the large wooden desk Ed's sitting at, the wall of books behind him—they are all very real.

"You're right," Dad says. I recognize this voice. It reminds me of Reece. When he wanted to get something from me, he'd use this same conciliatory tone. "I know this is difficult for all of us. We're all grieving. It's just that . . . what happens to my mother's house is important to me. And it doesn't make sense that she would do this. We've always talked about how the house would be passed on to me, as her only child. Perhaps her stroke impacted her judgment."

I shake my head. He's grasping at straws.

"She was perfectly lucid and capable of making this decision, Craig," Ed says firmly. "Besides, she made this decision before her stroke. When I visited her in the hospital, I did so as her friend, not as her lawyer."

"Oh. Well. Okay. But . . . Sabina is married. Her life is in Los Angeles. What's she going to do with the house?" He's lifting his hands and shrugging his shoulders, using big forceful gestures to make his case. I've seen this before. "It would be a lot of responsibility for her. The house needs a lot of work."

What is he talking about? Nana has kept the house in great shape. It might be faded in some places and a little saggy in others, but, overall, it's doing fine. And apparently he's forgotten—or is conveniently dismissing—the fact that Reece and I bought a fixer-upper. I'm not new to home ownership.

"Last time I checked, Sabina was a grown woman." Ed gives me a small smile. There are shadows around his eyes. As a longtime friend of Nana's, he's been touched by her death too. "She's very capable of making decisions about what to do with the house. She's free to live there, or, if she returns to LA, then she can sell or rent it. Really, the choice is up to her."

The choice is up to me. These words apply to so much more than just the house. If I can embrace them, that is.

I can't believe Nana never said anything about this in all the time we had together at the hospital. I wish she were here to defend her decision, to tell Dad in her own words why she changed the will. Perhaps she didn't say anything because she didn't have the energy for it. Then it hits me: she knew it would be left up to me to have this conversation. I bet she thought I needed to stand up to him—that what happened in this room would be part of my own Grand Reset. I resist smiling in the midst of this heated discussion. Still, my heart leaps at the idea of Nana still giving me advice, even after she's left this lifetime.

"Of course she's a grown woman," Dad snaps. He looks over at me, but he doesn't really see me. He sees what he wants to see. He always has.

I press a hand to my chest, feeling heat rise through my core. *Do not yell at him*, I tell myself. I take a breath instead. "Dad, what would you do with the house if Nana had left it to you?"

He brushes at some invisible lint on his button-down shirt. "Well, I . . ."

"You want to sell it, don't you?"

"I—no—I mean." He crosses his arms over his chest. "Yes. I had considered selling it. Given the market right now, it would do really well."

I take another deep breath, as deep as I can, given the pressure rising inside of me. The Angry Woman appears next to me. "Dad, you can't possibly sell Nana's house. It's . . ."

"It's what, Sabina?" Dad turns and waves his hand at me. "You think you know about taking care of a house on your own?" His voice is harsh. "It's a money pit. Taxes. Repairs. I bet you anything the foundation has never been fixed and the roof is a mess. I'm surprised it didn't cave in during the last winter storm. And it's just a house—one that would fetch a good price, since people seem to be flocking to this silly little town for some reason."

I detect something like a wince in Ed's eyes. If I recall correctly, he moved to Santa Cruz long before Pops and Nana did.

"Let's just come back to the facts, shall we?" Ed's voice is stern. "Cordelia has left the house to Sabina. There isn't anything that can be said or done to change that fact—unless Sabina was to sign the house over to you, Craig."

They both look at me, and I look down at my lap. "I'm not going to sign it over to you, Dad," I mutter, without raising my eyes.

"What, Sabina?" Dad asks. "I didn't hear you."

I look up at him. The Angry Woman's presence gives me strength. With a trembling but louder voice, I repeat myself. "I'm not going to sign Nana's house over to you."

His green eyes pierce me with rage. Then he blinks rapidly and turns away.

I did it! I can't believe it. I imagine giving Nana a high five. The Angry Woman smiles. I feel almost drunk on power. Dad's angry, but I don't feel afraid of him. Rather than looking away, I stare at his profile. For the first time, I notice his red hair is slightly disheveled. It's plastered to his forehead in the front but sticking up a bit in the back. I guess he's more impacted by grief than he's letting on. But I'm still not going to let him bully me. *No more locking away my fur.*

My father's silence is deafening. Ed clears his throat. I take that as a sign to ask Ed, "Is there more for us to hear?"

"There is." Ed meets my eyes and . . . is that a wink? "Craig, shall I continue?"

"Uh, yes. You can continue." Dad quickly sweeps his fury under some invisible rug, as though he's the master of his emotions. Maybe that's where I got my ability to tuck things away.

"Well, regarding the finances." He passes one piece of paper to Dad and one to me. "Each of your sheets details what she has left to you." I count the zeros on the page in my hands: one, two, three, four, five—she's left me six figures. Holy shit. I lift my face to Ed, my eyes wide.

He nods. "I know. Cordelia had a bit of a nest egg. There are other assets that she wishes to have donated to various organizations around town. We'll take care of that. She also made a detailed list of specific belongings of hers that she'd like to have given to the Library Ladies and, of course, Dora. Your mom is on that list too, Sabina, as are some other names I don't recognize." He hands me another sheet. "Lia expressed a desire for you to be the one to put those gifts together for each recipient."

Nana's generosity doesn't surprise me. I want to hug her, hold her hand, thank her. But she's not here. On second thought, yes she is. I look down at this list of people she wants me to reach out to. This is Nana, right here in my hands, doing what she has always done. The impact of that threatens to explode out of me in tears. I swallow hard, attempting to bury the grief. But then, I look over at Dad and remember him sweeping away his fury just moments ago. Where does that go? What does it do to someone? How many times have I buried my sadness, my anger, my rage, my everything? I don't want to live like that anymore. I don't want to swallow my tears when the grief they express—the sadness that's washing through me right now—is like a wave of appreciation for Nana. So I let them roll down my cheeks and turn to face my father. "Dad, Nana was the most generous person I've ever known."

He grunts.

"She was the most generous person I've ever known, too, Sabina," Ed says, genuinely.

As I take the box of tissues Ed offers, it dawns on me how, even though Dad has asked me how I'm doing, he hasn't really listened. It always ends up being about him: his upset, his plans. I'm so completely done with his bullshit. I'm ready to wrap this up and get the hell out of here. I've got some serious processing to do, and it's not happening in this office, that's for sure. "Thanks, Ed. Is there anything else?"

He looks down at the papers on his desk then back up at me. "We've covered it for now. I know this is a lot to take in. I'm here for you, of course, if you have any questions. We can check in again next week if you like, either by phone or in person if you're still in town. That goes for you, too, Craig." Only then does he look over at Dad, who still isn't making eye contact with either of us.

"Dad?"

"Hmm? Oh. Yes. That's fine. Then we'll be going now." He stands up abruptly.

Ed rises more slowly and comes around to the side of his desk. "Cordelia was a magnificent woman. She'll be missed." He reaches his hand out to Dad, who shakes it with a gruff up-and-down motion and then drops it.

"Bye, Mr. Townsend." Dad heads toward the door without looking at me. "Come on, we're going," he calls over his shoulder.

I stand up. "You can go ahead without me. I'll walk home." He doesn't turn around or make any sign that he's heard me. He just opens the door and walks out.

I hug Ed goodbye then make my way through the waiting

room and step outside, just in time to see my dad's car pull away from the curb. I guess he did hear me after all. I inhale a lungful of crisp air. And another one. The fog has lifted. All the palm trees, houses, and cars parked on the street look shiny, like they've been freshly washed. I look up at the sky and let the sun warm my face.

33

"GRAHAM?" I'M SURPRISED—AND GRATEFUL—THAT IT'S HIM. I only got back from Ed's office a little bit ago and am not ready to deal with my father's anger again.

"Hey, Sabina." Graham's eyes search my face. "I came by earlier and you weren't here, so I went to the hospital. I saw James. He told me about Lia." He takes a deep breath. "I'm so sorry. How are you doing?"

"I'm . . . sad." I hold the door open. "Come on in."

He steps inside, slipping his shoes off like he's been coming inside to visit every day. Which he did, one summer. "I can only stay for a few minutes. But I had to come see you, especially when I heard the news."

I curl up in the corner of the couch, tucking my feet beneath me. He sits down in the teal armchair, kitty-corner from me. The last time we saw each other—at the bar—feels like forever ago, even though only a few days have passed. Still, as my eyes drop down to his lips, I remember the taste and touch of his mouth on mine. I quickly look away, focusing on the crystals hanging in the window.

He's quiet, waiting for me to speak. "Dora and my dad were with her when she slipped away. I mean, when she died." I press my hand against my chest and look back at him. "I still can't believe she's gone. I keep expecting her to emerge from her bedroom with a book in her hand, wanting to read something to me. Or greeting me at the back door when I come in from the studio." I close my eyes for a moment, picturing her sitting with us. But then her image wavers and disappears. I slowly open my eyes. "We're scattering her ashes tomorrow. We rented a boat. Just a few of us. The wake is afterward. At Rosie McCanns—the Irish pub over on Pacific Avenue." I swallow before asking, "Can you come?"

"Sabina . . ."

He's not using his nickname for me. Is that because of the kiss? Or because I pushed him away? Maybe he's trying to reestablish that he can be just a friend. But I sense something else is going on, given the pained expression on his face. "Graham, what're you not saying?"

He sighs audibly. "I wish I could be at Lia's wake. And, of course you're sad. Your favorite person in the world just died. I know how the missing can ache so much." His eyes crinkle at the edges. He's clearly familiar with the terrain of grief.

"It does. So much." I reach for Nana's blue shawl, draped over the arm of the couch next to me. I bring it up to my face. It smells like her unique blend of vanilla, lavender, and a hint of The Wild, which is both crushing and comforting. How long will that smell linger? When it fades, will I remember it? And if I can't—will that part of her be lost to me? I lower the shawl into my lap and return my attention to Graham. "But something else is going on. What is it?"

He rubs his chin. "It's actually really good news. The timing isn't ideal, but . . ." I lean forward. "I got a call I've been waiting for . . . from National Geographic. They invited me to join a two-week expedition in Alaska, as one of their experts. It's a last-minute request. The photographer that was slated for it got sick. They're flying me home to Anchorage so I can get my gear, then on to Fairbanks, where the trip begins. My flight leaves this evening."

It takes me a moment to process his words and comprehend the look on his face. This is joy I'm seeing. This trip is something he wants, something he's been waiting for. But he's going to go, and I don't know when I'll see him again. He won't be here for the wake. His sister, Sam, could go into labor any day now, and he'll miss the birth. Isn't that why he came down here? To be with her? How can he just leave like this? Leave her, leave me?

My cheeks flush as I hear my own thoughts. The Abandoned Woman is sitting next to me. I look down at my hands, where I've threaded Nana's shawl between my fingers. I force myself to breathe. He's not leaving me. He's going toward something he wants—a creative adventure that will further his career by leaps and bounds. Nana would be happy for him. I can picture her patting his hand and telling him congratulations. I want to do the same, but, instead, a sob escapes through my lips. "I'm sorry."

Graham leans toward me. "What's . . . you don't have to apologize. But what's going on?"

"It's just . . ." I meet his ocean-eyes. Is this it then? Our goodbye? "I can picture Nana congratulating you. She'd be happy for you. I . . . I am too. I know it doesn't look like it!" I wave the shawl in the air. “But I am. I just . . . it’s sudden, you know? But it’s good. For you. So, what’s the trip about?”

As he tells me about the expedition, I listen—and try to really listen. When my mind wanders to my hurt, I remind myself that this is not about me. He is not leaving me. I want the people I care about to have experiences that bring them joy, exactly like this trip does for Graham. Sometimes, that’s going to mean that they’re far away from me. I need to accept that.

Though he keeps his voice subdued, I can feel his excitement as he describes the group’s itinerary. It includes both Denali and Kenai Fjords National Parks, as well as a wildlife-conservation center. It’s focused on photography, but there’s an educational element too, and the idea is to inspire these people to become conservation advocates as well. I reach out and rest my hand on his. “Graham, it sounds incredible, and like a really big deal. Congratulations.”

He puts a hand on top of mine. “I know you’re deep in your own grief right now. I don’t mean to make this about me.”

“You’re not.” I shake my head. “I’m glad you’re telling me. Life continues for the rest of us, and Nana would want us to live it fully.” I think I believe that. But it does feel a little like I’m trying to convince myself.

He squeezes my hand and then releases it. “Before I go, tell me something? About you? About Lia?”

I stretch back against the couch, considering. I’m not ready to talk about the visit to Ed’s office. I’m still processing what he told us and everything that happened there with my dad. But there is something. Something I haven’t told anyone yet. “On the day Nana died, I was with her alone and . . .” Am I really going to tell him this? Something nudges me to keep sharing. "As I sat with her, I sensed a presence in the room. It was in the corner above her and looked kind of like a cloud, just hovering there. It was white, but I got the sense—and I know this sounds really bizarre—that it was showing itself to me as a color, without any defined edges, so that I would register there was something there, so I wouldn't ignore it." I pause. How do I put into words the gift of that presence? As hard as it is, I feel like I need to try. "As I tapped into it, I got a sense of . . . something. I guess I would call it Divine Love. Whatever it was, it was with me, with Nana, waiting to receive her when she died. Like a mother receives her newborn baby in her arms, you know? And I also got this piercing shot of wisdom in that moment—that this presence, this Divine Love, is with us all the time. All the time, Graham. It's just, we don't . . . we forget. We don't let it . . . in."

There aren't any tears right now, not like when I perceived this presence in the hospital room. Instead, I'm filled with the same sweet thrumming sensation that I experienced that day. My cells are humming, vibrating, responding to some music that I can't hear but can feel down into my marrow. It's really subtle, but it's definitely present. "I was able to let go of Nana a little bit more then, as well as the fear I had of losing her to the mystery of death. I knew she would be held. And I knew I was held too. I was a bit of a mess—and still am. But, when I remember to let the presence in, it soothes me."

Graham doesn't say anything right away. I wonder what he's thinking. But then I realize, even if he thinks I'm crazy, it's okay. I know what I experienced was a gift. Finally, he says, "Sabina, what you describe . . . it's so beautiful."

"It is, isn't it?" I wrap Nana's shawl around my shoulders. Talking about it out loud, sharing this with him, helps it become more real for me.

He turns his attention to the wall across from us—the gallery of happier times. I'd found an empty antique silver frame in the attic for the picture he'd given us at the hospital and added it to the collection. He spots it and looks back at me with a small smile. Then he glances down at his watch. "I have to go. I'm sorry that I'm not able to stay longer. To hear more. To be of support to you." He leans forward, and for a moment I think he's going to take my hands in his, but he doesn't. Instead, he rests his elbows on his knees again. "It's meant a lot to me to reconnect with you."

"Me too, Graham." All the things I want to say gather in my mouth, making it hard to breathe. *I don't regret that we kissed*, I want to tell him. *And if things were different, if I was single—or divorced—I might be interested in exploring something with you.* I want to confess that. But instead, I muster up two puny words: "A lot."

He reaches out and squeezes my hand before getting up to slip his shoes back on. I untuck my feet from beneath me and walk across the room to stand with him by the door. And then we're hugging, our bodies pressed against each other. I tuck my face into his neck and breathe in his woodsy scent one last time.

We pull back from each other at the same time. He reaches for the door. I don't know when or if I'll see him again. And I don't know what to say, so I just wave as he turns to walk across the porch. I close the door behind him, slide down to the floor, and sob.

34

"WHAT ARE YOU DOING HERE, REECE?" I ASK IN A LOW voice. He's standing a few feet from the door with a bottle of beer and a sympathetic smile.

I've just come from Nana's burial at sea. It had been strange yet comforting to hold the remains of Nana's body in my hands. The ashes were a pasty white and gray color, and they felt coarse and gritty when I dug my hands into them. I tossed handfuls over the side of the boat and watched as some of the granules disappeared into the water and others flew away, carried by the breeze.

I focus on my husband. He's the last person I expected to see in this crowd of people at Rosie McCanns. "Your dad called me. And hello to you too," he says jokingly. Then his voice becomes somber. "I'm sorry about Lia."

His voice is warm and genuine, but his words sound like they're coming from the other end of a tunnel; muffled, far away. I sway slightly back and forth as though I'm still on the boat. He sets his beer down on a nearby table and takes me into his arms. Instinctively, I return the hug, but then I quickly release him and back away. Why is he here? Is this just another performance for him where he shows up to play the part of the supportive husband? "What are you doing here?" I ask again.

He reaches out to tuck a piece of hair behind my ear, but I brush his hand away. He pulls back and picks up his beer, taking a long swallow before answering. "Your dad told me about Lia, about the wake. He also said that you wanted me to be here."

I cross my arms over my chest. "That isn't true."

"Well it sure looks like a wake is going on here." He smirks and tilts his beer bottle to the folks gathered around us.

"You know what I mean." I can't keep the annoyance out of my voice.

The smirk vanishes, and he tilts his head. "Your dad said you'd say that. I know you're upset with me. But let me be here for you."

I scratch my forehead, considering what to say. *No more tucking things aside, remember?* "I don't want you here. Seeing you isn't comforting. It's triggering. It brings up all the reminders of how our marriage is dead. I can't handle that, this—you—on top of Nana's death. Please leave." My voice is firm.

"Sabina . . ." He tries to take my hand, but I pull it away. "Who said our marriage is dead? That's why I called you the other day."

"What?" And then I remember. He had called. That day at the hospital. But he hadn't left a message. And with everything going on with Nana, I hadn't given it much thought. "Reece, I don't have energy for this. Not here, not now."

"Okay, all right." He puts a hand up. "But would it be okay if I stuck around?"

"Reece." There's a tightness in my jaw. A big internal *no* resounds through me. "Please don't argue with me."

"I swear, I'm not arguing, Shug. I'm just trying to discuss this. I liked Lia. I care about you. And about your dad. I know he's hurting."

I glance over his shoulder and see Dora lifting a glass to me, waving me over to the bar. I look back at Reece. "Fine. You can comfort my dad. You two have a lot in common."

"What's that supposed to mean?"

Dad walks up to us then. "Reece, good man. You came." They shake hands. "Sabina," he says to me, nodding.

"Dad." I consider biting my tongue. But I can no longer stand the tension in my jaw—the actual physical pain of not speaking up. "Why did you call Reece? I didn't ask you to interfere in my life."

"What?" He puts his hand up just like Reece had a moment ago. Like I'm the one overreacting. "Reece is my son-in-law. I wanted as much family around as possible on this day. It's a hard day." The blank face he wore on the boat—stoicism or boredom or something else—has shifted into a mask of sorrow. Now that he has an audience, he's assuming a more appropriate expression. Reece reaches over and pats him on the back.

It's eerie to see them side by side. They're so similar, from their mannerisms to their beverage preferences—they're both drinking the same brand of beer. They even have the same look in their eyes, like they'd be shocked if I refused them what they wanted. I don't know what to say. Luckily, I hear Dora call my name. "I have to go. We're making a toast." I head toward the bar, relieved to have an excuse to walk away.

Dora hands me a glass of whiskey, neat. "In honor of Lia," she says. I take a swallow, relishing the familiar burn. "You ready?"

"Well. I wouldn't say 'ready.' But I'm here for it."

Dora taps her glass with a spoon to get everyone's attention. I feel a little lightheaded as I take in the faces of so many friends and loved ones. I spot Mel, Miguel, James, and Caleb at a table. Their presence reassures me, and reminds me to take a breath and feel my feet on the ground. There's a smattering of bright colors—Kelly green, ruby red, sunshine yellow—mixed in with the black clothing. Given what Nana had told us about looking for the rainbows after she'd gone, we'd invited people to wear bright colors instead of the traditional black garb. I'm wearing a cobalt blue dress I'd found when I went shopping for the fundraiser. Blue had always been Nana's favorite color, and buying it seemed like a step toward injecting a little color into my black LA wardrobe.

I welcome everyone, and we make a toast to Nana. Dora reads a poem. Then friends take turns sharing stories—calling them out from wherever they're standing or sitting in the room. Many of these people have known Nana longer than I've been alive, and while I've heard some of the stories before, I haven't heard all of them. My glass never stays empty for long. I drift around the room, from person to person, hugging, saying hello, listening to the boisterous anecdotes told loudly for all to hear as well as the somber ones, shared in small groups.

As the night wears on, the gathering thins out, and Dad seeks me out—with Reece at his side. "Pip, I've been talking with Reece, and we both want to know what you're going to do with your Nana's house. You have a husband and a home in LA.

Reece, tell her." He puts a hand on Reece's shoulder. "Tell her what you told me. Tell her you want her back."

My body tenses. "Dad," I warn quietly, "my marriage is none of your business. And now is not the time to talk about Nana's house."

"What? Why? Because you're sad?" He releases his hand from Reece's shoulder and gestures at the people around us. "Just because I'm not weepy and sentimental like everyone else doesn't mean I'm not hurting too." I feel his hot breath on my cheek and note his trembling lips. He sounds more angry than sad. As I count to three on an inhale, I remind myself we each cope in different ways. Maybe getting mad is his way of grieving.

Not sure what to say in response, I turn my attention to Reece. I look him directly in the eye and keep my voice steady. "We're not having a conversation tonight about anything related to you and me. I already asked you to go. Please leave."

"But—" Dad protests.

"Dad. No."

Reece bows slightly to me. I don't know if it's meant to be sarcastic or respectful, but I don't care. Then he turns to my dad. "Craig." They shake hands, and he leaves. My shoulders drop a few inches as I watch him make his way out the door.

I turn back to my father. "Tonight, we're celebrating Nana. I'm not talking with you about her house. I'm not going to change my mind. From here on out, I'm making choices about my life for myself. If I want your opinion, I'll ask for it. Got it?"

"Well . . ." He looks around, noticing a few people have turned to watch our interaction. I can sense him cringing. I know he doesn't like this kind of attention.

"Dad?" My heart is beating fast. I've never spoken to him like this.

"Yes." He winces, as though it hurts him to give me what I'm asking for. "But, Pip, you don't know the whole story."

I take the bait. "What whole story?"

He looks down at the floor. "I was relying on the sale of your Nana's house to get your mom and me out of a tight spot."

I stand completely still and exhale through pursed lips. "What do you mean?"

He looks around to make sure nobody is listening. "I made some investments that didn't turn out as expected." His face reddens. "The money Lia left us will only cover part of what I lost. I may . . . we may have to sell the brownstone."

There's a prickling sensation along the back of my neck. My father has never, ever mentioned any financial struggles to me. As far as I knew, there had never been any. If he and Mom had money issues while I was growing up, they were spoken of behind closed doors. It must be pretty bad if he's telling me this. I clear my throat, unsure of what to say. I feel a strange mixture of pride—like he's finally seeing me as an adult—and suspicion. Is he trying to get what he wants by tugging on my heartstrings? He knows how much I love the brownstone. After all, I grew up there. It doesn't have the same cluttered coziness as Nana's, but it has some really special places—a window seat in my bedroom where I spent hours curled up reading, banisters I slid down when nobody was watching, a front stoop where I hung out with our neighbors.

When he looks at me again, I notice his eyes are bloodshot. "I don't want to take anything from you, but you know how your mother loves that house."

I do. The brownstone is my mom's sanctuary when she's sick and her showcase when she has energy for entertaining. She worked closely with an interior designer to create the kind of elegant, classy home she never had growing up. And with dad gone so much of the time, the house is kind of like her companion—one she has to care for. There is always something to fix, restore, tend to. It's like the house gives her things to do to take her mind off Dad's absence, something to put her heart into.

But I can't imagine selling Nana's cottage. That feels so wrong. Even though Reece seems to think our marriage isn't dead, it is to me, which means I won't have anywhere to live if I part with it. I bite my cheek. I don't want to give him the house. Does this make me a horrible daughter? I should be offering up anything I can to help them save the brownstone, right? Isn't that what Nana would do? Give them what she could to help them out of this predicament?

But damn it. I bite down harder and taste the metallic sting of blood. Why do I have to keep giving up what's important to me? When do I get to have what I want?

I swallow the blood, wishing I still had a glass of whiskey with me, and reach for one of my curls. As I meet Dad's eyes, I drop my hand. From somewhere in my depths, I muster up a restraint I didn't know I had. I'm tempted to yell at him and stomp my feet, but I remind myself I'm an adult and, as an adult, know better than to try and talk about this any further right now. "Dad, we've had a lot to drink and it's an emotional night. Let's . . . table this conversation for now but revisit it soon."

He dips his head. "Okay."

While I am not exactly sure what Nana would do, I know

without a doubt that she would work this out without a blowup, and she'd want us to do the same. But right now, I don't see a way forward where one of us doesn't lose something important.

35

I SLIP OFF MY SNEAKERS AND CURL MY TOES INTO THE SAND before stepping into the water. "I'm setting myself free," I whisper, wishing I had a hood and booties to complete my Selkie-fur transformation. The waves are surprisingly serene. Like usual, I count twenty paces into the water and turn to swim parallel to the shore in an overarm crawl. "I'll always be with you," Nana had told me, so I imagine her by my side as I swim toward the lighthouse. Each stroke, each kick, feels labored, like my body is filled with wet cement. The hangover doesn't help. But I keep going, knowing that the only way forward is through.

Nana left her house to me. To *me*. Not Dad. Not anyone else. But she didn't know about Dad's financial situation. If she had, would she have left the house to him? I've been turning this over in my mind for hours, but trying to read the mind of someone who's no longer alive feels like being on a hamster wheel. I'm getting nowhere. And it really doesn't even matter if she would have given him the house or not. She made her decision. Now it's my turn to make mine.

As I lift my head from the water to breathe, questions that

Dora asked me the other day ring in my ears: *What have you locked away? Where have you betrayed yourself?*

Dropping my head back in the water, I think about how I quit swimming in LA. When Reece and I were living together in our apartment in Los Feliz, he always made a point to mention how much he enjoyed waking up next to me on the mornings I didn't go to the local pool. So gradually, over time, I stopped going. I was the one who gave up something I loved so that I'd be there for him, with him, in the morning.

I gave that up. Me.

In the moment, it seemed like such a small thing. A singular choice. But I made a lot of those kinds of choices, and now, several years later, all those moments have piled on top of each other like the tangles of seaweed on the beach. I can no longer deny how much I betrayed myself.

And it wasn't just with Reece. I did that with Marco. And with Dad.

But there are new scenes now, hanging before me like transparent pieces of film. The one from Ed's office—Dad's furious eyes as I told him I wasn't going to sign the house over to him—and from the wake, when I told him to stop interfering in my life.

You stood up to him. You didn't let him bully you.

I lift my head out of the water again, and a strangled laugh erupts from my mouth. So that's what not abandoning myself can look like. It was uncomfortable, but it was also intoxicating, in a way.

But what do I do now, in light of Dad's situation? There's gotta be a way to help him without giving myself away.

Bring your fur to the conversation.

I laugh at the thought of wearing a fur while talking with Dad, realizing too late that my face is underwater. I inhale a mouthful of seawater and jerk my head up. I tread water as the coughing turns into broken laughter. "You want me to bring my fur to the conversation?" I ask the empty air around me. "What, my wetsuit?"

And then I get it. If I'm being my own forever woman and not giving up my skin and what's important to me, I have to learn how to have these conversations in new ways. Whether I'm talking with Dad about helping him get out of this "tight spot" or Reece about our marriage, our house, and dividing up the finances of the business, I can't do what I would have in the past—give them each what they want to please them, to avoid conflict. But being a forever woman doesn't mean being selfish or not caring about the people around me either. I've so often seen these conversations as either-or situations, and I get the feeling that won't work anymore. I want to keep Nana's house. I need to do that for me. But that doesn't mean I won't help. I don't want to see my parents lose the brownstone.

I reach into the water and start swimming toward the lighthouse again. My body no longer feels laden with cement. There's a lightness in my limbs now. My mind is racing but it feels generative, helpful. What do I need to know from Dad in order to have a constructive conversation? I should find out how much money is needed to save the house. And if he intends it as a gift or a loan.

And Reece. Will we sell the house in Silver Lake? Will he buy my half of it? If so, maybe I'd have enough money to help Dad out and make sure I have enough to live on for the short term. How would this all work?

What was it Graham said at the bar, about how sometimes we get in over our heads and need help? Right; it's not a sign of weakness. And I'm certainly out of my depths when it comes to navigating these financial conversations and the dissolution of a marriage. Maybe the wise thing here is to recognize this and ask for support. Ed's kind eyes and mop of white hair come to mind. I could go see him and ask for his input. I bet Ed could refer me to a divorce lawyer. Or at least give me some advice on how to choose one. And how to handle this situation with my father.

Suddenly, the water around me feels warm. I stop swimming and lift my face to the sky. The presence I perceived in Nana's hospital room the day she died seems to hover all around me. It's a potent, loving energy. Closing my eyes, I take a deep breath and sense myself being hugged, by the water, by Divine Love, by Nana. That same thrumming I experienced in the hospital room vibrates in my cells, reminding me I'm not alone.

Words spill out of me. "No more giving my fur away. I can show up to these conversations with my fur on. I can be generous without giving myself away. I'm the Forever Woman. I can have what I want, without waiting for someone else to give me permission to have it. I will keep Nana's house. I will continue making art. And I will swim every morning if I want to."

In the Selkie myth, the fisherman is seen as the powerful one, the one who controls the Selkie by locking her fur away, keeping her onshore with him. She's only able to escape when she finds the key he accidentally leaves behind one day.

Now I see that, as the Selkie, I'm the powerful one.

And the key to unlocking myself is inside of me.

~~~

BACK AT the cottage, after a long, hot shower, I turn my phone on and stare at it for a moment. It's time to face what I've been putting off. I consider calling Reece but tap out a text instead.

> Reece, can you arrange to be out of the house for a few days, sometime soon, so I can come pick up my things? We can talk when I'm there about the business and the house and

My finger hovers above the keypad. And what?

I remember the wisdom I heard the night of my show. Although at the time it applied to my paintings, now it seems applicable to my marriage. *It's time to let go and move on.*

I finish the rest of the text.

> filing for divorce.

The moment I press send, a deep sigh moves through me. Tension in my upper back that I hadn't even been aware of melts. My shoulders drop. This is what I want. I want to stay here in Santa Cruz, in Nana's house. In my house.

My life in LA was built around Reece's music. I was there for him. It wasn't a waste of time, but it wasn't exactly what I wanted either. Now it's time to live my life for me—to make my dreams and art a priority.

And it's time to take care of my past in order to move forward into my future.
~~~

36

Los Angeles, California
Two Weeks Later

WITH A MUG OF COFFEE IN HAND, I WANDER DOWN THE hallway from the kitchen to our bedroom. My throat tightens as I stare at our California king bed. The geometrically patterned quilt that we bought together is pulled up over the pillows. An empty water glass sits on the nightstand on Reece's side.

We'd gotten the bed when we first moved in together, in our apartment in Los Feliz. Along with a new set of sheets and a thick pillow topper. It had felt so big to me, so luxurious. But last night, even after a day of driving and several hours of packing up my things, I couldn't bring myself to sleep in it. I slept on the couch, and I woke up off and on throughout the night with dreams of a roller coaster and both the Abandoned Woman and the Angry Woman talking to me.

I turn to head toward the front door, where the pile of

boxes and bags has been steadily growing. I stop and trace my fingers along the edge of a framed selfie we'd taken during our honeymoon on Maui. We're golden tan, and we're standing on Red Sand Beach. In the photo next to it, we're hugging the roots of a huge banyan tree. We'd asked an older couple to take our picture. They'd congratulated us enthusiastically when we'd told them we were on our honeymoon. "Good luck," the woman had whispered to me as they went on their way.

I remember the argument Reece and I had about the picture frames. He'd insisted all of our photos be in the same modern black frame. I'd wanted to use a blend of funky antique frames. But eventually, I acquiesced. I did the same thing with our honeymoon. I'd wanted to go backpacking through Italy. "We're not college kids anymore, Shug. We're adults. And why go backpacking when we can afford to stay at a resort and lounge at the beach or the pool all day?"

"Oh, Reece." I sigh. A photo from our wedding day catches my attention. In it, I'm wearing a long sleeveless white dress I'd found with Mel at a vintage shop. My hair is up, with a few curls hanging down. I'm leaning back into Reece, all handsome in his black tuxedo. He has his arms wrapped around me. Our faces, cheek to cheek, smile back at me. We were so in love. And we did have something special. What happened? I'm no longer sure how much of our drifting apart is a result of his work, his interest in other women, and his needing to be the center of attention and how much of it came from my pattern of giving up on my dreams, wants, and needs again and again. They're clearly intertwined and playing off of each other. And I'm not sure it matters.

I take a sip of coffee and scan the highlights of our happy

times together. Knowing all these framed photos are going to get packed up in a box and not come out again for a long time—if ever—is like a punch in the gut. All those years and shared moments . . . down the drain.

I look back at my younger self as a smiling bride. For a moment, there's a roaring sensation in my ears like I'm underwater. The Angry Woman's words from my dream pulse through me: *Forgiveness isn't a hall pass to keep doing the same old things.* I've been thinking she was referring to Reece. How many times had I forgiven him over the years when he crossed a boundary and apologized the next day? Then he kept on doing the same thing. And Dad sure seems to view Mom's forgiveness as permission to continue having the occasional affair.

But what if the Angry Woman was talking to me *about me*?

I lean back against the wall opposite the photos and groan. Then I look at my younger self, the one in the wedding photo. "I'm sorry for all the ways I abandoned you. I'm so sorry," I say to her. I close my eyes and breathe into a river of grief rising up from my belly, pooling in my head. I know I can't go back in time and change any of it—my mistakes, my self-betrayals—but that doesn't take the hurt away. That feeling is real.

I take a deep breath. And then another one. "I . . . I forgive you." My voice is a whisper at first, as I test out the words, seeing how they feel when I say them. The grief is still there, but it's not heavy. "I forgive myself," I say, a bit louder this time. The words create a soothing vibration throughout my head and chest. I open my eyes and focus on that young bride on the wall. The one who gave up her fur. She didn't know. She was in love and trying so hard to make this challenging thing called "marriage" work. And she thought that, to do that, she needed to keep making sacrifices. But now, I know better. "I'm not going to abandon you again. I promise. I mean, I might mess up. I might do it again out of habit. And if I do, well, Selkies, can you help me with this?" The request rolls out of me so naturally, reminding me I'm not alone in this. I step closer to the photo and kiss my own face in the frame. "Please show me how to stay with me. I'm rebuilding trust with myself, starting now."

37

I SIP THE SHAKE THAT REECE PICKED UP FROM THE Punchbowl—the juice bar near where we used to live in Los Feliz. We've been polite with each other since he arrived about fifteen minutes ago. Him getting my favorite drink—the "Power Mint" with coconut cashew cream, mint leaves, banana, and cacao nibs—seems like a peace offering. I look over at him, sitting on the other side of the kitchen island. "I guess this is better than shouting at each other."

Reece takes a swallow of his smoothie and says, "Yeah, Sabina. I didn't come here for that. I mean, if you want to shout at me, you can. You have every right to."

We look at each other then—like, really look at each other for the first time since he arrived. "Are you still with her?" I blurt out.

"I'm not." He sets his cup down. There's a look in his eyes I don't think I've ever seen before. "Sabina, I really messed up. I'm sorry. Leaving you was a huge mistake. I never meant to hurt you so much." He inhales slowly. "Can you—can you forgive me?"

My mouth falls open. Reece, admitting he messed up. But rather than feeling a sense of lightness, I feel a heavy weight in my gut. I can't answer his question yet. There's still too much I want to know. "What made you so convinced you had to explore something with her in the first place?"

He takes another deep breath. "You really want to know?" I nod. As I take another sip of my shake, I notice he's fidgeting with the pick he always carries in his pocket. "We had a lot of chemistry. Both on and off the stage." He speaks slowly at first, hesitantly. But then he seems to gather steam and speaks the words all in a gush. "Knowing we were heading into the recording studio together, I just . . . I got afraid that our recording might be jeopardized if we weren't free to follow that attraction."

I fiddle with my straw. "Wait . . . how were you up in Santa Cruz if you were supposed to be recording?"

He tucks his pick back in his pocket and lays his hands on the table between us. "Jaxon got sick, and we had to delay things to give him time to heal his voice."

"Is he okay now?"

"Yeah. He recovered, and the recording went . . . well, it was intense, actually."

Rather than ask him about that—I have a sense what made it intense was his dynamic with Fiona—I make myself ask the other thing I could speculate about or just ask. "Why didn't it work out? With . . . her?"

"It was too much too fast. Beyond the chemistry, we didn't share any kind of ground together. Once I got into it, I realized what an idiot I was. I mean, to throw away everything we built together?" He waves his hands around then drops them in his lap. "It . . . I ended it with her when I woke up and saw how I'd gotten it all wrong. I wasn't acknowledging how good I had it with you. I wanted to come to you sooner, but then, with Lia having a stroke and you asking for space, I just, well, that's why, when your dad called, I leaped at the chance to come see you." His eyebrows press together, and he leans forward on the island. "Can you forgive me? And more than that—do you think you could give me—give us—a second chance?"

For a moment, I feel like I'm falling backward. He's uttering words I was so sure I wanted to hear, back when he first left. But now that it's actually happening, I feel strange, like I'm in some kind of twilight zone. I grip the edge of the island and close my eyes.

When I open my eyes again, he's no longer across the island from me. He's pulled up the stool next to me and is looking at me earnestly. "Shug, I miss you. We were so good together. Look what we built together." He gestures to the room around us. "We turned this dump into a home. We transformed the fallen-down garage into a studio. We built my music into a career that's going places. I couldn't have done any of that without you."

It's hard not to notice that two of those three things are all about his dreams. "Oh." I move farther back on the stool. "So, you need me. Is that what this is?"

"No. Yes. I mean. It's not like that." He shakes his head. "I love you. I love us . . . what we were together. What we created together. I made some bad choices. I know they hurt you. I want to make it up to you." He reaches out and takes my hand, but I pull it away and stand up, holding the side of the island as my legs wobble.

"Reece. You left us. It seemed like you thought nothing of just walking away from me, us, our marriage, to explore another relationship." I cross my arms over my chest. "How can you guarantee that won't happen again? It's not like you're going to stop performing with other women or encountering other attractive women out and about in LA. You're a musician. There's always a chance for that chemistry to be there. How could I trust you again?" As I ask him these questions, even bigger ones about me buzz around: *Can I trust that I won't abandon myself again? Can I learn how to wear my fur while in a relationship with him? I don't believe that I can. And I'm not willing to take a chance. Not when so much is at stake.*

"We could go to counseling." He sits up taller. "I could go on my own. Whatever it takes, Sabina, to regain your trust."

This is all happening so fast it doesn't seem real. "So, what . . . you'd have me move back in and we'd pick up with marriage and business again?"

"Yes. That is what I'm saying. I want you back. I want our life back, just like it was before." He leans forward, his hands on the stool I just vacated. "I don't want to get divorced. I don't want to buy the house from you. I want to live in it with you. I want to share life together with you. I want to grow the business with you. If that's what you want, of course. Only if that's what you want."

The Forever Woman stands beside me. *What do you want, Sabina?*

"I'm not the same woman you married, Reece. I'm also not the same woman who left LA a month ago." I twist the tie of my wraparound dress in my fingers. I can hear the clock ticking—the clock shaped like a guitar I got him for Christmas the year we moved into this house. "I don't know if I want the same things anymore."

"But that means you might, right? 'I don't know' is different from no." He scoots the stool closer to me. "And I'm not the same person either. We've both changed during this time apart."

Has he? The Angry Woman appears next to me. Hands on her hips. Does it matter? Is this about him or me?

I tap my fingers on the island. That heavy weight in my gut shifts. Closing my eyes, I tune into the Forever Woman next to me. In her presence, I have the courage to say the things I need to say. I open my eyes and scan Reece's clean-shaven jaw. He's watching me, his dark brown eyes hopeful—the same eyes I once looked into before I said "I do." And I felt like the happiest woman on earth then. Maybe I was.

"Your apology, Reece, and what you're saying, is everything I thought I wanted to hear. But . . ." I let out a gush of air. "There's something I need to be honest with you about." I bite my lip. I need to get this out. It feels important that he knows this. "Even though it was you who left, physically, to be with, well, Fiona, I've come to realize . . ." I stop to take a breath. "It was me. I was the one who left myself first, in so many important ways."

He frowns. "What do you mean?"

I take a deep breath and try to put into words what I've learned about myself over these past several weeks. "I repeated with you a dynamic I have with my dad. I always wanted to please him, be what he wanted me to be, so I let go of what was important to me. That's why—how—I ended up getting an MBA instead of a master of fine arts. As just one example of many compromises I made. One of many ways I abandoned myself." I take another sip of my drink. "So with you, it seemed natural, familiar, to give up my painting to support you with your music. To use my MBA to help you build a business. I never really realized how much I was sacrificing to give myself over to what you wanted, the vision you saw for your future."

He shakes his head. "Sabina, I never asked you to make those sacrifices."

"In a way, you did," I say evenly, honestly. "You asked me to stay and support you in your business even when I expressed a clear desire to turn my attention to my art. You told me you needed me. So I stayed. But, yes, you're right. Ultimately, I was the one who chose to lock myself and my wants and needs away." *My fur*, I think, though I'm not going to use that term with him. Reece was never my captor, like the fisherman in the Selkie myth. I'm the one who gave up my life to enter his. Unlike the Selkie, I had a choice. And I made that choice because it seemed like the safer path.

"I chose what I did as a very scared, young version of myself who believed she couldn't survive on her own. Who believed she could only survive if she held on to a man's coattails and became who and what he wanted her to be. I . . . I can't believe my life has been driven by this dynamic for so long. But it's true." After all the purging I've done on canvases over the past several weeks, putting words to my revelations feels strangely empowering. Rather than being a victim to these patterns, I'm now aware of them and able to choose something else. And still, it's so sad. I can't avoid grieving what I've lost. So much time. So many opportunities.

"Sabina, all of this . . . it's good to know, right?" His voice is optimistic, eager. "This means you don't have to operate from the same place anymore. You've identified the pattern. You know better. We know better. Which means we can start over. Do it differently."

I shake my head. "That's not where I'm going with this, Reece. It's more that . . ." I trail off. Where am I going with this? I press a hand to my chest. "I don't blame you anymore. I forgive you, Reece. For sleeping with Fiona. For leaving us to explore something with her. I forgive you." I pause, noticing the heavy weight in my belly is no longer there.

"Shug, thank you." He stands up and puts his hands on my shoulders. "You'll see. It'll be different this time. We can start again."

"Reece, no." I slip out from beneath his hands. "I'm clear. I don't want to get back together. I want to file for a divorce." My heart is in my throat, adding a percussive drumbeat to my words.

"Wow. Just like that?" There's a thread of bitterness in his voice.

"It's not 'just like that,' Reece," I say. "I've given this a lot of thought."

"But it's only been, what, a little over a month? How can you be so sure in such a short time? We could hold off on the divorce. You could take some time to be on your own and consider everything."

I think about Nana and Jeffrey and Pops. But that was different, wasn't it? Pops was the love of her life. It's not that they made each other complete; they already were on their own. It's that they encouraged each other to live life the way they really wanted to. That's not Reece, and that's not us. I haven't learned yet how to trust that I can be complete on my own, and I need to do that. I won't be able to if I return to this dynamic. Reece looked to me to be his support, his number one fan, his cheerleader. I tried to control him to protect myself against the scenario that ended up unfolding—him leaving to be with another woman. Once upon a time I did fall in love with him, and I may still love him. But he's not the love of my life, and, no matter what he says, I don't believe I'm his either.

I recall Mel's comment from earlier today, when she came over to feed me lunch: "It seemed like Reece was always more interested in what you could do for him rather than what was best for you."

It's time for me to do what's best for me, to choose what it is I really want. To take time to be on my own. Follow my own path. To know, without a doubt, that I'm choosing what's important to me for my own happiness, not for someone else's.

"Reece," I say steadily. "I don't want to do that. I lost myself in you the way you lose yourself in your music. Only for me, that isn't a healthy thing to do. It's time for me to change this pattern. I want to move forward with a divorce now. I can't be who I want to become while in a relationship with you."

"Is there another man?" he asks so quickly I'm not sure he heard what I just said. "Are you leaving me to start something with him?"

"No. I kissed Graham. But that's all. I'm not asking for a divorce because of him or to pursue something with him. I'm just clear that our marriage is over, Reece. And not because you slept with Fiona or because I kissed Graham. The way I see it . . ." I pause. "Those are just symptoms. The real issue beneath all of this is that we haven't been truly happy for a while. At least I haven't been. And it's time for me to be honest about that and find happiness in myself and my art rather than seeking it in you and your music."

He looks at me through narrowed eyes. "You're sure this is what you want?"

"Yes, it is." My heart thuds in my chest like a drumbeat, only this time, it's reassuring, resolute. "We can come to an agreement on details related to the house and the business with the help of a couple of collaborative lawyers. I've been looking into this—it's different from mediation. We each have our own lawyer, but we settle outside of court. Look into it and let me know how that sounds to you." I press my palms into my thighs and notice a lightness in my chest.

He peers out the kitchen window and doesn't say anything.

"Reece?"

"Yeah."

"I'll be gone from the house within an hour." I know I could wait until tomorrow to leave, but all I want to do tonight is sleep in my own bed at Nana's, in a place that truly feels like home. "I'll text you this week with the names of a few lawyers. Nana's lawyer recommended them. You can see if you'd like to work with one of them. Then we can arrange a meeting."

"Fine." He won't look me in the eye. He turns to go. "I'll see myself out."

And then he's gone. The front door shuts with a quiet click. I push myself away from the island and remember how Reece made this same move right before he dropped the bomb about Fiona. I head to the front door and lock it. Although my legs are no longer wobbly, they feel weak, like I just swam in rough waters. I lean back and let the door hold my weight. What a crazy summer it's been. Talk about the shit hitting the fan all at once. Why did I have to go through all of this? I rest my head in my hands and feel a wave of self-pity wash through me. I look over and see the Abandoned Woman sitting on the floor. Not bent over. Not reaching her hand out. Just looking at me.

There's a fluttery feeling in my belly. An image of the Selkies flits in front of me. They shape-shift: human to seal, seal to human. They're so smooth, so fluid, as they transition from one form to another, one perspective to another. Then a question emerges, as if coming from the Selkies themselves: What if I shape-shift my view of this experience?

I think through the order of events again. The truth is, I didn't have the courage to physically leave my marriage until Reece did. Had he not had the affair and told me about it, I might have stayed. How much longer would I have lasted, supporting him and betraying myself? Another year or two? Even more? I press my fingers to my lips. I can't believe this, but I'm actually grateful for Reece. And Fiona. Their affair rocked my world, and that betrayal hurt like hell, but it also woke me up. Now I know what I want. And I'm way more motivated to put energy into my life, my art, my business.

The Angry Woman, leaning against the wall nearby, stretches her arms back behind her head and gives me a wide grin. Heat streams from my belly out to my fingertips and down to my toes. What used to be anger now feels like strength. Power. *I survived.* The sadness didn't drown me. The rage didn't destroy me. I'm not pissy or bitter. My hand slides down from my lips to my chest. Through all of this, I found my way home.

The Forever Woman sits on my boxes, beaming at me.

38

I PULL OFF THE PACIFIC COAST HIGHWAY AT A CAMPGROUND south of Big Sur to use the bathroom. There are several tents set up and a few campers moving about. As I open the car door, the roaring ocean tickles my ears and its tangy smell fills my nose.

After using the restroom, I walk to the edge of the cliff and look down. Each wave splashes the rocky shore as though it's greeting the land before retreating. Their repetitive, percussive rhythm is hypnotizing. Rather than looking scary, like they once did in my nightmares, they're beautiful.

I pull my wedding ring out of the pocket of my pants. I wasn't sure what I was going to do with it when I retrieved it from the broken birdhouse. But now I know.

Wrapped in my hand, I feel its solidness, its roundness. Until just recently, I'd been thinking that all these years with Reece were a waste. But now I'm beginning to see that's not true. These years have taught me so much about what not to do going forward, about not letting go of my fur. And rather than being ashamed of my time working on his business, I can acknowledge all the success I helped to build. I'm proud of that, and that accomplishment will serve me well as I move forward with creating my life. If I helped him get a label and put out two albums in less than five years, what's possible now for me and my art?

As I hold the ring up, it catches the light of the setting sun and sparkles. I remember a simple yet powerful Hawaiian forgiveness practice Dora once taught me, called *ho'oponopono*, and say the words out loud: "I'm sorry. Please forgive me. Thank you. I love you." I pull my arm back, like the Angry Woman's pose. Only, I'm not angry. I feel . . . capable. Awake. Energized. I toss the ring as far as I can into the water.

The sea swallows my gift, and the waves continue their timeless dance of intimacy with the shore.

What do you want now, Sabina?

EPILOGUE

One Month Later

THE BLACK PAINT SURGES FROM THE ROLLER BRUSH LIKE velvet, transforming the cement wall into a midnight sky. I'm standing on a stepladder to get the uppermost corners of the wall. Up and down, back and forth, I stretch my arm as far as it can go.

A warm sensation radiates through my body. *I'm doing it.* I keep mentally chanting these three words like a drumbeat. *I'm doing it. I'm doing it.* My stomach rumbles. *I know, I know. Food's on its way.* I was so excited to start painting this morning that I didn't even take time to eat something after my swim.

I set the roller brush in the tray of paint and lean back to look at the whole wall. The Selkies, in their human form, seem to wave at me. I've outlined them in pencil; it'll be a while before I get them all painted in. There are four of them, dancing around a large fire. The flames are leaping out as though joining in the dance. To the right of them, waves lap the shore, wild yet inviting. The Selkies' furs, which will be painted in various shades of grays and browns, lay in a pile to their left, in the foreground. Beyond the furs rise the golden sandstone cliffs. And above the women, a full moon has risen, shining down upon them and illuminating what will be the white frothy edges of the waves.

I swipe a stray curl out of my face, realizing too late that I've smeared some black paint on my cheek in the process. I get down off the stepladder and smile at what I see. At eleven-by-fourteen feet, this is the second-largest canvas I've ever painted on—the first one being The Wall, up at Dora's barn. But this experience is so different from exploding all of my emotions onto The Wall. At The Wall, there's no prep. It's all about letting go of what's inside of me, however it comes through. There's no goal or final image. But for this one, I've already spent hours crafting the final image on a smaller canvas, playing with the composition of the different elements. Then I spent hours—days, really—transferring that image onto the wall—after having prepped and primed it. And who knows how many days it will take me to fill in the details.

A warm breeze caresses my face, bringing with it the scent of the ocean—a scent that's steadily becoming more familiar to me. I breathe in deeply and, as I do, get a glimpse of the Forever Woman, dancing with the Selkies around the fire. I laugh. "Oh yeah? You wanna be part of this creation too?" Her presence reminds me of what it was like to paint the three women for the fundraiser. It was a different kind of process painting. Like this. I wonder what these women, the four Selkies dancing around the fire, will evoke from within me as I give life to them in the mural.

I wrap my hand around the small, antique golden key that rests on my chest. I'd come across it while going through Nana's jewelry box after I returned from LA. I slipped it onto one of her necklaces and started wearing it around my neck. I'm not sure what it opens, but I like it, and it reminds me that I hold the key to my own fur, my own freedom. It's not easy, switching up my whole way of being, and I need all the reminders I can get. "Nana," I whisper, "I'm finally doing it. I bet you're getting a kick out of how this all turned out."

"Hey, Bina Bell!" I look over and see Dora standing next to my boxes and buckets. "I see you've finished outlining the mural. It looks fabulous!"

"Morning, Dora." I smile at her. "Yeah. I finished that last night. Couldn't wait to start painting this morning. Maddie helped me get all set up." Dora's assistant was at the gallery already when I arrived today at eight. She'd helped me pull out all the supplies from their back room.

Dora lifts a small brown bag in one hand and a tray with two coffees in the other. "As promised, I swung by The Buttery on my way here. Got your favorite—blueberry cheese twist."

"Aw, thanks, Dora." I wipe my hands on a rag and take the coffee she indicates is mine.

"How are you feeling?"

"Well, my cheeks ache from smiling so much. I just . . . I'm so happy to finally be painting this mural after what—almost seven years?" I suddenly feel really emotional. "Thank you for your patience. Better to show up for my life now than never, ya know?"

She leans over and kisses my cheek—the one that doesn't have black paint on it. "Achy cheeks are a beautiful thing." She glances back over at the mural and studies it for a few moments as I breathe into the emotion, letting myself feel it all before taking a sip of coffee. Then I dig into the bag for the pastry. "Already, it has such promise of movement, of coming alive, like your recent paintings. With the Selkies' hair lifting in the wind. The way the flames seem to be dancing too. Amazing. I can't wait to see this when it's all done." Dora looks back and forth between me and the mural. "And are those keys on each of the Selkies? Like your own necklace?"

I smile at her, savoring the bite of flaky goodness in my mouth. "Yeah." I swallow, brush the crumbs from my mouth, and look at the Selkies. "I figured if I'm going to share the story of the Selkies with all of Santa Cruz, it's going to be the updated version of the myth. The one where each woman knows that the key to her own fur—you know, her own treasures, her own freedom—belongs to her and can never be taken away."

"Oh, Bina Bell. I love that."

We stand side by side, sipping our coffees, our eyes on the mural. The black of the sky seems full. It hints at the mystery of the Selkies and the power within each of them . . . each of us. And the keys. I can picture the bright golden color they'll be. I'll even add some mica so they'll glitter in the sunlight. An image of my wedding band bursts before me, along with the rays I'd painted coming from the Angry Woman's hands. What started off as a promise of forever to someone else has evolved into a key that set me free.

Fire doesn't just destroy, it also transforms, I hear again, just like I did at my show.

So true, I whisper silently in response. Just like the Selkies when they shape-shift, transforming from one form to another.

Just like what Nana had said about death. "I'll let go of my skin. Not gone. Just different. Like the Selkies."

Nana is never far from my thoughts. I miss her every day. And there have been moments while out here alone, sketching the mural, when I've felt her with me. Sometimes, it's in the way the sun peeks out from a cloud to shine on my face; other times, it's like the caress of the wind—like a little while ago.

"What will go in there?" Dora's question pulls me out of my reverie. She's pointing at the circle in the lower left corner of the mural that's about the size of a large beach ball.

"That's reserved for when I'm all done with the rest of the mural." I link my arm through hers. "I thought, if you'd like, we could paint that together. It will be the dedication. I think it's going to say, 'For Cordelia Bell, Daughter of the Sea,' and 'All good things are wild and free.'"

Dora looks at me, her teary eyes mirroring my own. "Oh, Bina, I love that too. So much."

"And we'll know, every time we look at this, that the keys on the Selkies also represent Nana's legacy: that we are responsible for our own happily-ever-after."

The sound of tinkling bells reverberates through my body like laughter. *Yes, you are,* I hear. *Yes, you are.*

ACKNOWLEDGMENTS

This book may be complete now, but its journey started long before the first sentence. Here are my big, heartfelt thank-yous to the many people who played a key role in bringing my novel to you.

I start with the women who have supported me throughout my journey—beginning with my own divorce and continuing through the writing of this book and beyond . . .

My besties:

Merryl Rothaus, thank you for catching me and for introducing me to the cathartic power of process painting. Thanks also for guiding me in navigating and writing about challenging relationships and for inspiring me in so many ways as a real-life artist.

Isabell Fearnsby and Missy Singer-Dumars, thank you for inhabiting Sabina's story along with me and for being sounding boards and creative consultants throughout its many iterations.

Isabell, thank you for your advice over the years on painting, the soulful language of art, and the creative process. You also inspire me as a real-life artist.

Missy, thank you for being with me through it all—from giving me a wall on which to spread out my Post-it Notes and flip chart paper to helping me dial in the back-cover copy, as well as all the moments in between.

My writing mentors:

Andy Couturier of The Opening, thank you for inviting me to pause and breathe on our first call together. Thanks for your guidance on "writing open the mind," for helping me go to places I hadn't gone before, and for your enthusiastic leadership of our Book Completion Group . . . I did it!

Laura Munson, participating in your Haven Writing Retreat in September 2019 fundamentally altered something for me. I left there with a commitment to *be all in* and believe in myself as a writer and author even more. Thank you.

I also want to thank my second-grade creative writing teacher, Mrs. Guaranski, for introducing me to the play of putting words to the world of my imagination.

My editors:

Bridget A. Lyons, thank you for helping me turn my 150,000-word manuscript into a 75,000-word publisher-ready one! I'm grateful for how you showed up just as I was ready to find an editor. I'm in awe of all the synchronicities too: You live in Santa Cruz, California, you surf, and you know music. Thank you for getting my book and helping me tell Sabina's story in the truest way.

Sheila Trask, thank you for taking my publisher-ready manuscript and turning it into a reader-ready book. I'm grateful that you also got my book and helped Sabina's story become even stronger.

My beta readers:

Jennifer Walrod, your belief in me and insightful feedback buoyed my next steps, yet it's been sharing this journey with you as a sister that's meant the most to me. Thank you for your support all along the way.

Susyn Reeve, confessing to me that Sabina's story inspired your own life journey was music to my ears and affirmed my sense of what this book is capable of. Thank you.

Jaclyn Gruber, your high praise partnered with Barbara Edward's constructive feedback created a dynamic tension that gave me further clarity for my way forward. Thank you both for your honesty and different perspectives.

Thanks also to the members of my writing groups with The Opening and Laura's Haven retreat who heard me read early versions of parts of this book. It's a vulnerable thing to share first pages. Thank you for receiving them with such grace. Your feedback and encouragement gave me the fuel I needed to keep going!

My publishing team—Brooke Warner and everyone at She Writes Press:

Thank you for pioneering new pathways in the publishing world and turning my dream into a reality. I'm honored to be partnering with you.

My mom and dad:

Thank you for instilling a love of reading and writing in me from the very beginning. Thanks for encouraging me, as a young girl, to keep writing when I read my short stories to you and for showing me, as published writers yourselves, how writing could be a way to express myself while also influencing and contributing to the world.

My online author community:

Thank you for being part of my path to publishing over the past year plus. Your support, input, and encouragement continue to inspire me to *go for it* in even bigger ways.

The people who generously supported me in my pre-pre-order:

Kavita Arora, Carol Daly, Susan Kerby, Sage Lavine, Kate Niebauer, Lisa and John Sutherland, Kendra E. Thornbury, Jennifer Walrod, and Mary Wong—thank you for believing in me!

Sabina, Nana, Dora, Graham, and the Big Magic that cocreated *It's Always Been Me* with me:

Thank you for knocking on my door and inviting me to play. Thank you for showing me what I'm capable of, how to show up for myself, how to surrender into your support, and how to become the Forever Woman for myself.

And last but certainly not least . . .

My readers:

I couldn't do this without you! It's your hearts and hands that I've been eagerly waiting to get my book into. Thank you for reading *It's Always Been Me.* I hope Sabina's story contributes to your own journey long after you read the last sentence.

ABOUT THE AUTHOR

Photo credit: Lucinda Rae

MEGAN WALROD is a writer, women's empowerment coach, and founder of Live Your Yes, LLC. Over the past sixteen years, she's supported thousands of women to break free from their "good girl" training and create fun, fulfilling lives, unapologetically owning their true selves. Megan brings a playful yet powerful approach to personal transformation and has a thing for mermaids, cupcakes, and skinny dipping. *It's Always Been Me* is her first novel.

Visit Megan's website or scan the QR code below for reflection questions, book club discussion topics, and more ways to explore the book's themes as they resonate with your own life. www.MeganWalrod.com/book.

Looking for your next great read?

We can help!

Visit www.shewritespress.com/next-read
or scan the QR code below for a list
of our recommended titles.

She Writes Press is an award-winning
independent publishing company founded to
serve women writers everywhere.